WELCOME HOME

Jimmy's mother's decapitated body lay on the stairs, neck-stump hanging off the bottom step so that gravity helped exsanguinate her more completely. By now Jimmy's body was going haywire: heart hammering but blood pressure dropping, brain screaming to get out while his body threatened to faint.

He began to blink, then his brain started firing again. He realized:

My mother's been murdered.

And it had to be that mailman 'cos he told me he'd just been here. . . .

The house was totally silent. He blinked some more, began to think some more, and then:

I have to call the police. . . .

He ran to the phone in the kitchen, saw what was there, then screamed. Yes, the mailman had left a package for him, all right. His mother's head was neatly propped up on the kitchen counter, right next to the phone. Her eyes were open, and she was looking at him. It almost seemed as though she were smiling.

Jimmy stared.

His mother *was* smiling. Her lips turned up and her eyes widened further when he looked at her.

"Jimmy," she said in the softest, kindest, sweetest voice. "How are you, honey?"

Other *Leisure* books by Edward Lee:

INFERNAL ANGEL
MONSTROSITY
CITY INFERNAL

EDWARD LEE

MESSENGER

LEISURE BOOKS NEW YORK CITY

For Kathy Rosamilia.
WUMUITIFAY

LEISURE BOOKS ®

August 2004

Published by

Dorchester Publishing Co., Inc.
200 Madison Avenue
New York, NY 10016

ISBN 0-8439-5204-0

The name "Leisure Books" and the stylized "L" with design are trademarks of Dorchester Publishing Co., Inc.

Printed in the United States of America.

Visit us on the web at www.dorchesterpub.com.

ACKNOWLEDGMENTS

As always, I am in debt to many, but I'd like to particularly acknowledge the following for their support, inspiration, and friendship: Tim McGinnis, Dave Barnett, Patti Beller, Wendy Brewer, Rich Chizmar, Doug Clegg, Don D'Auria, Kim and Tony Duarte, Dallas, Teri Jacobs, Tom Pic, Bob Strauss, Karen Valentine. Perennial thanks to Amy and Scott, Christy and Bill, Charlie, Cowboy Jeff, Darren, Julie, R. J., and Stephanie, and of course, Audrey Craker and Kathy and Kirt Rosamilia; also to all the cool folks at Philthy Phil's and The Sloppy Pelican. Last but not least, for technical stuff on this one, thanks to Rich Underwood and John Grubmeyer—the author assumes all responsibility for mistakes!

ACKNOWLEDGMENTS

MESSENGER

Prologue

Death was in the package. Of course, it would've been impossible for Dodd to know that, unless he'd been psychic—which he wasn't—but either way it scarcely mattered. He never would've been able to guess. Why would he? It was a simple fact that he would discover soon enough: The odd box he'd just picked up off the belt contained his death.

Dodd sorted packages. That was his job. He was a package handler. It wasn't a bad job, as far as jobs went. Great benefits, good pay and retirement, paid vacation, plenty of available overtime when he needed some extra money, and the location, of course. When he picked up the package in question, there wasn't a whole lot on his mind. By now, his tasks had become so ingrained, most of his mind switched off; he became an automaton, sorting all these packages.

Day in, day out, in this same place. The same scenery, the same noises, the same tasks. He paused by the belt, and thought: *I've still got nine more years of this before I can retire.* That truth often overwhelmed him, even though, for the most part, he didn't mind his job. He didn't want to try to guess how many packages he'd picked up and moved in his career. Enough to circle Earth? Enough to reach the Moon? Abstractions were of little value on the line. It was easier to just throw the packages into the proper zone bin and move on to the next one.

Day in, day out.

Sometimes his mind would stray, though, usually to some image that involved sex. Dodd was married to a loving and rather drab wife. She was not attractive, nor unattractive, just . . . drab, as drab as Dodd's package-handling life. On the rare occasions when his mind strayed, he never thought of her. He'd think fleetingly, in freeze-frames of local women he'd see on the street; living this close to a beach town, there was much to fill his mind when he became bored or anxious. Yesterday, for example, he'd stopped by the drugstore for cigarettes and saw a beautiful woman—thirty, perhaps—buying a beach towel and a tube of suntan lotion. Dodd got tunnel vision standing behind her in line. Her hair shined, chocolate brown, shoulder length, fragrant. She was wearing white shorts and a stunning rose-pink bikini top. The top was a bit small on her; it buoyed her breasts like blushing satchels. Her skin wasn't tan at all, though; like Dodd, perhaps she had a job that kept her out of the sun. But her beauty seemed focused, very compact. To see her standing there, voluptuous yet nonchalant, felt like an impact to Dodd. The vision was a lovely punch in the eye.

Did she sense him looking at her?

She turned and smiled at him.

More impact.

"Hi," she said.

"Hi," Dodd replied, nearly faltering. "Hitting the beach, I see."

"Yeah." She sheepishly held up the towel. "Can you believe it? I've lived here almost a year now, and I don't even own a beach towel, haven't even been out to the beach. Well, today I fix that. I'm pale as a ghost."

"I don't get out much, either," Dodd replied.

"A postman?" she said, noticing his work uniform. "All that walking around, delivering mail?"

"I'm not a carrier. I work inside." *I'm a package handler . . . and you are one package I'd like to handle. . . .*

"Oh, that's too bad."

"Not really. I get to stay inside in the air-conditioning while everyone else gets the heat."

"Good old Florida." She was turning the tube of lotion around in her fingers. "But that's one thing that doesn't bother me. I love the heat. I love it when it's hot."

She smiled at him again, very discreetly.

"Me too," Dodd said.

The tunnel vision intensified. She was radiant in curves, long legs, and fresh white skin that shined. He imagined what her nipples were like—large and dark, the kind that pucker a little, he decided. He imagined kissing her. He imagined being pressed up against her, both of them naked, sharing each other's body heat, arms entwined. Her hands ranging across his body . . .

"Would you like to go?"

The impact of the vision fractured. He blinked. "Go?" he muttered.

"To the beach, with me," she said, still smiling. "We could go to one of those beach bars by the hotels. I've never been."

"I . . ." His hand tightened around his wallet. "I'd really like to, but—"

Then she saw his wedding band; however, the smile didn't abate. "Oh, I see. Don't feel *that* bad about it." She held up her hand. "I've got one of those too."

Dodd's breath shortened. *Go,* he thought. *Just go . . .* But he said, "I . . . I'm sorry. I wish I could, but I can't."

Her lashes batted. "I understand. You're a good man."

He couldn't stop looking at her as she paid for her towel and lotion. *I could be putting that lotion on her,* he reminded himself. Her buttocks in the tight white shorts couldn't have been more perfect. He wanted to spread the lotion over that, too, and everywhere else. They could go to the nude beach out past the campgrounds. He'd spread the lotion all down her legs, up her back, then turn her around. All up her perfect stomach and breasts, up the insides of her thighs.

Everywhere.

" 'Bye," she said. A final smile, which seemed sad now, as sad as Dodd's life.

" 'Bye. Have fun."

She walked out, calves flexing as her flipflops snapped.

God . . .

The vision was gone. Dodd was back at the post office, sorting his interminable packages.

That's when he picked up the package that would be his death.

He hit the stop button on the conveyor. He didn't know why. He didn't think, *Why did I do that?* or *I'm going to stop the belt*. He just did it. He stood there. He looked at the package.

It was an oddly shaped box, oblong. It was wrapped in plain brown paper, like the paper grocery bags are made of. There was no return address, and the postmark appeared smeared; Dodd couldn't make out the city, state, or zip code it had been mailed from. He looked at the top again. The box read:

DANELLETON POST OFFICE

DANELLETON, FLORIDA

It had been written by hand with a red felt-tip, marker in an erratic scrawl.

Due to its nature—no return address, shoddily wrapped—a package like this was an instant red flag to the original handler. But it wasn't a bomb. It contained no anthrax, no poison gas nor germ warfare agents. It had already been x-rayed and bomb-scanned at the central distribution depot in Orlando. Even in this day, before the Unabomber and before the anthrax scare of 2002, a package this suspicious would be vigorously scrutinized. This one had been and it was cleared. Nevertheless it still contained his death. But it wasn't anything from a terrorist or psychopath.

Since the box wasn't addressed to a resident or business, Dodd's next job was to deliver the package to the branch manager, who wouldn't be in until later. Instead Dodd did something that he was clearly *not* authorized to do.

He opened the package.

More crinkling as he peeled the paper off. Did the box feel hot? No, that was ridiculous. He opened it slowly, not in fear or hesitation but in some undecipherable adoration. His eyes were wide and unfocused. He wasn't really even looking at the box, he was adoring it in his hands.

As he did so, part of his mind drifted. He thought of the woman who'd invited him to the beach. He did not think about kissing her now, he thought about killing her. About holding her down on the floor by her throat and cutting off that rose-pink top and the white shorts. No, he didn't want to make love to her anymore, he just wanted to slit open her belly and haul out her guts while her legs kicked and her body bucked. That's what Dodd wanted to do to that fussy big-tit bitch with the shiny chocolate-brown hair and white shorts. He wanted to turn those shorts red. He wanted to scalp that shiny brown hair right off her head.

Dodd opened the box and looked inside.

Jimmy O'Brady was fourteen years old and had lived in Danelleton for all fourteen of them. He delivered papers in the morning and mowed lawns most days after school—an industrious kid. Better yet, school was out for the summer, so he could work even more. Florida sunlight bathed the long street—the street he lived on—and right now he was briskly pedaling his bike to the next block, where another lawn waited to be mowed. Money was what made the world go around;

Jimmy knew that even at his young age. He couldn't wait to turn sixteen and get his work permit. Then he could get a job as a busboy at one of the beach restaurants, really haul in some cash. Another thing he couldn't wait for was adulthood. Jimmy already knew what he wanted to be when he grew up: He wanted to work for the post office.

And there was the mailman now. Mr. Dexter was cool; he delivered the mail on this street every day, and he'd always stop and talk to Jimmy. He'd tell Jimmy all about working for the post office.

Mr. Dexter was walking away from the front door of the neighboring house. That's when Jimmy smiled, stopped his bike, and waved. "Hi, Mr. Dexter!"

The postman turned at the sidewalk, smiled back, and began to walk toward Jimmy.

That's when Jimmy noticed that it wasn't Mr. Dexter.

Dodd approached the kid on the bike. *No, no, not in broad daylight,* he was wise enough to decide. Kids needed adults to look up to, they needed role models—just like President Reagan said. Dodd almost laughed out loud. *Yeah, I guess if I cut the kid's head off, he wouldn't have ANYTHING to look up to!*

"Hi, there, Jimmy. How are you today?"

"Fine, sir." The tow-headed kid gave Dodd a scrinched-up look. "How did you know my name?"

"I'm the mailman. You're Jimmy O'Brady, and you live at 12404 Gatesman Lane." Dodd pointed to the house at the corner. "Right there. See, when you're the mailman, you know everybody's name."

The kid squinted against the sun. "But you're not the

regular mailman. Mr. Dexter is our regular mailman. Do you know him?"

"I sure do, Jimmy. I'm filling in for him because he's sick today." *You ain't kidding he's sick. I strangled the fat son of a bitch with the strap on his mail pouch and put his body in the Dumpster before the first shift came on.* "I usually don't deliver the mail myself, haven't in years. I'm a package handler. But it's fun to take a walking shift every now and then. I just delivered mail to your house."

"Really? Was there anything for me?"

"As a matter of fact, there was. You got a big surprise waiting for you when you get back home."

Now the kid was really beaming. Dodd felt wonderful. Indeed, there'd be a *big* surprise for the kid.

"What is it?"

"You'll see when you get home. It's great being a mailman. You get to deliver nice surprises to people every day. And you know something, Jimmy? I've got a funny feeling that you want to be a mailman someday too."

"How did you know that?" the kid asked, impressed.

I know a lot of things now. "Um, Mr. Dexter told me."

"It's true. I really wanna be a mailman when I grow up." But the kid was impatient. He looked at his watch. "I'm supposed to mow a lawn right now, but—"

"Can't it wait a few minutes?" Dodd suggested. "You could ride back to your house right now and see the surprise first. Your mother's home. She'll show it to you."

The kid tapped his sneakered foot. "Yeah, I think I will. Thanks, sir! Hope to see you soon!"

"Me, too, Jimmy. Have a great day."

But just before the kid pulled away on his bike, he

paused for a last squint at Dodd. "How come you're wearing that? Aren't you hot?"

Dodd was wearing his long-tailed official post office raincoat. "Me? No, I like the heat, Jimmy. And there's supposed to be a thunderstorm in a little while."

Jimmy looked up at the cloudless sky, then shrugged. "If you say so. 'Bye!"

"See ya later, Jimmy," Dodd said and turned for the next house. He started walking. He'd only gotten five houses on the street so far, but he was determined to get all of them before the police came. The hubbies were all at work, leaving only their wives, and the wives were easy and the most fun. *Hell, with any luck,* Dodd thought, *I could take out a couple blocks before I get caught.* . . .

At the very least he'd give it his best.

He walked up to the next house, the McNamaras, at 12408. He rang the doorbell, and when the door opened an inch, a pretty face peered out.

"Hi, Mrs. McNamara. It's just me, the mailman. I've got an Express Mail delivery for you to sign for."

"Oh, okay. Here. Come on in," the woman said and opened the door the rest of the way.

Dodd smiled, thanked her, and entered. He was just inside the foyer, out of the view of the street, when he took out the machete he'd been hiding under the raincoat.

Several seconds after Jimmy O'Brady rushed into his three-bedroom colonial on Gatesman Lane, he couldn't move, he couldn't scream, he couldn't blink. He could only stare and shiver. He was suffering from

9

what a clinician would call reactive psychogenic adrenaline shock. In layman's terms, however, he was suffering from being scared shitless.

Red liquid glazed the fieldstone foyer. Subconsciously, he knew it was blood. Consciously, his brain would not acknowledge that, especially because the only other person in the house, he knew, was his mother. Therefore, that's whose blood it must be.

It was a lot of blood. It looked like the time his father had accidently tipped over a gallon of Sherwin-Williams's No. 10 Cinnabar-Red enamel in the garage. It was a veritable pond of red.

His mother's decapitated body lay on the stairs, neck stump hanging off the bottom step so that gravity helped exsanguinate her more completely. By now Jimmy's body was going haywire in a mode of metabolic opposites: heart hammering but blood pressure dropping, adrenaline dumping but knees weakening, brain screaming to get out while his body threatened to faint. Defense mechanisms pitted against a psychological overload that wanted to shut him down.

In spite of his age, after another minute or so, some aspect of reason returned. He began to blink; then his brain started firing again. He realized:

My mother's been murdered.

And it had to be that mailman 'cos he told me he'd just been here . . .

The house was silent. He blinked some more, began to think some more, and then:

I have to call the police.

He ran to the phone in the kitchen, saw what was there, and screamed. Yes, the mailman had left a package for him, all right. His mother's head was neatly propped up on the kitchen counter, right next to the phone. Her eyes were open, and she was looking at him. It almost seemed as though she were smiling.

Jimmy stared.

His mother *was* smiling. Her lips turned up and her eyes widened further when he looked at her.

"Jimmy," she said in the softest, kindest, sweetest voice. "How are you, honey? Aren't you supposed to be cutting someone's lawn?"

"Muh-Muh-Mom?" Jimmy stammered.

"Such a fine, fine boy," his mother said. "Did you know that your father and I weren't going to have children? He didn't even want to marry me. So I stopped taking my birth control pills so I'd get pregnant. I knew that if I got pregnant, he'd marry me. He makes a lot of money and I didn't want to work anymore—he was the perfect sucker. Shit, I didn't want kids, I *hate* kids. But I hate working more, so I figured one rugrat wouldn't be too bad."

Jimmy continued to stare.

"But you're a good boy, Jimmy. I guess you got that from your father 'cos I sure as shit ain't a good person. Don't worry, you'll grow up to be just like your father. A perfect dupe, a sucker."

Jimmy began to feel dizzy.

"I cheated on your father every chance I got—"

Jimmy ran to the next house, the Norahees. His shock and his horror dazed him; he couldn't really think now. It was just instinct driving him. The front door was open an inch, so he barged in—

The foyer was full of blood, just like his. Mrs. Norahee lay decapitated on the stairs, and when he ran to the kitchen—

"Your mother's in hell now," Mrs. Norahee's head told him. "I ought to know. I'm right there with her."

Close to psychotic now, Jimmy checked every house on Gatesman Lane, and found the same thing.

He collapsed in the last yard. His brain felt on the verge of shutting down. Part of him heard a quick scream from the house across the street at the corner. Then a moment later saw the new mailman walk out the front door and head casually to the next address. Before he knocked on the next door, the mailman turned slowly, smiled at Jimmy, and waved.

Chapter One

Twenty Years Later

(I)

The scissors *snipped!* as the brand-new stainless steel blades sliced through the yellow ribbon. When the ribbon parted and fell, the small crowd that had gathered began to cheer.

That was simple, Jane thought. She handed the scissors back to the mayor. Flashbulbs popped and the applause grew loud. There were even some writers and photographers from the local papers in the crowd. It wasn't that big a deal but it looked like it. *All this hoopla,* Jane thought, *and all for what? We're opening a new post office, for God's sake.* In a small town, however, even something like this was an event. Jane didn't go for cameras and publicity—she was all business. She was almost ill at ease.

Yeah, she thought again. *This was simple. Now the hard part starts.*

"Thank you, Jane," the mayor said into a microphone. It was possible that he'd had a vodka tonic or two before the opening ceremony. "And now that the ribbon is cut . . . let's go inside for cookies and punch!"

"Jesus," Carlton Spence said under his breath. "Cookies and punch. Is this corny or what?"

Jane whispered back, "Don't be too sure. You haven't tried the punch."

Jane smiled and nodded, shaking hands with the people in the crowd as they filed into the post office. *I am so bad at this game,* she told herself. When most of the crowd had filed in, Carlton sighed. Carlton was Jane's assistant now, amiable, early forties, often quick with some good-natured sarcasm. He was as good at his job as Jane was at hers, and that's why she knew they'd make a great team. He was also very perceptive sometimes.

"Either your dog shit in your shoes this morning," he said, "or this whole grand opening thing is making you very uncomfortable."

"I don't have a dog."

"I know."

She made a weary smile. "I just want to get on with it. Get all this foolishness over with and get on with the job."

Carlton scratched the beer belly he'd been working hard on for the last twenty years. "Small-town politics and all that. Opening a new post office in a little burg like Danelleton is like opening a skyscraper in a big city." A photographer snapped a quick picture of the two of them, then hustled inside. Carlton frowned. "Besides, we gotta give the local papers something to write about, don't we?"

Jane was grateful for the implication. Danelleton had one of the lowest per-capita crime rates in the state. *I guess I should be happy this is the big story of the week instead of a drive-by shooting or crack cocaine bust.*

"Oh, and one other thing," Carlton said, "congratulations on the promotion, Jane. You'll do a kick-butt job running this place."

"*We'll* do a kick-butt job, Mr. Deputy Assistant Postmaster."

"Isn't that kind of like the assistant to the assistant to the assistant of the assistant secretary of state?"

"Sure. You're the one who makes the coffee, and I'm the one who delivers it."

They both laughed but they knew it wasn't that bad.

Carlton looked up at the sun. "Things will be great, just you watch."

"I hope so," she said. "But I still don't quite understand why Danelleton needs a *second* post office."

"Are you kidding? In the last twenty years, the town's population has quadrupled. The main post office at the town square just isn't enough anymore. It's progress, Jane. That's a good thing. More people moving here means more money for the local economy." Carlton shrugged. "More mail to be delivered. And lemme tell ya—" He looked up at the sun again, the perfect cloudless sky. At the same moment, a group of lorikeets flew by. "There are worse places to work for the post office."

"I know, we get Florida paradise, and the other chumps get to deliver mail in the South St. Pete ghettos. Don't worry, I'm not taking things for granted, and I really am looking forward to this—"

Jane paused to look at the small but well-designed building. *It's mine,* she told herself. Suddenly her discomfort over the grand opening was displaced by pride. *I'm the boss. This little post office annex is my baby.* Cool air swept their faces when the automatic doors parted. They walked inside, ignoring the continued grand opening formalities over by the gift shop—where the mayor appeared to be getting drunk on spiked punch—and turned toward the clerk stations.

"So much for punch and cookies," Carlton said.

Customers were lining up to buy stamps, send packages, get mail metered. "Yeah," Jane said, "I guess we better get inside and start taking care of these customers. Jeez, look at them all."

Carlton scratched his beer belly again. "Aw, don't sweat it. I'll bet half of them are only here for the newest Elvis stamp."

Jane could only hope so. *No time like the present,* she thought. "See ya at the end of the shift, Carlton, and don't forget to have someone clear all those old records out of the basement. We don't want the fire department writing us up for fire hazards the first week we're open." Then she went through the half door to head into the administrative wing. It was quiet in back, but if she listened carefully she could hear the trucks pulling up in back at the loading dock. Her footsteps ticked across the brand-new tile. In a lost moment, she caught herself peering at her reflection in an office window. *How do you like that?* she asked herself. *Thirty-five years old, and I'm still not half bad looking.* The knee-length navy blue skirt and patched sky-blue tunic notwithstanding, Jane's looks, if anything, had improved as she'd grown older, as if her desirability had seasoned and maximized. *Boobs not sagging yet, stomach's still flat, even after two kids. I really can't complain.* Noon-blue eyes looked back at her; the uncertain expression changed with a confident smile. Her hair was too bright to label her a brunette, but it wasn't auburn either—something more like cinnamon—a little shorter than shoulder length. The bright shine to her hair was augmented by a rich nut-brown tan, an overall glow of vitality. Bodywise, Jane was happy to see that all the right curves had remained in all the right places. Her breasts filled the top of her tunic, ghosts of nipples showing through the light fabric, and when she cocked her hip and grinned, she even looked sultry. *Somehow that look isn't me,* she laughed to herself. *The Hussy Mail Chick.* Instead, she simply looked like a beautiful, self-assured modern working woman, still in good shape and still at her peak. *I've got a lot to look forward to, and even better than that—* She laughed to herself again—*construction workers still whistle at me!*

The good day had just gotten better, with a positive acknowledgment of herself. It hadn't always been like that, not since the move . . . and the loss of her husband. Sometimes being a widow with two young children seemed impossible. It was impossible to do everything right, too many obstacles seemed to have dropped on her, too many hardships. She'd felt very insecure at times, very doubtful.

But she'd persevered, and now things couldn't be better: the promotion, the new post office, the kids adjusting better to school and their lives without a father.

And now this . . .

Jane's eyes roved up the office window that framed her reflection, to the words stenciled in black letters near the top: JANE RYAN, STATION MANAGER, DANELLETON WEST BRANCH.

(II)

Idyllic wasn't the word; it didn't suffice. To call the town romantic, picturesque, or quaint proved trite but at least accurate. Danelleton had grown, yes, but it hadn't lost any of the traits that made it so unique in this day and age. Once just a little suburb in central Florida, now it was incorporated, flourishing, progressing without giving up its honest luster. Perhaps its location kept it isolated—off a major thoroughfare beyond an old county road that appeared rural—or perhaps something even spiritual protected it from the corruption that tended to follow real estate development near tourism hubs. Who knew? It existed between Tampa and St. Petersburg—big cities with big crime waves—yet Danelleton boasted almost no crime. Last year, for example, the most serious crimes to be committed were one stolen bike, some graffiti spray-painted in a Main Street alley, and a tipped-over Johnny On The Spot at a construction site. No drugs here, no rapes, no armed robberies.

Just a ten-minute drive to the beaches of the Gulf of Mexico. Excellent schools, superior municipal services, an abundance of community organizations and charity groups. Real estate costs had miraculously remained reasonable when they'd skyrocketed in other towns. Plenty of day care, plenty of activities for kids. Families were close-knit; everyone looked out for everyone else. There was little riff-raff. There was no "bad" part of town. In essence, Danelleton proved the model for middle-class Florida life.

And the beauty.

Palms trees lined well-groomed streets of plush green lawns, colorful gardens, and humble but immaculate homes. More plush green served as a backdrop for the east side of the town: the rise of the forest teeming with fern and Australian pine trees. To the west spired the tall lemon-yellow water tower emblazoned with bright pink words: IT'S A BEAUTIFUL DAY. The town square radiated sedate charm while boats rocked quietly in bayside slips, mooring ropes chiming against their masts. The sun always seemed brighter in Danelleton, the sky more expansive, the air more pure.

What more could anyone ask of a place to live? Who *wouldn't* want to live here? Danelleton was as close to perfect as any town could ever strive to be. Beautiful, civilized, and safe. No drugs, no rapes, no armed robberies, no murd—

Well, there were some murders once.

But that was a long time ago.

(III)

In the basement.

God, what a mess, Carlton thought. He kneed his way into the dark cubby, clumsily wielding the flashlight, extricating decades-old boxes with his other hand. The only way to get to the end was to dig everything out. But Jane had been right about one thing: *This basement is a fire hazard,* Carlton realized, dust-covered now. *If the inspectors saw this, they'd make us close down until we got it all cleared out.* The refuse consisted mainly of old boxes of records, antiquated sorting machines and spare parts, old uniforms, and out-of-date packing items. Carlton figured if he took all these boxes outside he could build a pyramid out of them as high as the post office.

I'm second-in-charge of this place and look at me. I'm hauling junk out of the basement. Carlton doubted that these tasks were in his government job description.

He laughed through it, though, a good sport, even as cobwebs spread and stuck to his face. It was a dull process: crawl in, grab a box, drag it out, then crawl back in for the next one. It would take the rest of the day more than likely, but at least he could look forward to the end of the shift when he could stop by the bar—covered in dust and cobwebs—and celebrate the first day of his promotion.

Carlton had no sour grapes that Jane had been named branch station manager instead of him, even though he had more time and grade. He was better at the dirty work anyway, keeping the employees on their toes, while Jane could deal with the red tape and management duties. In truth, he was happy for her, and he was happy that the town had opened this second postal facility, because it proved that Danelleton was prospering. More residents meant more homes, hence, more mail than the main post office could handle on its own anymore. Carlton and Jane, in fact, had both begun their careers at the main facility at the town square, and the place didn't exactly bring back good memories. *Christ,* he thought as an image from his past swept through his mind. Suddenly he paused at a twinge of despair.

He took a breath, counted off a few moments, then grabbed another box and began to drag it out.

The main post office was where he'd thought he was starting his family life, but in truth it had been where he'd ended it.

Don't think about it, he warned himself. *It's over. It's done. You got a new life here so get on with it. The past is the past, good and bad.*

He rarely *did* think of it lately, even over the past handful of years. He'd gotten over it, with the help of time, reason, and a good shrink.

Get off that shit! Grab another box and do your job!

Subconsciously, he supposed, he'd never be rid of it. How could he be? How could anyone? And what he couldn't figure, as he dragged yet another box of old post office records out of the crawlway, was why now? And why here, of all places? He'd never been in this building before his promotion. The Danelleton west branch had originally been closed and abandoned for the past twenty years. For that time period all mail was processed through the main office at the city dock. This just reopened facility meant nothing to Carlton.

He shook his head in the musty darkness edged by the flashlight beam.

What was it about *this* building that triggered the worst memories of his life?

He forcibly tried to shut his mind off, and dragged another box from the cubby, grunting. Sweat darkened his collar. His heart was beating faster.

First Mariel, he thought. *Then Belinda.*

It had all happened so fast, sometimes it still seemed like a dream. After eight fine years of marriage—and with no warning signs—Mariel had lost it. Totally. In layman's terms, she'd gone off the deep end. In psychiatric terms, she'd suffered a systemized psychotic break with paranoid ideations, amine-related mania, and traits of something called Capgras syndrome. In other words, Carlton's wife had begun to believe that nobody and nothing around her was genuine. She believed that Carlton, for instance, wasn't really Carlton but an identical impostor. She believed the same of the neighbors, her friends, and her parents, anyone close in her life. They were all fakes. She even believed it about the house, the car, and eventually, the entire neighborhood. Everything had been manufactured as part of a plot to fool her. After the fact, Carlton had read about the syndrome on the Internet. It was rare but very real, spurred by either an organic brain defect or microtumors. Untreatable, in other words. Carlton had lost his wife in the wink of an eye.

And his daughter, Belinda, too.

Seven years ago, he realized. Belinda would be going on nineteen now—and then he reminded himself: *Not "would be." She* is. *She* is *going on nineteen now.*

One thing Carlton would not give up hope on was the prospect of Belinda still being alive. Mariel's body had been recovered from the wreck but Belinda's body had never been found. There was no blood of her type in the wreckage, no forensic signs that she'd been injured. She'd been eating Cracker Jacks in the car and the fingerprint people found Belinda's prints and traces of corn syrup and sugar on the seat belt buckle and passenger door handle, so she'd clearly been buckled up.

For whatever reason pertaining to her illness, the one person Muriel *didn't* believe was counterfeit was Belinda. So one night, she'd put her daughter in the family station wagon and left town—in her mind believing she was saving herself and her daughter from the "plot." She'd made it as far as Baltimore before a drunk driver had crashed into them on Interstate 95. Muriel had been vaulted through the windshield—she always forgot to wear her seat belt—and broken her neck on impact. Instant death.

But Belinda's body was not to be seen.

Don't think about it, don't think about it, don't think about it. The words kept pounding in Carlton's mind.

But something—for some reason—*forced* him to think about it.

The drunk driver had been killed too, so there was no living witness directly on the scene. Maryland state police, however, told Carlton a motorist who'd pulled over to help had seen another vehicle leaving the shoulder just as he'd stopped. In the back window the motorist thought he'd seen two adult men and another shorter figure. "Shorter, sitting lower, like a kid maybe," he'd reported.

"I know this is very difficult for you to accept, sir," an FBI agent had later told Carlton, "but it's our speculation that your daughter was abducted from the scene by an illicit party."

Abducted? Illicit party?

No. This would never be something he could ever "accept."

Surely, Belinda, traumatized by the crash and witnessing her mother's death, had gotten out of the car in a state of shock and was seen by another passing motorist. Not an *illicit party*. Just some normal decent person who'd seen the wreck and spotted a little twelve-year-old girl in the road. He'd picked Belinda up and taken her to a hospital. Surely, Carlton would hear from the authorities that Belinda was safe, recovering, and soon to be returned home.

After a couple weeks, part of Carlton knew that that was not the case. And after a couple of months, another part of him suspected that he'd never see his daughter again. She'd been abducted by an illicit party.

For God knew what purpose.

Eventually the authorities apprized him of the worst possibilities, but Carlton didn't listen. He could not think about his precious daughter in such terms. Instead, he clung to the best possibility. That some otherwise decent people had taken Belinda because they couldn't have a child of their own. "I mean, it's possible, right?" he'd practically begged the FBI agent. "Something like that *could've* happened. Right?"

"Of course, sir. Things like that happen every day . . ."

That's all Carlton needed to hear, and that's where he'd left it. He'd left it all with that stray hope and no reason to believe otherwise. And then he'd put it all aside, to the best that any man in the same horrible situation could.

Until now.

Until he'd come down into this dark old basement to clear out a bunch of twenty-year-old boxes that posed a fire risk.

Oh, Belinda. Please be alive. Please be okay. Please be with people who are taking care of you. . . .

He'd read about things like that all the time, and seen it on television. Otherwise well-meaning couples who were miserable because they couldn't have kids. So they'd take someone else's. And in *that* situation? Seeing her mother killed? Crawling out of the car in a state of shock? It was feasible that Belinda would've blacked the memory out. The new parents would tell her that not only her mother had been killed in the wreck but Carlton too. Or maybe she wouldn't remember anything of her past, including Carlton. Delayed stress reaction. Amnesia. Things like that. Carlton could only pray that that's what had happened.

Belinda, came the final thought.

One last box, full of clanky sorter parts. Carlton dragged it out, huffing, filthy in dust. *That's it. The last one.* He sleeved some sweat off his brow, then shone his light down the crawl space to make sure he hadn't missed anything.

Something glimmered.

I wonder what that is . . .

No more boxes remained in the cubby. But something—he was certain—glimmered on the floor when he angled his flashlight in.

Oh, what the hell? One more trip won't kill me. And it ain't like I can get any dirtier.

Carlton crawled back in, the end of the cubby blooming with light as he neared the end. But his eyes bloomed too. The object that glimmered was a bracelet . . .

A bracelet that looked very familiar.

Carlton picked it up.

And stared.

This is impossible.

. It was a silver-chain bracelet ringed with shiny dolphins. It looked exactly like the bracelet he'd given Belinda seven years ago, on her twelfth birthday.

Impossible.

Maybe it was just his imagination. Yes, that had to be it. It was just some old bracelet laying there, and because he'd been thinking about Belinda, he was subconsciously convincing himself it was the same as his daughter's.

That had to be it.

His hands began to tremble when he flipped over one of the silver dolphins and saw the inscription:

TO BELINDA, FROM DAD.

Then he heard—

Carlton's head shot up.

He was looking right at the butt-end of the crawlway, which appeared to be nothing more than a square of Sheetrock.

But there was a sound—

What the . . . ?

—a sound coming from *behind* the Sheetrock.

Scratching.

It sounded like someone on the other side, scratching on the Sheetrock with their fingernails. Carlton put the flashlight right up to the corner and saw that the square had been chalked into the frame. He pressed his opened hand against it, pressed a little harder, and the panel gave a little.

Hair on the back on his neck stood up.

The scratching on the other side grew frantic.

It's . . . probably . . . a rat or something . . .

Carlton gave the panel a hard thud with his palm.

Thump!

The corner nudged out another inch, and then the scratching stopped and gave over to rapid taps.

Not a rat. A rat couldn't do that.

But a person could. A person rapping their knuckles against the other side of the panel. Carlton couldn't deny what he was observing.

There's somebody behind this panel!

"Who's there?" he shouted. "Is someone there?"

Finally he drew back and rammed his fist against the Sheetrock, banging the panel completely out of its frame. Darkness swallowed it, and foul air gusted out of the opening.

"Is somebody there? I KNOW there's someone there! I can hear you!"

He picked up the flashlight, meaning to thrust its beam in the hole, when—

Darkness fell on him like an avalanche.

Carlton froze. The flashlight had died in his hand. He smacked it in the most cliched desperation, hoping it would snap back on, but it didn't.

Blind now, he thought of crawling backward out of the cubby. It would be easy. He could do it quickly. He could be back in the light. But he didn't.

He didn't move.

"Is somebody there?" he whispered into the dark.

He already knew the answer, before the faint but familiar voice replied:

"Hi, Daddy. It's me. It's Belinda."

Carlton's heart didn't seem to beat as much as squirm in his chest. The foul air continued to eddy into his face, evil fetors like rotten meat and bodies unwashed for weeks. Again, part of his senses thought to back up, get out of the cubby and be away from this hallucination or nightmare or whatever it was, but his muscles wouldn't respond to the commands of his brain. He simply remained there on hands and knees, staring into the rank darkness.

"You should see where I've been, Daddy," his daughter's voice flowed. "It's not like in the Bible."

"What?"

"But I can only be here for a few minutes. He let me come up, to talk to you."

He?

"He's the Messenger. He wants me to tell you some

things." The pretty voice seemed to dip up and down. Carlton wasn't sure but as his eyes were acclimating to the darkness, he thought he could make out the dimmest shape just beyond the opening, an indistinct silhouette.

"Who is . . . *he*?" Carlton croaked.

"I can't say. His name's a secret, and someone like me isn't allowed to speak it."

"Someone like you? But you're just a teenaged girl. What do you mean, someone like you?"

"I'm just a low-level myrmidon, Daddy."

Myrmidon? Carlton had never heard the word.

"I'm, like, a sexual acolyte. There's lots and lots of sex down here, Daddy."

"But you're not even twenty! You're just a teenage girl!" Carlton bellowed back into the insanity.

"Not anymore. I might as well be ten thousand years old, Daddy. I'll live forever down here. You know where *here* is, don't you?"

"You're my daughter! You're an innocent little girl! This is a trick! It's stress! I'm hearing things and seeing things because of the stress of your mother being killed and you being taken! I know you're alive somewhere, being cared for by good people, people who couldn't have a child of their own but wanted one so much they took you!"

"Oh, I was taken, all right, Daddy. But not by people who wanted a little girl to raise. When Mommy crashed, some men pulled me out and put me in their car. They drove me to Baltimore. They got me on crack right away, so I'd do anything they wanted. They tricked me out mostly, and made me be in movies. The scat movies were the worst but after a while it wasn't so bad. I got used to it, just as long as I got my rock. And they used me for a lot of kink johns, special jobs, stuff like that."

Carlton's mouth hung open.

The tiny voice in the dark continued. "Then I began to wear out from all the dope, started to look beat. Shit, in that business once a girl's past sixteen, she's no good for kiddie flicks and pedophiles. So about a month ago, the guys were shooting another movie, a four-way, and one of the stuntcocks got a little carried away. Fuckin' asshole was big as a rolling pin to begin with, and he was all methed out. Anyway, I had a massive hemorrhage and died."

Carlton's eyes felt lidless.

"And then I came down here."

Did she giggle?

"Now I'm an odalisque, Daddy. That's what they call a prostitute down here. I'm kept by the wardens of Grand Duke Belarius of the Drakonia Prefecture. He commands four legions—that's about 12,000 conscripts. There's a big war going on now in the Lowlands, so I'm in the field a lot. We have these big tents that they cycle the troops in and out of—you know, for sexual relief. Sometimes I'm on my back for a week at a time, one conscript after another, until the campaign's over. There's no sleep here, either. It's an endless night, and that's all I do. Like I said, Daddy, there's a lot of sex down here. That's pretty much what it's all about in hell."

"You're not in hell!" Carlton roared so loudly he nearly blew his vocal cords. "You're an innocent teenage girl! Even if you *did* die, you wouldn't have gone to hell! You'd have gone to heaven!"

The responding giggle fluttered, then seemed to be absorbed by darkness. "Are you sure? Things aren't always as they seem. Mommy's down here too, but she's not an odalisque. She works on a chain gang in one of the waste furnaces in the Industrial Zone. Everything's recycled here, Daddy, including shit. They bake it in furnaces and turn it into bricks. That's where Mommy works, and she'll continue to work there until the end of time."

"This is a nightmare! That's all it is!" Carlton shrieked, spit flying off his lips.

"Think what you want. I have to go back now anyway. This is only a partial discarnation. But there's a reason why he let me come here today, even for just a few minutes. He sent me to tell you something."

He, Carlton thought again.

"He sent me to give you a message. This is the message: Behold the Messenger. The arrival of the Messenger is at hand."

Now the darkness seemed to howl.

"I have to go now, Daddy. It's been nice talking to you. But before I go, I want you to look in here. I want you to see me as I am now. I'm not a teenage girl anymore. I'm a seasoned odalisque."

Carlton's mind was spiraling. All he could make out was the splotched silhouette. "I can't! It's too dark!"

Suddenly the flashlight snapped back on. The light blared all around him.

Then he screamed when he pointed it into the hole.

Belinda was no teenage girl now, she was a mature

woman—a woman, yes, and more. She lay naked within the recess, her sleek body and long legs stretched out lazily over what first appeared to be a couch but as Carlton let his vision focus he saw that the couch was formed of severed hands. Some of the hands appeared to be human, some clearly were not. Some sported more than five fingers, others had just two or three. Some were taloned. Some were flaked with snakelike scales, some covered with tumors, mold, or nameless filth, while still others were mummified or decomposed down to bone.

Then Carlton noticed something else: the hands were moving. This demonic couch of hands was alive.

Belinda's heavy breasts sat flawlessly erect even though she was lying down. Sweat coated her body thick as glycerin; her poreless perfect skin shone white as summer clouds, a stunning contrast to large, blood-red nipples and flame-orange eyes. Her hair seemed luminous, hanging in yard-long, sun-blond tresses off each shoulder. She moaned, closed-eyed, grinning like a cat. Her buttocks, legs, and back squirmed in the most erotic luxury—it was the hands, all those severed but living hands caressing her from underneath, kneading her flesh. Carlton's eyes roamed up his daughter's elegant body to her face.

Blushing-pink horns sprouted from her forehead, and in the pre-orgasmic grin, Carlton saw fangs and a slender forked tongue. Eventually she pulled two hands from the moving mass—a demonic hand and one that seemed octopod—then sighed when she placed them on her breasts. The hands kneaded her independently, coaxing more waves of writhing pleasure. Finally she picked up a third hand—a large human one—and began to masturbate with it.

The image blared bright as headlights in his face.

"Good-bye, Daddy. I'll see you again some day. And remember what I said. Remember *his* holy message."

Carlton's heart felt like a dying lump.

"The arrival of the Messenger is at hand . . ."

And then she was gone.

The vision vanished, leaving Carlton alone in utter silence. The cubby seemed cold, like a walk-in refrigerator, and the flashlight's beam reflected off the narrow walls so brightly it was hurting his eyes. *I must've fallen asleep or something,* he told himself, *and had a nightmare.* And what a nightmare it had been, the cruelest invention. How could his mind manufacture something so awful?

The imaginary bracelet, too, was gone. None of it had been real. All that remained was the square hole in front of him, the panel of which he'd knocked out previously. He took a few moments to still his mind, to let the remnant images of horror evaporate, then looked at the hole again.

I can't leave it like that. Gotta put that panel back in.

He crawled forward, moved his head and shoulders into the opening, and roved his light around. The space beneath the post office seemed vast but totally empty. No pipes, no wires, nothing he might expect. He didn't even see the panel. It must've fallen below the opening.

For whatever reason, and as hard as he was trying to forget the illusion of his lost daughter, the vision's strange words dripped back into his head for a mere second:

Behold the Messenger. The arrival of the Messenger is at hand.

When Carlton leaned farther into the opening, he saw the space wasn't *totally* empty.

There was something there. He reached forward to touch it.

It looked like a box.

Chapter Two

(I)

Marlene always had to have her morning coffee, a big one. Always black, no frills. So that's what she got today, at the Qwik-Mart two blocks down from the main post office.

The only difference between today and any other day was this:

Marlene didn't work at the main post office anymore. She worked at the west branch office, which had only opened yesterday.

She looked the same. Short, pretty, mocha-brown eyes, and buffed straight hair that could be called dark blond or light brunette, depending on the light. She was in excellent physical condition, after a decade with the post office; half of her delivery shift had always been in a vehicle, but the other half was on foot, which left her legs toned and tan. Many an eye regularly glanced back at her official post-office shorts, and at the light blue top that always seemed strained across a more-than-adequate bosom. In her mid-thirties now, Marlene looked as desirable as any woman in town a decade younger.

"Marlene," said Marvic, the gray-bearded proprietor of the Qwik-Mart. He was from the Balkans, and had an interesting accent, which sounded part-German and part-Arabic. "Please do not take this the wrong way, but you do fine justice to those shorts."

Marlene smiled, nonchalant, as she pulled the plastic cut-out tab from her coffee lid. "Thanks, Marv. My husband tells me the same thing every morning but he has an easier way of saying it. He just tells me I've got a killer ass."

"I would definitely concur with that."

"Well, I better go, Marv. Work's two blocks away, and I'm late."

"But wait. I thought you mentioned yesterday that you no longer work at the main post office."

"That's right, Marv. I got reassigned to the west branch."

"But that's on the other side of town, isn't it?"

"Sure is. I just have something to drop off here first. Have a good day!" Then she left the store, knowing Marvic's eyes were following her. Marlene appreciated the compliment. It made her feel positive about herself. It made her feel complete.

A few minutes later, she was parking in the front lot of the main post office. She paused a moment in the sun, to look at the long and rather sterile brick building. The west branch looked so much nicer even though it was so much older. The west branch was quaint, its drab bricks painted a vibrant white, with pastel blue trim, and children's art work from the local elementary school adorning the front windows.

But this place . . .

This place looks like shit, Marlene thought with rare profanity. It wasn't even her own voice in her head, but she wasn't capable of comprehending that. It was something else.

And the people inside . . . are shit.

The voice darkened.

It's time, my lovely Marlene. It's time to deliver a message, isn't it?

"Yeah," Marlene replied to herself in a hushed voice.

The motion-sensitive front doors parted; Marlene walked into cool air, so cool in fact, her nipples seemed to pucker. The sensation struck her with such intensity that she thought obliquely of her husband—the way he'd come up behind her by surprise, slip his arms around her, and tweak her nipples. Yes, yes, that's exactly what it felt like—

Someone standing right behind her. Right up against her. Pinching her nipples.

But that was impossible. Even Marlene, in the strange daze that had struck her since yesterday when she'd gotten off her first shift at the west branch, knew that no one was standing right behind her.

"Hi, Marlene!" said Emmy, her friend at the first teller window. The line of familiar customers looked over, too, and all smiled and waved. "How was your first day at the new office?"

"Oh, it's great. I love it."

"But I'll bet you miss this place don't you? Just a little?"

Marlene shot her friend the warmest smile. "Of course, and I miss working with you guys too. A lot."

Really, really? she thought in that weird voice again, the voice that seemed like her own but with another voice hissing behind it.

You don't miss this place. You don't miss these people.

Marlene frowned to herself.

And they won't miss this world . . .

"Well, we miss you too," Emmy went on, stamping a postmark onto a customer's package. "But it's all for the best. Opening the west branch really takes a lot of the workload off us. I still can't believe how much Danelleton has grown in the past year."

"Yeah," Marlene muttered.

She was just standing there. Staring.

"So what are you doing out our way?" Emmy asked.

Marlene almost felt as though she were hovering. It took her several moments to answer: "Oh, I just . . ." Then a long pause.

Emmy cast a concerned look past the register. "Marlene? Are you all right?"

Now Marlene's eyes felt hot, like coals punched into her eye sockets. Her words droned from her mouth. "I just stopped by to say hi."

Emmy was squinting over, and so were several customers in line.

"Plus I needed to drop off this package."

"A package?" asked another teller. "For us?"

"Yeah. Special Delivery," Marlene said.

Marlene stood wavering in place, yet she felt quite secure in what she was about to do. That voice in her head, too—part hers, part someone else's—etched with confidence. *I am the Messenger. Bring my message . . .*

Again, she felt as though someone were standing right behind her, surely a male figure, for she could still feel his incorporeal hands running up and down her sides and sweeping up over her breasts. Were someone to be looking closely, they'd be able to see it, the most minute indentations sliding up against the fabric of her work shirt.

"Marlene, what is wrong with you?" Emmy said more sharply now. "And what's this about a package? What, something of ours got misdelivered to your branch?"

"No," Marlene said, now swooning at the invisible touches. For the briefest moment, she cast an eye aside, at the long front window, and in it she glimpsed her reflection.

She glimpsed someone else's reflection too.

Someone standing directly behind her. A man, or something *like* a man. With his hands on her. The image was almost translucent, like an outline in distant fog. Then the nearly shapeless hands of that outline slid down Marlene's arms, to her own hands. The figure began to move her hands down.

"No," she repeated. "Not really a package. It's a message."

From her mailbag, Marlene withdrew an Ingram MAC-11 submachine gun. It was compact, weighed just over three pounds, and was scarcely larger than a typical pistol.

Until she snapped in the high-capacity forty-seven-round magazine. No one screamed at this point, they simply stared through a paralyzing hush.

Marlene yanked back the charging handle with a metallic crack.

"Behold the Messenger," she said, and that's when everyone in the lobby began to scream. She fired in controlled bursts, three 9mm rounds slammed into Emmy's chest, then three more at the second teller, who'd been ducking but not quite in time. The bullets took off the top of his head and sent it across the room like a hairy Frisbee.

Yes, she heard in her head. *Yes. Yes.*

With the tellers dead, Marlene grinned and turned about. Her technique was tactically sound: she stood at the entrance door, the only exit for the remaining customers who were all screaming and backing up. Several tried to vault over the counter but when they did so, Marlene picked them off.

Then she opened up on the crowd in the corner.

She fired bullets as though she were spraying a garden hose. Her once pretty face was now twisted up like a grinning wooden mask. For some reason she didn't hear the weapon's earsplitting reports, and as she swerved the spray of bullets into the crowd, their screams faded to a muffled silence.

Gun smoke rose like tear gas. The smoke amplified the details of the mirage standing behind her; at one point she looked down and saw bony yellow-skinned hands with long-manicured black nails wrapped around her own hands as she grasped the gun, the long triple-jointed yellow finger pulling her trigger finger back.

Marlene emptied the clip into the mass of humans, then she smacked in another forty-seven-rounder and emptied that. By the time she was done, the pile of collapsed post-office customers looked as though they'd been run over by an aerating machine. A puddle of blood the size of a kiddie pool oozed out across the floor.

Bring my message to them all . . .

Marlene smacked in the next clip, then walked calmly around the counter and entered the office and processing areas.

More staccato gunshots rang out, more gun smoke rising. Empty cartridges sprayed into the air in a golden arc. A few minutes later, the police charged in.

(II)

The blond newscaster looked more like one of those girls on an E! Channel beach show. The smart burgundy business dress didn't work with the implanted breasts, platinum hair, and rich tan. Yet she held the microphone like a stoic, and spoke like one too, as ambulance and police lights flashed in the background, vehicles all parked askew in front of the main branch.

"*. . . an unimaginable tragedy today at the Danelleton main post office on Rosamilia Avenue. Longtime* *employee Marlene Troy allegedly entered the office at approximately 9 A.M., withdrew an automatic weapon, and opened fire . . ."*

One after another, EMTs exited the building, bearing stretchers laden with black body bags. Trails formed of dots of blood tracked out to the lot, along with bloody footprints. The next shot showed the inside of the lobby after the bodies had been extricated: more footprints and gurney marks running out of a pool of blood that stretched nearly to the front doors. Gallons of blood must have been spilled there. Higher, on the back walls, more dots could be seen, not dots of blood but rip-stitch lines of bullet holes.

"Authorities are mystified as to what might have caused the frenzied slaughter," the newscaster went on. Next, the scene cut back to the front of the main branch, where more police hovered with clipboards and evidence-collection material. And in the foreground, more EMTs loaded covered stretchers into ambulances. *"The official death toll is twenty-six, with no survivors of this hideous and inexplicable rampage."* To highlight bad taste, the camera homed in closer on one of the stretchers. By now, authorities had run out of body bags and resorted to sheets. The sheet over the current body was nearly saturated with blood, and when the stretcher was hoisted up to be pushed into the ambulance, an arm flopped out from under the sheet. The top of the sleeve was patched with the emblem of the U.S. Post Office.

"The alleged assailant, Marlene Troy, is said to have opened fire first in the crowded lobby, trapping over a dozen residents and killing everyone in a matter of min-

utes. *Then Troy reloaded, swept the rest of the facility with gunfire, and killed the remaining occupants, all postal employees. Danelleton police responded shortly thereafter and gunned Troy down in one of the loading bays. She was reported dead on arrival at South County General Hospital."*

Jane Ryan bowed her head, finally looking away from the television screen. Her expression had gone from appalled to mystified. The brand-new office she sat in felt like an isolation chamber. She was unable to believe what was happening just a few miles away at the main branch.

"Marlene was one of my best carriers," she said. "We worked together for five years in Pasco County. She's always been one of the most stable people I've known, not just a quality employee but a wonderful person."

Jane wiped a tear from her eye, then snapped off the television with the remote. An older man sitting at the side of the desk seemed to be commiserating: Buchanan, the county postal superintendent.

"I know how you must feel, Jane," he said. "When I got my first PM promotion in California, I had a carrier walk off his route and kill four people in a fast-food joint. Turns out he'd been cracking up for months over his wife leaving him, then he got into cocaine. Nobody knew. I guess sometimes people just snap. Doesn't matter why. Stress, mental illness, drug and alcohol problems. No town is immune to it—it can happen anywhere."

The words didn't allay her grief and confusion. Nothing could. It just didn't make sense. Tragedies like this always happened somewhere else. All Jane could do was nod, repressing the her sobs.

"Anyway, we're all done here with the paperwork for now. If you need anything let me know."

"Okay."

Buchanan was about to leave, to carry on with his own arm of the investigation, but he stopped just short of the door. "Oh, and there's a cop out here who'd like to talk to you. One of the local ones. You feel up to talking to him? I'm sure you probably don't but you're going to have to eventually."

Dread swept over her, but she forced herself to straighten up. She wiped her nose with a Kleenex, fixed her hair as best she could.

"I'm fine. Go ahead and send him in."

Buchanan cast her a last consoling glance, then quietly left the office. A few seconds later, the door clicked back open, and a shadow crossed the floor.

"Ms. Ryan?"

The man Jane looked up at stood tall and lean, in dark slacks, white shirt, and a tie. He looked far more like an engineer or computer executive than a police officer; in fact, the only hint of his actual profession was the police badge clipped to his belt. Jane guessed him to be in his early forties. Short sandy hair, perennial Florida tan. Something about his eyes—intense and bright blue—seemed contrary: The hard-line cop was either confused or damaged.

But damaged by what?

"I'm Steve Higgins, chief of Danelleton police," he announced. "I know this is a bad time, Ms. Ryan, but I guess there never really is a *good* time for such things."

Jane shook his hand from behind her desk. "No, there isn't."

"I'm sorry we have to meet under such unpleasant circumstances, but I need to ask you some questions about Marlene Troy."

Simply hearing the name in the context of this aftermath shocked her. It reminded her that this was all real. *An employee and a friend just went on a killing spree*, she had to keep telling herself. *There's just been a mass murder in our town, and the killer was someone from my post office* . . .

"Had Ms. Troy ever exhibited any . . . strange behavior in the past? Mood swings? Outbursts? Things like that?"

"No, no. I was just telling my district supervisor that Marlene was an exemplary carrier as well as a very nice person."

"Any disputes with other employees?"

"No. Everybody liked her."

"Any problems with the law that you know of? I mean, before working here? Her Florida record's clean but are you aware of any infractions in the past? Anything she might've mentioned, even just in passing, say, from her teens, early adulthood, college? We're particularly interested in any history of drug use or alcoholism."

Jane just shook her head no.

"Do you know anything about her religious beliefs, Ms. Ryan?"

Jane peered up at him. What a strange question, but come to think of it, she didn't recall ever hearing Marlene mention any spiritual beliefs. Odder than the question, though, was the tone with which Steve had asked it. As though it were a loaded question of some kind. "I'm totally unaware of any of Marlene's religious beliefs," Jane finally answered after a bit more thought. "I can't ever remember her saying anything about it. For all I know, she *had* no religious beliefs."

Steve looked puzzled, withdrawing a slip of paper from his pocket. He unfolded it, looked at it a moment, then passed it to Jane.

"Does this design mean anything to you, Ms. Ryan? Have you ever seen it in relation to anything that might have to do with Marlene Troy?"

Jane gave the paper a look of puzzlement. It was a drawing, a sketch in black ink, crudely but deliberately formed, clearly not by an artistic hand. It looked like a cup with a flanged edge, and hovering at the top of the cup was a single asterisk-like star. The drawing, in fact, seemed manic, desperate.

"I don't get it," Jane said. "A sketch of a cup."

"Sorry, other way," and he quickly took the paper, turned it around, and gave it back to her. "Not a cup, we don't think."

No, Jane saw. Now that the sketch inverted, it was easier to guess what it was. "A bell?"

"It would seem so."

"A bell with a star at the edge," she observed. "How strange. There's just something about it . . ."

"Yes, there is. Hard to say what, but I know what you mean."

It's just . . . creepy.

"Is that design familiar to you in any way, Ms. Ryan?"

Jane snapped out of a fog. "No, Chief Higgins. I've

never seen anything like this before in my life. What *is* it?"

Steve paused, almost as if he were hedging something. "It's best that I just say this design pertains to the evidence on the scene."

"You found this at the main post office?"

"No, no, I mean secondary evidence. We found it at Marlene Troy's house after the shooting."

Jane gasped, a shock seizing her. "Her house . . . my God. I didn't even think of it until now, but Marlene has a husband and a son in grade school," and then an edgy despair set in. *They'd have to be told right away, if they hadn't been already.* How do you deliver a message like that? It was always the same, she supposed. A police officer would come to the house, grim-faced, and say something like *I'm sorry to have to tell you this, but. . . .*

To this, Jane could relate quite well, forced to recall the time not so long ago when a state trooper had come to *her* door. To notify her that her husband was dead.

"Have you already notified her husband and son?" she asked.

Another pause from Steve, and a discomfited look on his face. "That's what makes all this even worse—no notification will be necessary. It appears that Marlene Troy stabbed both her husband and son to death this morning before she left for work. Both were mutilated." Steve closed his eyes for a moment. "It looked like she'd painted the walls with their blood."

Jane felt numb for the rest of the day; the shock was wearing off, replaced by a cold disillusionment. Details of the case haunted her, the murders of Marlene's husband and, even more particularly, the son, Jeff, who knew Jane's own children. A mass murder of adults was awful enough, but the murder of a kid? It just made the worst thing seem that much more insane.

When she locked her office at the west branch, the rest of the building was grimly silent, even though the crew in back was still working. She pulled out of her parking spot and switched on the radio, hoping for some cheerful music but instead got: " . . . *the latest on today's horrific murders in a Danelleton, Florida, post office, where an employee in good standing opened fire on a crowd of customers with an automatic weapon, and then proceeded to kill everyone else in the building—*"

Jane changed stations: " . . . *thirty-six-year-old Marlene Troy, known to coworkers as a friendly, diligent, and level-headed postal carrier, carried out the most tragic one-day killing spree in Florida histor. . . .*"

Jesus! Jane punched another button: " . . . *stabbed and mutilated her husband and young son in their beds before killing twenty-six people with a machine gun . . . *"

Jane snapped the radio off, grinding her teeth.

She drove through downtown, hoping it would clear her mind, but the peaceful city, and its appearance of sheer normalcy, only reinforced the horror of the day. Things were *never* as they seemed. People were *never* as they seemed. Danelleton *seemed* like the most tranquil—and sane—town anyone could imagine. *But look what happened*, she thought. Insanity could be the only explanation—and insanity was undetectable in most cases.

In *this* case.

The street along the pier, faced by its row of shops, looked abandoned. Only few passersby could be seen strolling, but they were all sullen, hunched. *This town is a mask*, Jane thought, *just like any town could be. Normal on the outside, but who knew what was really on the inside? Anyone, any of these normal-looking people, could snap, could go out of their minds the same way Marlene did*.

She shoved the thought away. Ordinarily she would've driven straight home to see her children, who'd be home from the recreation center by now, but something unbidden steered her away from the main road out. She was driving around the block, pulling in and parking at the main branch post office . . .

The EMTs were gone, all the bodies had been carried off. Several police cars remained, along with an evidence van. The long brick building looked monotonous, cold, even in the blaze of sun, nothing like Jane's cheerful, brightly painted west branch facility. Again, it was appearances that miffed her: true. The main post office looked like a lot of federal facilities—rather somber—but it didn't look like the site of a mass murder. Jane couldn't come to terms with what had happened here this morning.

A uniformed police officer stopped her, noticing her postal uniform. "Sorry, ma'am. This is a restricted crime scene."

For a reason she couldn't place, Jane felt that she

needed to go inside. She'd worked at this building for years but now, after what had happened, she felt she *had* to go back inside. "I'm Jane Ryan," she said, distracted. "I'm the postmaster at the west branch." She showed the cop her ID. "I knew a lot of the people who were killed. Could you let me go in for just a minute, please?"

The cop contemplated her request. "Sure, Ms. Ryan. But there are still a few evidence people inside, so try to keep out of the way. And try to make it quick, too. When they're done, they're going to seal the building."

"Thank you."

He let her pass the cordons, and then she was wandering into the lobby.

Dead silence stared back at her when the doors swooshed closed. It was very cold; Jane shivered as she walked disconcertedly past the stamp machines and the P.O. box coves. Then she heard voices.

The glass door to the customer service area had been propped open. Jane began to smell something that reminded her of disinfectant. Two men in blue utilities meandered within, one holding a large plastic evidence bag heavy with spent bullet cartridges, the other holding something that looked like a tackle box.

"Guess that's it," one of the technicians said. "The cleanup crew did a hell of a job with this place, huh? They should get a fuckin' trophy."

"Shit, all that blood?" the one with the cartridge bag replied. "I hope they wore hip-waders."

A detached laugh. "Better them than us."

"You got that right. And it's hard to believe there was a pile of dead bodies in here just a few hours ago. I've been working CES for ten years, six of 'em in Miami, and I've *never* seen that many bodies in one place. They'll be working overtime at the county morgue tonight, you can bet your ass."

"You see the one chick they were hauling out of here—one of the last ones? It was one of the employees working in back."

A grim dip in the response. "Oh, the pregnant one . . ."

"Man, I could shit my pants when I think about what this world is coming to. And this one was a *woman*. How many times you see that—a *chick* on a shooting spree?"

"Never. Chalk up another one to PMS."

"It's getting so you can't tell the crazies from the normal people. Christ, *my house* was on this woman's route."

"Makes ya wonder, you know? She carves up her hubbie and kid like lunch meat, then comes here and rip-stitches the place like it's the fuckin' Valentine's Day Massacre. Shit, man."

"And you gotta wonder . . ."

"What?"

"This sort of shit can happen any place, any time."

A laugh broke the profane solemnity, but it was a strained laugh. "Next time it could be me. Could be you."

"Could be anyone."

A pause, for a last look around, then: "Come on, man. Let's get out of this fuckin' slaughterhouse."

Jane's distracted daze snapped when the morose banter ended. She didn't want to be seen by them, and she didn't want to be here anymore. In fact, she still wasn't sure why she'd come in at all.

She grabbed her cars keys and rushed out of the building, hoping to never have to enter it again. Even though all the bodies had been transported out hours ago, it felt to Jane as though she were fleeing a mass grave.

Chapter Three

(I)

The two children would've otherwise been a perfect picture. Standing quietly, respectfully, hands folded before them. The eight-year-old boy—his name was Kevin—dressed neatly in a navy blue blazer with gold buttons, gray slacks, a blue-and-gold-striped tie. His almond-brown bangs were combed just right, not a hair out of place. Kevin was a well-behaved boy (at least most of the time) and even though he didn't fully understand what was going on here—or what had happened—he knew that it was important for him to be good today. Not a peep was heard from him.

Standing next to him, just as tidily, was his eleven-year-old sister, Jennifer. Tall and slim, with the same eyes as her brother, she looked like a perfect young

lady in her navy skirt with a gold butterfly-chain belt
and flowered slate-blue sleeveless top. A coffee-
colored ponytail hung down to her belt line, held with
a pretty hair band. But Jennifer *was* old enough to
know the importance of remaining quiet and being
good at this place.

They were in Winter-Damon Cemetery, just outside
of Danelleton.

She'd been to a graveside service in a cemetery
once before, to see her father buried.

Finches chirped obliviously in the tall shade trees
surrounding that section of the graveyard. A high sun
shone through the trees, in a sky blotted snow-white
with trace clouds. A refreshing breeze slipped through,
taking some of the heat out of the air.

A stoic minister stood before the three coffins, his
voice resonating:

"Remember thy servants, O Lord, Marlene and
Michael and Jeff, according to the favor which thou
bearest unto thy people—"

Jennifer took Kevin's hand, gripping it reassuringly.

"—and whosoever liveth, and believeth in Him shall
not perish but have everlasting life—"

The minister closed his tasseled prayer book, then
extended his hands without missing a beat.

"—through Jesus Christ, to whom be glory, forever
and ever. Amen."

In unison, the standing crowd around the triple
grave responded, "Amen."

Jane put her arm around the two well-dressed children, hugging them close. Jane was their mother.

Yes, she knew Jennifer was old enough to comprehend the funeral, and she hoped that Kevin was too. Kevin had been too young to attend her husband's funeral, but now, after much delicate explaining, the boy had a concept of death. Jennifer had been a trouper about this, perhaps grasping more. She recalled her father's burial and she specifically asked to attend this one. The first fact of life was death—all children had to learn about it. But what bothered Jane were the *circumstances* here. Her children had known Marlene's son. Now the son was dead, and it had been his mother who'd killed him.

How could children ever fully understand that?

"It's all over, kids," Jane said softly. "We can go home now."

Jane led the children down the winding path toward the cars, nodding briefly to other mourners she knew. Jennifer and Kevin kept silent, still confused by the day and the redundant comments by others as they left, like: "Life goes on," and "They're all in a better place now." Blue-haired old Mrs. Baxter, one of the town's fussbudgets, limped contentedly by on her cane, observing, "It's all God's will, we can't question that. The Lord works in mysterious ways." Jane smiled curtly, hurt by her son's perplexed expression. How could she ever explain anything—especially anything about God or spirituality—on a day like this?

I just want to get out of here, she thought. From far off, a bell tolled, and its lonely peal snagged her. It made her think of that bizarre sketch Steve Higgins had shown her.

A sketch of a bell.

What had that been all about? Something the police

had found at Marlene's house. Even more bizarre was Steve's tone of voice when he talked about it. So ambiguous. It seemed as though the police chief didn't want to reveal everything he knew about the sketch.

The service was disbanding. Not too long from now, Jane knew, the three coffins would be lowered into the ground and buried, Marlene and her family gone forever. More facts of life in death.

"Look, Mom," Jennifer finally cut into the silence.

"What, honey?"

"There's Carlton."

Jane saw her new manager standing between several parked cars on the path. He stood alone, in a somber dark suit, and was staring off.

"Carlton's cool," Kevin said. "He knows all the cheat codes for *Tech Warrior*."

It was the name of some video game; Carlton would sometimes come over and entertain the kids with his gaming skills.

"Hi, Carlton!" Kevin called, waving.

But Carlton didn't notice their approach. He remained there staring off into the distance.

"Hey, Mom, is Carlton okay?" her son asked.

"He looks a little out of it," Jennifer added precociously. "I guess he's depressed about Marlene too."

Jane squinted as they got closer. *Yeah, he looks out of it, all right.* More than that. Was he drunk? Carlton stood awkwardly, as if tilted, hands limp at his sides. He seemed to be squinting up at the sky. At one point, he grinned, muttered something inaudible to himself, then his face reverted to a blank stare. The kids noticed this too.

"Hi, Carlton!" Kevin said again.

And again Carlton didn't hear him.

Jane walked up to him. "Carlton? Are you all right?"

The man blinked, winced, then abruptly acknowledged her. "Oh, hi, Jane. Hey, kids."

"You looked off in space. Are you okay?"

"Yeah, sure. I'm just a little . . ."

"Out of it?" Jennifer said.

Carlton smiled, then patted Kevin's head. "Yeah, I guess you're right. Not feeling too hot is all, and then all this . . ."

"I know, Carlton. We're all a little out of sorts. Who could figure something like this?"

"Yeah. I still can't believe it."

Jane looked at him more closely. *He really doesn't look well.* Carlton's face looked drawn, pale, eyes tired. "Look kind of sick, Carlton," she said. "If you want to take a few days off, that's fine with me. No offense, but you look like you could use it."

"No, no, I'm fine. And, after all, we've got a brand-new post office to run, plus we'll be doing double-duty while the police have the main branch closed. Besides, I want to work. It keeps my mind off things."

Jane knew what he meant. "I guess the only thing any of us can do is pick up the pieces and move on."

Kevin tugged at Carlton's jacket sleeve. "Carlton, can you come back to the house and play me in a *Tech Warrior* death match?"

Jane frowned. "Honey, I don't think Carlton's feeling up to video games today."

"Nonsense," Carlton said. "Come on, Kevin. I can always go for a death match."

"And you can watch me feed Mel," Jennifer said. Mel was the family's pet toad.

Jane shook her head. "I can't believe how much you guys enjoy feeding crickets to that thing."

The four of them headed back down the path, still uncomfortable but coming to grips with the fact they'd never see Marlene or her family again. *Jeez*, Jane thought. *What can you do?*

"Hey, Mom"—suddenly there was a tugging at her belt—"who's that weird-looking guy over there?" Kevin said.

"Where?" Jane and Carlton said at the same time.

Kevin pointed toward a stand of trees, then lowered his finger, confused. "He was there a second ago."

"I saw him too," Jennifer said. "He had long hair and a beard."

"He looked really creepy," Kevin added.

Carlton walked over to the trees, looked behind them. "There's no one here, kids. No creepy guy with long hair and a beard."

Jane frowned, urged the children toward their car. "He was just someone attending the service. Forget about it, honey."

Carlton caught up with them. "He probably got in his car and left."

Kevin kept looking over his shoulder as they moved off, unconvinced. "It was really weird, though, Mom."

"What, honey?"

"That man. . . . he was staring right at you."

(II)

He was staring right at her. Actually, *through* her, not at her, with that strange hinge-like noise in his head. Everything he felt was wrong—he didn't know which auguries to trust and which to dismiss. It always came to him in his mind and dreams.

He knew that the Messenger was near.

God in Heaven, he thought and almost laughed out loud.

His name was Dhevic. He was a large man. He came from many places but felt rooted to no place in particular. Location was relative. For him, his life was a mission that ignored geography, society, and even culture. He had his instincts and his blood; he needed little else.

Worse for wear now, gray etching his beard and shoulder-length hair, he moved off, doubting that he'd even been seen by the woman. Would she be next? The blood in his brain gave him no inkling. Or would she just be more fodder? It was hard to tell these days—Dhevic was getting old.

He slipped away quickly, light on his feet in spite of his height. He didn't like to remain in graveyards long— the dead soured his visions. They sometimes whispered the most forbidden—and atrocious—things.

Have to get out of here . . .

Dhevic drove off, wondering about the attractive woman named Jane Ryan. *Maybe I'm just reading too much into things,* he thought. It was always so hard to tell. He shouldn't be thinking at all, because it was the thinking that made him see.

In his mind he'd seen the other one and the ensuing bloodbath, a festival of carnal horror. Marlene. He saw what she saw, felt what she felt. She'd cut her husband's throat to the bone while they'd been having sex, riding him like a gasping beast, thrusting down on him as blood shot from the riven throat. Then she'd finished herself off in her glee, masturbating wildly over his corpse. She'd rolled around in his blood, covering every inch of herself: hair drenched red like a mop, grinning face smeared red, her breasts erect and shining in bright, bright red. She'd already butchered her son but for her husband she took extra care. Her scarlet hands wielded the knife not with rage or hatred but with great passion, great love, and as she worked, taking out parts and opening him deeper, she felt caressed from behind by someone who felt that same passion and love for her, or at least it seemed that way. Marlene couldn't see this person but she knew he was there almost as though he were part of her, almost as though his hands were on hers, guiding them in her tasks. She would be caressed later by the same entity, when she delivered her message and machine-gunned the main branch post office.

There wasn't much left of her husband when she was done—a carved carcass, innards placed all about the room, face deftly removed and hung on the bathroom doorknob. She stood up and cast a final glance at her work and wished she could bring him back to life, just to fuck him and kill him all over again. Cut him up all over again because she knew how much it would please the Messenger.

Everything was messages. Everything was secrets. It had been Carlton who'd delivered that first message to her . . .

Carlton, Dhevic thought. The name invaded his mind, then the vision skewed, that familiar sound in his head—like the tiniest whine—that would not abate. The faint but steady ache in the pulp of his teeth.

Who was Carlton? *Wait!* The man he'd just seen back at the cemetery, with Jane Ryan and her children. That was the inkling Dhevic suddenly received, and he pulled his vehicle over to the shoulder, stopped, and closed his eyes to struggle through the pain.

The man in the cemetery.

Carlton.

Him, too, and then he began to see it all behind the lids of his eyes. A basement, cluttered. The man crawling out of some storage cranny. Sweating, patched with dust, knees and elbows scuffed and dirty. "What are you doing here, Marlene?" "I came to get my sorting boxes. What's . . . that?" No more talk, just vicious sex on the basement floor, each just short of strangling each other at the sweat-drenched moment of their climaxes, and that was how fast it happened. The Messenger had touched them both.

In Dhevic's mind he could see what was in *their* minds as they wrapped themselves up in one another: the most detestable images, images from someplace else, a charnel house the size of a thousand cities. A sound like crashing waves but then Dhevic realized that the sound was screams, hundreds of thousands of them, millions, squalling from every direction. The sound was endless.

Chaos. A living nightmare that never ended. Dhevic saw in flashes, white-edged images catapulted into his mind's eye. Things flying in the sky, things that were not birds. The sky was the color of arterial blood—it even seemed to *pump* like blood, behind soot-colored clouds and a black sickle moon. Figures in black armor marched in ranks down smoking streets, dismembering any poor soul who dared be out. Great swords and halberd shafts sang through the air in graceful arcs, lopping off heads, arms, severing bodies at the waist, cleaving others in half from head to crotch. On the ledges of the hundred-story ghetto blocks, griffins and gargoyles waited patiently for mongrel infants to be thrown from windows, tender meals to say the least. Infants were thrown from these windows quite regularly, in fact, by destitute mothers who were either damned humans, or demons, or mixes of both.

The Outer Sectors were uncharted but existed abstractly, in various dimensions, outside of the center of the Abyss. Parched fields of corrupt soil and infernal vegetation stretched for . . .

Well, no one knew. Mile-long chain gangs were a common sight in these regions, emaciated stick figures fettered together by welded cuffs and forced to work until there was nothing left of them but bones. Closer were rivers more vast than the Amazon, and bays and lakes larger than any ocean on Earth—only these bodies were filled with waste, filth, corpses, and

blood instead of water. The most unspeakable creatures lived in these depths.

Another image flashed, snapped into Dhevic's mind
with a sound like a stout branch cracking:

Marlene again. The living world behind her now, she
was entering her new eternal home through a field of
flames. She was naked, hair flowing and bright-eyed,
as beautiful as she'd ever been. A figure was waiting for
her, and when she saw it, she rejoiced. She ran to the
figure with open arms, her now-immortal heart beating with love.

The Messenger.

"Thank you for delivering my messages, Marlene,"
the entity said in a voice that was cosmic. "And you will
reap your reward now, as promised."

Marlene's expression went from one of love and total devotion to an expression of utter horror. The Messenger stood and watched as a horned, slug-skinned
demon came up from behind and chopped off Marlene's head with something like a cleaver. The head
was placed on a spiked stake alongside many, many
such heads. The heads were all still alive, some talking,
some drooling, some grinding their teeth or chewing
through their cheeks, all with their eyes still open, all
still seeing.

Marlene's head looked down from its perch and
watched more subordinate demons frolicking sexually
with her decapitated body.

The Messenger sighed, in bliss . . .

Dhevic passed out in his car seat. He wouldn't re-
gain consciousness for several hours.

(III)

Dinner was absolutely morose, but Jane expected that. *What do you talk about with your kids at the dinner table when you've just come back from a funeral? When one of the people buried was someone you knew, and that same person murdered her family and almost thirty other people?*

What did you talk about?

Everybody picked at their food, even Kevin. Jane had made his favorite meal, teriyaki meat loaf and deep-fried asparagus, which he usually devoured with gusto. Not tonight, though. Jennifer, on the other hand, always picked at her food (she was on a skinny kick lately, something going around school), but tonight she scarcely took a bite. Carlton had left earlier, after playing a game with Kevin and helping Jennifer feed the toad. Mel, a horrendously ugly horned toad, was actually Kevin's pet, but he let Jennifer feed it. (Kevin didn't want to admit that he was too squeamish for the feeding chores, which always required the sacrifice of a live cricket or mealworm.)

"So who won the game?" Jane asked, finally breaking the silence.

"No one, really," Kevin said. "Carlton wasn't really into it, and neither was I, I guess."

"What was wrong with Carlton today?" Jennifer asked, picking at an asparagus spear with her fork.

"Yeah, Mom. He was acting funny."

"And every now and then he'd kind of just . . . stare off," Jennifer said. "Sometimes I'd look at him and he'd have this weird look in his eyes. Did you notice that?"

Jane tried to rouse herself from her stupor. "He was just upset, honey. When things like this happen, people react in different ways. Carlton's worked with Marlene for a long time, just like I have. And there's another thing. The funeral probably reminded Carlton of something really bad that happened to him a long time ago."

"What, Mom?"

Oh, Jesus, why did I mention that! She fumbled for a way out but knew there was none. "Well, Carlton had a family, too, a wife and a daughter. I think that daughter was about the same age as Marlene's son. Anyway, his wife and daughter were killed one night in a car accident," and she didn't feel too bad about the white lie. They didn't need to know that the daughter was never found, probably abducted.

"Oh," Kevin said, thinking about what Jane had said, trying to understand. "But this is different. Marlene wasn't killed in a car crash. She was shot by the police."

Jesus, Jane thought once more.

A pause, then Jennifer said, "Why did Marlene do it?"

"Yeah, Mom. Why did Marlene kill all those people, and Mr. Troy and Jeff, too?"

All Jane could do was sigh at the impossible questions. "It's hard to explain. Sometimes something happens to people that makes them do bad things. Something happens in their brains. It's called mental illness. It makes a person's brain stop working right, and when that happens, sometimes people just—"

"You mean they go crazy?" Kevin said at once.

"Like that guy who killed Dad?" Jennifer added.

Jane faltered. Now the two tragedies were meeting on common ground, and that common ground was her children. Again, she didn't know what to say. She felt lost.

Oh, Matt, she thought.

Five years ago. She remembered it had been raining that night; she could hear it pattering on the roof. And she had a headache because it had been a week when she'd tried to swear off coffee. She remembered the door knocker clacking, irritatingly loud, which made the headache worse.

It was late. The kids were asleep and she'd been lounging on the couch. In spite of the headache, though, she'd felt wonderful. She was happy. She was in love. She had a good job, a beautiful home, and lived in a nice neighborhood. She had a wonderful husband and wonderful children. She had everything she'd ever dreamed of, everything a woman could ever want. She even remembered telling herself that. *How did I get so lucky? What did I do to deserve this? Thank you, thank you.*

Her husband, Matt, had just gone to the twenty-four-hour Qwik-Mart store, to get her some instant decaf. Before he'd left, they'd made slow and luxurious love right there on the couch, with the rain pattering in the background. She loved being that close to him, his heat beating into her—the contact, the passion—his touches revitalizing her. She squirmed beneath him, his hands ranging her body, then his mouth covering her, tending to every special spot until she was dizzy. When she couldn't stand it anymore, she'd opened her legs to him and dragged him into her. It didn't take long after that; Jane was already there, she was coming the moment he'd entered her, then more climaxes un-reeled when he stepped up his thrusts and came him-self. Slow, easy ecstasy. That's the way it always was for her when Matt was with her.

Afterward, she felt slaked. She couldn't get off the couch if she wanted to; she felt lazy and sleepy and full of his warmth. "I'll have you know," he said, dressing haphazardly in front of her, "I don't run out in the rain to get decaf for just *any* woman." "Just shut up and hurry," she replied. Her nipples tingled. "When you get back . . . we'll do it again." Matt nearly stumbled step-ping into his loafers and grabbing his keys. Jane had to laugh. Did he have his shoes on the wrong feet? He was gone a moment later.

Yes, I'm very, very lucky, she remembered thinking. Matt had landed a job with a good advertising firm downtown, which made the neighborhood even more perfect. Her own job was close, and the schools were right here too. She listened to the garage door go up, heard the car leave, then listened to more rain, revel-ing in the joy of her life.

The headache was a minor annoyance. She'd quit smoking, too, several years before, and it hadn't been that bad. She drifted in and out of sleep, seeing Matt in snatches of quick dreams, always smiling, his eyes al-ways so full of love for her. And—

RAP! RAP! RAP!

Knocking on the door jerked her out of the half-sleep. The headache flared. That's when it all came tumbling down.

". . . very sorry to have to tell you this, Mrs. Ryan, but it seems that your husband has just been killed . . ."

Killed. The word that had just come out of the state trooper's mouth sounded impossible. He stood there poker-faced in the doorway, his badge dripping, rain slicker glittering. No, he hadn't just said that word, not *that* word. Killed.

"Murdered, Mrs. Ryan. I'm very sorry to have to give you this news."

The next half hour she didn't remember at all. Like a dream that dragged on and on—a very bad dream—with pockets of blackouts that kept her doubting that there was any reality at all to this. She'd been taken away, in the state police car, to the county hospital. Batches of words kept flowing in and out of her attention: "... terrible time for you and your family ..." "... need you to come down to the county morgue ..." "... will be calling you shortly to ask you some questions ..." "... crisis counselors are available for you and your children ..." "... we need positive identification of the body ..."

Harsh white lights beat down on her, but the light felt cold. She could hear them buzzing overhead. Her raincoat dripped as she looked down.

A sheet flapped.

"Is this your husband, Mrs. Ryan?"

Jane stared. Just an hour ago, they'd been making love on the couch. His semen was still in her, she could feel it there, still vaguely warm—and now here was the same man. Dead on a morgue slab.

"The perpetrator escaped from the Danelleton Clinic. It's a private psychiatric hospital just outside of town. Raped a nurse and killed her, then killed two guards and somehow got the time-locked entrance door opened. From there, he escaped on foot. This was about ten o'clock this evening, Mrs. Ryan."

Jane was barely hearing him, but it was enough. Matt had left the house around eleven . . . *to get my decaf,* she thought, and just wanted to collapse and die right there on the spot.

"Fortunately the perpetrator was apprehended by the state police at approximately eleven-thirty. But by then . . ."

The trooper didn't finish. Jane knew what he meant to say. She finished for him. "By then it was too late. By then, Matt was already dead."

"I'm afraid so. It appears that your husband had just pulled into the convenience store near the town dock, that twenty-four-hour place. There were no other customers in the store at the time. The perpetrator had already entered and killed the cashier with a hunting knife he'd stolen from another store. Then he just waited for the first customer to walk in."

"Matt," Jane whispered, her face washed with silent tears.

"A silent alarm had gone off, and the police had already been dispatched. When they arrived, the perpetrator was attempting to start your husband's car."

What more need be said? Her entire life had been shattered in the space of an hour. By some psycho with a shoplifted hunting knife. The sheet over Matt's body was black plasticized fabric, not cotton, so there was no evidence of blood. Only his face had been uncovered, which she was grateful for, but a very dark part of herself was wondering: How exactly had he been murdered? Where had he been stabbed? Was it slow or quick, and how much pain had he suffered?

What had been his final thoughts in life?

These horrible things ran around Jane's head until she was nauseated. She was barely sentient when she scribbled her name at the bottom of some identification form for the coroner's office, then the state trooper was helping her out of the cold, harshly lit morgue suite. She staggered out, choking on sobs, dreading the horror that awaited, the horror of having to tell Jennifer and Kevin why Daddy was never coming home again. The worse horror was knowing that she'd never see him again, and that her last vision of him hadn't been when they were making love on the couch: It was Matt on a slab, dead, shrouded by a black sheet, his wounds unrevealed. When the trooper was helping her out she took a stray glance to her right and saw something in a clear plastic bag lying on a lab counter. It was a hunting knife—its blade covered with blood.

And then the memory was over and Jane was sitting at her kitchen table with her children, over food none of them wanted to eat. *These kids are to young too have to see murder again*.

Jane forced herself to eat another stalk of fried asparagus, acting as though she liked it, acting as though this were a normal dinner like everyone else in the world was having. "Well, yes, honey," she eventually answered her child's troubled question. "Like the man who killed your father. The man was very sick; he was mentally ill. And sometimes these things happen. Nobody knows why, really. Sometimes people are born that way, and sometimes something happens to them, in their minds, and they start doing really bad things. That's what happened to Marlene."

She looked at both their faces, hoping her explanation would help them but also knowing that it didn't. It didn't even come close. *If anything*, she realized, *they're just more confused now*.

"Anyway, kids, you both better get started on your chores before it's TV time."

"Okay, Mom," Jennifer said.

Kevin jumped up, ran to the other room, and returned a moment later holding a plastic terrarium. "Mel's gonna help me with mine, okay?"

Jane smiled meekly, glancing at the spiky horned toad. "Sure, honey."

"Cool! Then we can watch TV!" Kevin said. "I think that guy who wrestles alligators is on at eight!"

The boy's got reptiles on the brain, Jane thought. She smiled after them as they zipped out of the kitchen. *Thank God I have good kids*. She only hoped the whole ordeal with the killings didn't scar them for too long.

She picked up the dishes, elected to do them later, and meandered into the living room. She collapsed on the couch, then cringed, recalling what it would symbolize on a day like this: the last place she'd made love to Matt. What a mistake coming in here, but how could she get rid of the couch? All the images flooded back to her; they submerged her in the beauty of that night. First Matt's whispers of love into her ear as he kissed her neck, his hands touching very faintly at first, then so smoothly and firmly he could've been making a sculpture, forming every curve and every contour, every inch of her breasts. Desire pushed her nipples out, their tips so aroused they tingled as if pinched by tweezers. His kisses deepened, his heart stepped up as all that love began to surge for her. He was pushing her legs back, opening her first with his mouth, then entering her again, just as he had that night, her bliss reemerging as a crescendo.

Then the memory crashed.

It was all a lie. The last thing she saw behind her closed eyes as she lay on the couch was Matt's dead face in the county morgue.

The smallest gasp of despair escaped her throat.

Next, her eyes darted; she heard something, lightly at first, then with increasing volume. Pattering on the roof.

It was starting to rain.

Chapter Four

(I)

Carlton awoke as he normally did—alone. He hated it after all these years, but by now he was used to it. In fact, the idea of *not* waking up alone seemed alien. The clock glowed 4:12 A.M., yet it felt as though he'd only been asleep for fifteen minutes. *I wasn't drinking last night, was I?* he asked himself. The inside of his mouth and his lips tasted awful. His eyes felt like they had sand in them. *God, I feel like shit.* But he hadn't been drinking, had he? He'd been cutting down at lot lately. *Christ, if I was drinking last night, I'd remember . . .*

Wouldn't I?

He lay back, muggy in the bed. The air-conditioning droned yet his skin was clammy, stale with sweat. Something nagged at his brain, the notion that something bad had happened, a subconscious terror that cruelly refused to reveal itself, like a hideous face behind a dark veil. Had he dreamed it?

He fought to remember, gritting his teeth. Then, in visual wafts, like smoke, it replayed in his mind, image by grueling image.

He'd dreamed about Marlene.

Oh, God. It was true. How could he feel more ashamed? And the dream itself?

Carlton felt ill.

If dreams could have a smell, this dream *stank*. It made him mentally recoil, just as someone would physically recoil after stepping in wormy road kill on a hundred-degree day. In the dream, he hadn't been making love to Marlene, he'd been fucking her. Using her body as a receptacle for pleasure, not a person, a *thing* to placate his sex drive. He also knew that he didn't care about Marlene at all in the dream—it didn't matter that he knew her, it didn't matter that they were friends. Carlton discarded all that; in fact, he even hated her in the dream, hated her for being more than simply a luscious physical body with a hole for his needs. The soulless lust and hatred made him think of serial killers who murder the women they raped after they'd had their orgasm. Marlene's hands were at his throat as he thrust into her, and his were on hers. They were strangling each other as they bucked, and when Carlton came and looked down at her—expecting her to be dead—she grinned up at him in lust as perverse as his own. "Do it again," she panted, "do it again. Do it real hard this time, do it to me till I pass out. You can even kill me if you want—I don't give a shit. Just do it to me again." It was awful, it was so wrong, and in the dream part of him knew this—and was repulsed—but it didn't matter. The sexual Mr. Hyde in him had been tapped and was unloading full force—on her. They did it again and again and again, just like that, spending themselves and bringing each other to near-death at the brink of each demented climax.

Carlton had chuckled after finishing. She'd been on top for the last one, and he simply shoved her off on to the dirt-flecked floor, his handprints throbbing on her throat. Had he actually killed her this time?

He didn't care. He'd had his fun.

An even more forbidden idea began to occur to him as she lay there unmoving, but then her puffed eyes opened to slits, and she frowned.

"You are one dull lay, Carlton, Jesus Christ," she griped, and then she was up in a huff, beads of sweat flying off her flushed skin. Stomping away, putting her postal uniform back on, grabbing her route gear. Carlton particularly noticed her carrier bag, and . . .

What appeared to be the wire-stock of a small machine-pistol sticking out of it.

"Now I'm gonna go have some real fun, you asshole," she said, and left.

The dream's fringes were throbbing, like the choke marks on her throat, pinkish-blue around the edges. That's when Carlton noticed where the demented foray had taken place: in the basement of the newly re-opened west branch.

Awake now, head thumping as if hungover, he shivered at the nightmare in disgust. How could his mind create such a scenario? *Marlene was a friend, a coworker, and I just dreamed about having sex with her. Hard-core sex, like nothing I've ever had or would ever want to have. She'd been married, had a son. She'd been a good person.* Carlton had never felt so ashamed in his life. The shame tripled when he made this next observation: He was outrageously aroused.

What the hell is wrong with me?

A final image nagged him. It was something from the nightmare, but the nightmare had changed. It had changed places. The humid night beat down on him. He was standing outside, and could hear crickets. Mosquitoes buzzed around his head, some landing on his skin to taste his sweat and drink his blood. The moon shone behind him and in its light, when he looked down, he realized where he was.

A cemetery.

But not any cemetery. Winter-Damon Cemetery.

He realized what he was looking at.

Marlene's gravestone.

For a moment, just a single moment, he brought his hand to his erection in the most ultimate shame of all. But he stopped at the effort: His hand came away . . . gritty.

He jerked himself to one side, hugging the pillow, as if to turn away from all that disgust that his brain had produced. But . . .

The pillow felt gritty, too.

The awful taste in his mouth raged, and when he licked his lips . . .

They felt gritty.

Gritty as if with flecks of soil.

(II)

What a flippin' week, huh, Bobby? Bobby asked himself. He had a way of having conversations with himself, after so many years of first shift. *Who's on the mound for the Yanks tonight? Hmm, Bobby, I don't really know but I'd guess it's Mussina. Oh, yeah, I guess you're right.* Like that. He was a little screwy.

Bobby Weaver wasn't a carrier or anything. He was the maintenance supervisor for West Branch, more title than function, though. *Pretty funny, huh, Bobby? You ain't kidding, it's funny. Yeah, like who the flyin' flip do we supervise when we're the only maintenance employee in the flippin' building!*

You got that right, Bobby.

Bobby was typically the first employee in the building. Arrival time? 4:30 A.M. Bobby didn't mind. He made sure all the lights worked, prepped the sorting machines, cycled the circuits, that sort of thing. Not a hard job, but essential in its own way. The first dropoffs usually started coming in around five o'clock, so he had to get ready for that, too.

No biggie, right, Bobby? Naw, it's a walk in the park.

He whistled, going down his daily checklist. This building's unfamiliar look comforted him; until very recently he'd worked at the main branch, and nobody would ever forget what had happened there. *Yeah, can ya believe that shit, Bobby? Flippin' broad*

MACHINE-GUNS the main branch! Yeah, but AFTER offing her hubby and kid! No, neither of them could believe *that* shit.

Bobby didn't know her, really, he'd just seen her coming in each morning to do her pre-sort. Never saw her when she got off because his shift'd be over by then. *Seemed nice enough, though, huh, Bobby? Sure, and a looker too. Nice little apple-dumpling cart up front and not a bad bucket in back, either. Cut that shit out, Bobby! The broad's DEAD and you're rapping about her bod for chissakes! Yeah, sorry . . .*

Proof that it was a nutty world, though. A sure-fire, whacked-out flippin' world.

Bobby sighed. The last item on his checklist was always the kick in the tail. *Come on, Bobby. Let's go reload ALL the flippin' stamp machines out front. Aw, Christ, I HATE doing that. There's TEN machines out there!*

Tell me about it, Bobby.

Three-cent, thirty-seven-cent, Priority, Air, dollar stamps, ten packs, twenty packs, and hundred-stamp first-class rolls—all these slots had to be filled, the change removed, the changers topped off. Pretty tedious.

But there was nothing tedious about the rest of the day when Bobby waltzed into the vending lobby, keys in one hand, sack of packed stamps in the other, whistling *Dixie*.

He walked around the counters, passed the first rank of P.O. boxes, then stopped cold.

Dropped his keys.

Dropped the stamps.

Then all the blood drained out of his head from the vision of horror that stared right back into his face.

A woman was standing there in the corner of the vending cove, her arms spread out as if in wait for Bobby. She was naked and very pale. Hair that was a blend of blond and brunette straggled to her shoulders. Bobby thought for sure that some nutty homeless woman must've gotten into the post office, or some drug addict or something like that. What else could explain this woman being here, and in this state? Naked, ragged, pale?

But then Bobby recognized the woman . . .

It was Marlene Troy, who'd been killed by police a few days ago, and who'd just been buried.

Bullet holes full of clotted blood pocked her torso. Dirt clods hung in her hair, while more grave dirt peppered her skin. The woman was *dead* but she was standing there on her own. Her eyes were open, mortician's glue unseated, their whites jaundiced by embalming fluid. Bobby knew it was impossible but for a split second it seemed as though she'd blinked.

And her smile glimmered like newly honed cutlery.

These were the details Bobby noticed in those first few seconds. Then he fainted and collapsed to the floor. What he hadn't noticed, though, was the bizarre design scrawled on the floor at Marlene's feet: something that looked like a bell.

After Bobby fainted, Marlene Troy's arms fell limp at her sides, then the cadaver collapsed right on top of Bobby.

Chapter Five

(I)

Jane imagined what it must be like for some to, for instance, be standing on a street corner in broad daylight and suddenly witness a fatal car crash just yards away in the road. Instant death and calamity right before her eyes. That's how she felt at that moment in her office. The initial shock was gone now, leaving something worse, something like a colossal mental hangover, her disbelief colliding with the horror of what someone—someone in this same town—had done.

This . . . is . . . crazy, she thought.

Steve Higgins, the police chief, sat grimly opposite from her, a notepad on her desk, leaning over, jotting things down.

"This is absolutely disgusting. How could somebody do something like that? Digging up a dead woman and propping her body up in the lobby? What kind of a sick prank is that?"

"It could be more than a sick prank, Ms. Ryan," Steve said. "And it's pretty clear that Marlene Troy was into some stuff that no one knew about—some pretty off-the-wall stuff."

"Stuff," Jane repeated. She still couldn't believe it. "You mean occult rituals, satanism, demonology. *Stuff* like that."

"That's what it's looking like, isn't it? This isn't like some punk egging a bunch of cars or knocking over garbage cans. Somebody exhumed a corpse, brought it here, and drew occult markings on the floor."

"And they did it here, they brought the corpse *here*, to my post office," Jane said. "First, the tragedy at the main branch, and now this, here. It's crazy."

Steve nodded. "Calm down. At least we'll be able to keep this one out of the papers. The evidence team got the body out of here before any residents showed up. It's possible for the body to have been seen through the front window, but that early in the morning? If somebody *had* seen it—some guy walking his dog or out for a jog—then he would've called the police immediately. That didn't happen, so it's very important that all parties keep quiet about this."

"You sound like the mayor," Jane said with some bitterness. "Worried about the beautiful town of Danelleton getting a bad reputation."

"I couldn't care less about that, Ms. Ryan. It's simply that the fewer people who know about this, the better. We don't want to have to deal with the media; all that'll do is reduce the effectiveness of our investigation."

When Bobby Weaver had regained consciousness in the vending cove, half out of his mind, he'd shoved Marlene's body off and called the police. Steve and some subordinate officer arrived at once. The body was removed before any other postal employees had arrived. Steve had called Jane directly and now here she was, at 5:30 in the morning, just when the carriers and processing staff were coming in. When she'd arrived, Bobby was still being interviewed by a lieutenant, and Jane couldn't help but overhear some of the conversation.

"What's your explanation," she asked, "about what Bobby was saying before he left? He said the corpse *fell* on him. He said that Marlene's eyes were open, she was grinning at him. She was standing there holding her hands out, like she was still alive."

"She was in the ground for over twenty-four hours, Ms. Ryan. I guarantee you, she wasn't alive. She was killed by multiple gunshots—one of the bullets destroyed the left ventricle of her heart."

"But Bobby said she was *standing* there," Jane countered. "On her own. Then she collapsed on him."

"Let's not go off the deep end here. The medical examiner will be getting back to me later with a list of physiological prospects, but there are a lot of possible explanations right off the bat."

"Like what?"

"Postmortal rigidity, rigor mortis, things like that. Things like temperature, humidity, length of time that's passed since death, even ingredient concentrations of embalming fluid can determine the extent and duration of rigor mortis."

"You're saying that the body was still stiff and somebody propped it in the corner of the cove and it just stood there like a storefront mannequin on its own? Eyes open? Arms out? Grinning?"

"It's possible. Then the rigor wore off and the body collapsed."

"It collapsed *on top of Bobby?*"

"Why not? He'd already passed out from the trauma, he was already on the floor."

Jane frowned.

"Then we have to consider the reliability of the witness in the first place. That's quite a scare, isn't it? Wouldn't you be scared, wouldn't you be *terrified*, if you walked in here by yourself one day, turned the corner, and saw a dead body propped up in the corner? Wouldn't you be terrified?"

"Of course, but—"

"Traumas like that can do strange things to the human mind. Bobby was *terrified*. Bobby *thought* she was standing there with her arms out. Bobby *thought* her eyes were open and she was grinning. Some kind of trauma-based hallucination. Maybe the body had simply been left on the floor."

"Bobby said it was on top of him when he came to!"

Steve pitched a brow. "Bobby probably just thought it was. He was stressed out to the max, he was close to a clinical state of shock. The mind plays tricks on people in situations like that."

Jane eased back in her office seat. "I don't know. Maybe you're right. I guess I'm still not over the shock myself. Marlene killing her family then going on a shooting spree? Now this."

"I know." Steve seemed to be uncomfortable in his seat. "But let's talk about something else right now, okay?"

His tone and poised bothered her. "All right."

"For one thing, Marlene's body was exhumed. And the county forensics people knew right away that it was done with a shovel. That's *hard* work. That's a lot of effort for someone to go through, so that's how we know this isn't just a prank. And look what happened after that: The body was then transported from Winter-Damon Cemetery to your post office. That's a lot of risk."

"What are you getting at?"

"The body wasn't just dropped off out front, it was brought *inside* the building, supposedly before Bobby Weaver came on duty."

"Yes?"

"There are no signs of a forced entry. We've checked top to bottom. So that can only mean one thing. The person had access to the building's keys."

Something snapped in her mind. "I didn't think of that . . ." Another snap, and some alarm. "No, no way. You don't think it was Bobby Weaver? He's harmless. He's a little flighty sometimes, but I just can't see him doing *anything* like this."

Silence for a moment, then: "Let me ask you something. Is it possible that Marlene may have belonged to some sort of religious cult?"

The comment pissed Jane off. "I told you the other day. *No.* The idea is totally absurd. She was a mother, a resident in good standing, and a diligent, hard-working employee. She was probably the most normal, level-headed person I've ever worked with. A cult? What makes you ask that? The drawing of the bell you found at her house? It sounds to me like, if anything, she was the *victim* of some kind of cult. Maybe somebody abducted her, gave her some psychedelic drug that made her do those things. And as far as that design goes, do you even know that she was the one who drew it?"

"No, not yet, but we're checking. The Danelleton police department is pretty small; we're a municipal department, so we don't have our own crime-scene units and evidence techs. We have to rely on county and state services for that, and it takes a while. But the county graphologists are examining the first sketch right now. And don't forget, the same bell-shaped design was found here, too, this morning. Drawn on the floor in blood."

Jane couldn't help a little sarcasm. "Well, I guess we know she didn't draw that one, huh?"

Steve smiled faintly but just for a moment. "Yes, we definitely know that. But there are a lot of things we still don't know. For instance, who was the last person to have sex with her."

More sarcasm. "Well, I do know for fact that she was happily married, so—I don't know—I'll gamble here and say that her *husband* was the last person to do that."

"So it's inconceivable to you that Marlene Troy was seeing other men?"

"Yes. Very inconceivable."

"According to the county medical examiner, there were abundant traces of seminal fluid in her vaginal vault."

Jane pursed her lips as if she'd just sucked a lemon. *Seminal fluid. Vaginal vault.* "God, you really have a way with words, Chief Higgins."

"Sorry. What do you want me to say? But we know she had sex on the morning she murdered her family and killed everyone at the main branch. With *two* men."

Jane felt like a door had just been slammed in her face. *Two men?* "Are you sure about that?"

"The evidence doesn't lie," Steve remarked. "There was semen in her, two different secreter types. Two different men. The Medical Examiner says he's sure she'd been with both men within hours of her death. Marlene's husband was in the Naval Reserves; since 1990 all military personnel have DNA profiles put in their medical records. One of the seminal types matched her husband. All we know about the second semen traces is that they're from a person with A-negative blood."

By now Jane was feeling naive. Infidelity happened all the time, she knew, amongst the people you'd least expect it from. "The post office does have medical records of all employees, for their health plans. I guess you want to check and see what Bobby Weaver's blood type is."

"We have to get a court order for that, and we're in the process of doing that now," Steve explained. "But it's not Bobby Weaver we're interested in checking."

"Who, then?"

"A man named Carlton Spence."

Another door in the face. A big door. "Now, *that*, Chief Higgins, is inconceivable. I've known Carlton longer than I knew Marlene. He doesn't belong to any *cult.*"

"But didn't he go through a severe tragedy recently?"

"Not recently. That was a long time ago. His wife and daughter were killed in a car accident. He had an alcohol problem for a while but got over it."

Steve nodded again, not looking at her. "The information I have is a little different."

"What?" Jane paused. "Well, yes—the daughter. She wasn't killed in the crash—"

"No, she was abducted from the accident scene, according to the FBI and Maryland state police. The potential there, especially in this day and age, is pretty horrific: child pornography, child prostitution. Children are abducted for those pursuits all the time; that must take a tremendous toll on a parent, right? It would for me, I'm sure. And Carlton Spence was a devout Catholic. A tragedy like that? It must really challenge a person's faith. If there was ever a reason to turn your back on God, that's got to be it."

Jane reflected on that. How could she not agree? *He's right, but* . . . "Not him, not Carlton. He isn't capable of something like this. He just *isn't*. If you want my opinion, you're wasting your time even considering it."

"Really? Maybe. Tell me this, what exactly is his job here?"

Jane sat back. This was going to be a long interview. "In the post office, we don't have jobs, we call them crafts. Clerks, carriers, handlers, maintenance. Carlton went through the ranks in all those crafts, and recently—when my west branch opened—he was promoted to delivery supervisor. His pay grade is level fourteen. You can think of him as part personnel manager and part operations manager. He basically makes sure everyone else is on duty and getting their individual tasks done. He maintains the route schedules, transfer deliveries, overtime assignments, and a lot more. He's been a quality employee for as long as I've known him."

"Is he on duty right now?"

"Yes."

"How about calling him in here."

Jane frowned. She didn't have any worries that she might be wrong about this—she felt *certain* that Carlton would never have anything to do with cults—but she supposed she had no choice. After all, Steve *was* the chief of police. *It's my civic duty to cooperate—and prove him wrong.* "One second." She picked up the phone, hit Carlton's office extension, and waited. Then she hit another extension, and waited. "Hmm. Can't find him," she muttered. "Let me try the service area." One more extension. "Doreen, is Carlton up there? I need to see him. . . . Oh, okay."

Jane hung up. "Carlton's not here right now. He's out on a delivery."

"I thought you just said he's basically a personnel manager. You mean he also walks a mail route?"

"In emergencies, everyone in the pecking order has to go out," Jane explained. "If the service area is crowded with customers and all the handlers are busy in back? Sure. There are times when even a station manager like me, or even a postmaster will have to grab a mailbag and pick up a route. Anyone in management. Other times we have to go out and empty relay boxes and the regular mail boxes. Especially in emergencies, like this."

"Oh, I see. With the main branch closed for the time being, your branch has to do extra duty and pick up all their slack."

"That's right, Chief. And right now, Carlton is in the field. We got a late Express Mail package and all the carriers are out. So he took it."

Steve looked right at her, quite serious. "I need to know where he is. As in *right now*."

Jane's impatience smacked into her confusion. She made another call out to the front, jotted something down, and hung up.

"It's in the scan log. Carlton left a half hour ago to take that Express Mail to the Seaton School for Girls."

"Great. Thanks." Steve rose, gathering his things. He seemed distracted.

"Chief Higgins! What's going on?" Jane blurted. "You're wrong about Carlton, I'm telling you—"

"I hope I am," he said.

"There's something you're not telling me—"

Steve looked down at her, a look of total skepticism. "Yeah, there is. It's not definite proof of anything, but we have to check it out. And it's probably cause for a search warrant."

More shock. "What are you talking about?" Jane almost shouted.

"It was just a basic incident report, Ms. Ryan. In a quiet, laid-back town like Danelleton, not a whole lot happens. So we notice even the most minor incident reports, stuff that in a big city like Tampa or St. Pete would be overlooked because it wasn't deemed crucial."

"What incident!"

"Last night at about 3 A.M., a man pulled into the Qwik-Mart, walked in, got a coffee, and left. The man was acting peculiar, so the guy at the register called us to report it. Just a routine suspicious persons report. We get them a lot, and ninety-nine percent of the time they're nothing. Just someone mad at someone else, or someone overreacting. You know what I mean?"

Jane's face was getting warm from aggravation. "No, Chief Higgins, I don't. I don't have *any idea* what you mean. At this point, you're practically driving me nuts, so would you *please* get to the point?"

"When I came in this morning, first thing I do is look and see if there are any incident reports filed by the night shift," he continued. "There was only one, this one. Then I get the call about what happened here, so I'm juggling two things at once but it occurs to me that the two could easily be connected."

Now Jane was just plain mad. "What was the incident?" she seethed.

"Look at what happened, Ms. Ryan. Last night somebody dug up Marlene Troy's corpse and put it inside your post office. And last night, we get an incident report about a suspicious person at the Qwik-Mart. Follow me?"

"No!"

"The clerk at the Qwik-Mart said the guy was 'peculiar.' Want to know why?"

"Not if I have to wait till I'm fifty to find out."

90

"The guy was covered in dirt. It was all over his clothes, smudged on his face, his arms, had dirt in his hair—"

"Dirt," Jane said.

"As in soil. Covered in it. Anyway, the clerk at the store recognized this man. It was Carlton Spence."

Chapter Six

(I)

Carlton enjoyed driving the LLVs. They looked cumbersome and uncomfortable but they actually rode well. Manufactured via contract by the Grumman Corporation, the van-like vehicle's initials stood for Long-Life Vehicle, and that was no lie. They almost never broke down and when they did, service was efficient and easy. The only feature that carriers complained about was the steering wheel on the right side, for mailbox access. You either got used to it or you didn't. Most did. Those who didn't caused many a fender bender. But driving it down Danelleton's serene streets made Carlton feel like a genuine mailman again.

It made him feel like a messenger.

He drove almost as if someone else were driving, someone guiding him—a guiding dark light. He was beginning to understand that light now, a little more with each hour. It was as though his heart no longer beat solely for himself. It beat for someone else, someone great, with an important plan for the world. Knowing that this light was in his heart made Carlton feel important. *God never made me feel important*, he reminded himself. *No. God let my wife go fuckin' psycho and get killed in a car wreck. And God looked the other way when a bunch of sick fucks took my beautiful daughter and put her in porn movies and made her turn tricks and then killed her. God's done nothing for me. God is my enemy.*

I believe in someone else now.

Someone who makes me feel important. Someone who will never turn his back on me . . .

Carlton's eyes stared ahead.

I will worship him to the ends of the earth . . .

The LLV coursed through more sedate streets. Tall trees—some palms, some Australian pines—threw down great, comforting blocks of shade. The houses lining each street all stood neat and bright, with vivid green lawns and front gardens bursting with delirious colors. Carlton saw Old Man Halm out for his daily walk. Amiable enough of a guy, always stopped to say hello, ask how you're doing. Would even loan you money in a pinch. White hair shining in the sun, Halm hobbled happily down the street with his cane; then he looked up and waved to Carlton.

Carlton waved back and thought, *You crotchety old fuck. I could take your old head off with this machete, watch it roll down the street. Then I'd take that fuckin' cane of yours and kill some people with it . . .*

Carlton had a machete in the LLV. His hand reached down for it—he could see the head flying, blood sailing up from the stump in red strings—but then that increasingly familiar voice told him, *No. That's not the message for today.*

Carlton nodded.

You'd get caught by the authorities before you got to where I need you to be.

Carlton nodded.

He waved at Old Man Halm as he passed.

Yeah, you're lucky today. . . .

Next house, there was Margarita Poole, on her hands and knees in the garden. She was pulling weeds. *What a fox*, Carlton thought. *I would do her up so right . . .* Five-two, a hundred and ten, and tan, tan, tan. She could be an Hawaiian Tropic model with all that flowing bronze hair and those grapefruit breasts. The gardening gloves didn't mesh with the rest of the look: flourescent green bikini top and jeans cut off so high they could've been a denim thong. *Christ.* Carlton wanted to take her down right there in the garden, put those dirty gardening gloves on and strip her and feel her up but good. Then he'd give it to her *hard* in the mulch. *Yeah, those gloves are a nice touch*, he mused. When he was done with her, he'd strangle her with them. Then he'd chop her up in the yard, play with her pieces. Let all the neighbors see him, wearing only her blood as he danced in the sun.

Carlton waved at her when he passed, and she shot him a great big white smile.

I work for the Messenger now, he reminded himself. *I can't let myself get distracted . . .*

No, the voice in his heart said, agreeing with him. *But there's no harm in pondering.*

Pondering. Dreaming as he drove. What a luxury. He turned the LLV at the next corner. Somebody mowing their yard waved. Then a FedEx truck drove by in the oncoming lane, and the driver waved. *Everybody knows me,* Carlton felt secure. *Everybody likes me. But they won't for long . . .*

He was being manipulated. He was being *guided.* Someone else's hands were on the wheel, someone else's spirit sharing his psyche. It made him feel exultant, it made him feel elevated. Carlton's heart just kept singing as he drove, not even consciously aware of his destination.

At the corner a group of kids were waiting at the crosswalk, the old lady crossing guard holding up her hand for them to wait. The kids were all gradeschoolers, a little rowdy as kids would be, laughing. Good kids. Going places when they got older because they were diligent and they obeyed their parents and they did their homework every night. Yes, six of them, waiting for the guard to let them cross.

Oh, it would be sweet, wouldn't it?

The guard held her hand up to Carlton's lane. Carlton stopped, just ten feet from the line. The kids were coming across now.

Time it just right . . . just right. He *knew* he could do it! His booted foot fidgeted over the gas pedal. If he waited two more seconds and then floored it—

He'd get them all.

There's where I want you, kids. Under my wheels . . .

He could mow them all down in one bunch, drag

their bodies under the chassis. Wouldn't necessarily kill them all, but he could turn around, couldn't he? Finish the job. Or maybe not. Maybe just drive away and leave some of them crippled.

Carlton shook his head.

No, no. You have a more important message, the Messenger told him.

Carlton knew the Messenger was right. He'd have to put his human weakness away and be strong. . . .

But just as God tested Job, perhaps someone else was testing Carlton, dangling temptations before his eyes.

Carlton sighed at what he saw next.

When he turned another corner, to the last road before he'd be heading out of town limits, he saw Joanne Malloy getting out of her Mercedes wagon. She was like a lot of the rich bitches out here: well-tended, well-jeweled. Her husband made a fortune suing nursing homes and convalescent centers. *Ooo,* Carlton thought, slowing down. *And it looks like the twins are home from school—Harvard, of course.* Joanna was cut from a familiar mold: forty years old but looked thirty from a distance. Kerchief around her head like she was Jackie Kennedy on vacation in Cape Fucking Cod. The face-lifts got rid of the wrinkles and crow's feet from thousands of days lounging on the beach. Augmentation from the best plastic surgeons in the county took care of the saddlebags and boob sag. *She looks like a million bucks*, Carlton thought, which was probably what her husband had spent on her. Not very friendly, a stiff bitch. Nose in the air. Better than everybody else. And of course her spoiled-rotten nineteen-year-old twin daughters had the same disposition. *Like mother, like daughter* . . . They were in their first semester in college, and Carlton could bet they spent the whole time turning heads. *And I'll bet they fuck their professors for grades, and pay them off with Daddy's money.*

They'd just come back from the beach, all in matching designer bikinis and flowing sarongs, hundred-dollar flip-flops and sunglasses that probably cost half a g-note a pair. *Yeah, there's a threesome, all right,* Carlton mused again. He imagined the most debauched things, scenes that beggared description. All under force, of course, under the threat of death. *Naw, I'm afraid there wouldn't be much cuddling.* . . . He eyed their perfect contours, the outlines of their perfect breasts, six long tan legs all walking in unison around the half-circle driveway. The front door to the house could've been the front door to an embassy. *You know,* Carlton thought, *I'll bet that fucking door cost more than my car.*

It did, his guide replied. *And there's something you must know.*

What?

They hate you. They think they're better than you. They think you exist simply to serve them. You're a servant to their falsehood and gluttonies.

Oh am I, now?

Carlton waved as they passed.

Joanna turned and looked at him, soulless in the sunglasses. She didn't wave. She didn't even smile. All that returned Carlton's greeting was the blankest of looks—a look of *non*acknowledgment—which Carlton deemed a worse insult than a frown. Hell, she could've given him the finger, and it wouldn't have been as mocking. The two snooty twins turned their heads, too, with the same looks. One of them shielded her eyes, gazing more intently: "Who's that, Mom?"

"Oh, it's just the flunky mailman," her mother said.

Carlton heard that one. *Oh? Just the flunky mailman?* He'd go in there and show them the flunky mailman. Oh, yes. Carlton pulled over to the curb and stopped the LLV. He turned the engine off. In all the delectable musings of these past few minutes, one suddenly occurred to him that easily ranked superior to the others.

I'll go in there and bust them up. No, not kill them. Just give 'em all a good shot to the head to knock them out. Strip them all down—no, cut their little bikinis off—then have a little party. After that, drag the three of them into the garage . . .

And what then?

Carlton knew in an instant. He'd hog-tie the twins and wake 'em up. Then he'd hang the mother upside-down by her ankles. He'd ensure that her legs were spread good and wide, like a wishbone. And he'd make the twins watch as he slit the mother open from crotch to sternum. Flap her guts out onto the floor. Maybe even put a bucket under her to catch the blood.

Then drink the blood right in front of the twins.

He'd only kill one of them. Real slow. Maybe put a wire-wheel on her, or a soldering gun. Something to really get her making noise. He wanted it *loud*. Because he wouldn't kill the other twin. Maybe he'd put a tourniquet around her wrists and chop her hands off, or wreck her face with the soldering gun. But, no, he wouldn't kill her. He needed the other twin to remember her sister's eardrum-ripping screams. Traumatize her for the rest of her life. Ruin her.

He'd have a little more fun with her one last time—put a bun in her oven, too, if he was lucky—and maybe leave her sister's head in her lap and dump the rest of her mother's blood on her head, and then he'd leave, but before he left the house, he knew what he would say to her.

He'd say: *Take a look, Miss Priss. Pretty good work for a flunky mailman, huh?*

Yes. That's what Carlton would say to her when he was finished.

He was looking at their front door. He was about to get out of the LLV and walk to the house but before he could do so, something stopped him. His legs pulled back inside as though someone else were controlling them.

Carlton knew who. And he knew why.

He pulled away, content, resolved.

All these things in his mind he knew he could do. He could do them easily and without hesitation. All of these messages he would be thrilled to deliver—Old Man Halm, Margarita, the kids at the crosswalk, Joanna Malloy and her twins—but that, he knew, would be selfish. Carlton's guide had instructed him well. There was a far more important message to be sent today.

It was only a few more minutes until he got there. Right before the turnoff, however, he began to feel sick. Nauseated. Edgy. But was it Carlton who was getting sick, or was it his guide?

He jerked his gaze to the left and there it was. The sprawling white building with black trim, the big sign out front. The sun shot the shadow of the steeple across the road, a dark ghost.

ST. MARY'S EPISCOPAL CHURCH, the sign read, along with a quote from Luke: "HERE AM I, THE SERVANT OF THE LORD; LET IT BE WITH ME ACCORDING TO YOUR WORD."

Carlton couldn't help but stop the vehicle. He was about to throw up. It wasn't the church—the Messenger had trod through many churches throughout history, to desecrate them. No, it wasn't the church at all. It was something *about* the church . . .

Carlton felt panicked when he looked upward. Atop the steeple was a simple cross, as anyone might expect. The cross had no power against him, nor the Messenger. But just below the cross, something jutted. Carlton stared, sickness boiling up.

A gold statue stood there: an angel with a trumpet.

The Archangel Gabriel, the messenger of God.

Carlton snarled at the figure, hurled some invective in a language that had never been spoken on Earth. The profanity fired into the air loud as a cannon shot. Birds lifted off from trees en masse. Carlton wasn't sure but it seemed that even the statue itself rocked at its base.

The hands controlling his hands gripped the wheel. The foot controlling his foot stomped the accelerator. Carlton and the Messenger sped away.

The vision of the Messenger's nemesis left Carlton feeling crazed and depressed—but mostly crazed. It would all work out for the best, though—he knew that.

It would help him deliver the message more effectively. His mentor's rage was being shared with Carlton, it was becoming *part* of him. The Messenger's heart beat in synchronicity with Carlton's heart. The Messenger's lust was now Carlton's lust. Carlton and the Messenger were now essentially one.

The sedate private school and its plush grounds shimmered in the sun. There was an opened gate access but no guard, no one to sign in with. The sign read THE SEATON SCHOOL FOR CHRISTIAN GIRLS. A cement fountain gently gushed at the center of the entrance court.

Nice place . . .

A hush seemed to spread across the grounds when he drove the LLV through the gate. Carlton drove past the administration building and St. Agnes Hall, which was the main classroom facility. A few moments later he was parking in front of the long, front-pillared dormitory building.

"Why, hello!" the nun at the front desk greeted him.

Carlton smiled.

Sister Katrice was not a clichéd nun; in other words she wasn't elderly, bowed, and wrinkled. Instead the woman in the habit who smiled back at Carlton was attractive and vibrant, mid-thirties, a pretty face.

Carlton's smile deepened as he approached with his package. "Behold the Messenger," he said jovially.

Sister Katrice's brow furrowed. "Pardon me? Oh, you mean you have a package for us."

"Yep. It didn't get out on the first run so I brought it over."

The nun seemed excited, something to break up what must be a very dull post. "Who's it from?"

101

It's from the deepest crevice of hell, the Messenger's voice creaked in Carlton's heart, and Carlton himself would've loved to say that but instead he simply looked at the return address and said, "Let's see. Local address, no name, same zip code. Whoever sent it didn't really need Express Mail. Still would've been same day. Oh, well." Then he chuckled. "The post office needs the money anyway."

Sister Katrice grabbed a pen. "Do I need to sign for it?"

"Actually, yes. There's a return-receipt request." He pulled off the tab and gave it to her.

"I wonder what it is," she said with enthusiasm, scribbling her name.

"Hmm, look at that . . ." Carlton looked at the edge of the box. The flap was unsealed. "It must must've come open so let's see." He stuck his hand into the box.

Sister Katrice was frowning but she didn't say anything. From the box Carlton withdrew a carpenter's hammer. It was a quality one: fiberglass handle, anodized stainless steel head, one end flat, the other beveled.

Sister Katrice squinted at it. "A *hammer?*"

Carlton hefted it in his hand. "Sure looks like a hammer to me."

"Why on earth would someone send us a *hammer?*"

"Here's why," he told her.

And that was just the beginning of a glorious day.

(II)

Jane was too perturbed. When Steve Higgins left her office, she sat there a moment and just shook her head. Yes, the situation was curious, but there could be many explanations.

Next thing she knew she was up and out of her office, trotting out to the parking lot. "Chief Higgins! Wait!"

He'd already gotten into his patrol car, and rolled down the window. He seemed to be putting his radio back in its slot when he looked up at her.

"You can't just go *arrest* Carlton because someone at the Qwik-Mart saw him last night with dirt on his face. That's ridiculous."

"It's not ridiculous, Ms. Ryan," he said. "It's probable cause. We'd be negligent not to investigate."

"So where are you going?"

"To the address of the delivery he's on, Seaton School for Christian Girls. And I've already dispatched a uniformed unit."

"Would you please *wait* a minute!" she insisted. "This is a mistake!"

"If it's a mistake, then we can make that determination after questioning. So if you don't mind, I've got to get out there now."

"I'm going with you," she huffed.

"Ms. Ryan, please. It's police business. You can't—"

Jane slipped around to the other side of the car and got in. She slammed the door closed.

"You're persistent, aren't you?" Steve observed.

"I'm Carlton's boss. It makes sense for me to be there."

"All right, fine." He pulled off. "But I don't want you getting in the way, I don't even want—"

"Besides, I want to be there to see you eat your

words," Jane added. "For goodness sake. You're all up in arms because someone saw him *dirty*. Did you ever think that maybe he had a flat tire."

"What was he doing out at that hour?"

"It's a free country, isn't it? He's got to be to work by six in the morning anyway, which means he's up by five at least. We *all* get up early in this job. Maybe he was simply out for a drive. You ever done that?"

"I've never done that only to be reported later to the police as being covered in grave dirt," Steve replied.

"He didn't say *grave dirt!* He said he was dirty. So what?"

"The clerk said the man had bits of *soil* on him. And he positively identified the man as Carlton Spence."

The more Jane thought about it, the more laughable the situation became. Of course, there was nothing funny about what had happened, but the idea of a low-key guy like Carlton getting involved in some cult and digging up a grave was preposterous.

Steve didn't say anything as he drove. The silent type? For some reason, though, he didn't strike her that way except for maybe when he was at work. *He's a good-looking man,* she caught herself thinking. Intense eyes. Lean, not overtly muscular but in shape. In spite of the heat, he kept the air-conditioning off and the window down, his blondish hair waving in the wind. When he put his sunglasses on he looked even more attractive—enigmatic, perhaps—but more like a cop.

She smirked at herself. *What am I thinking?* The nip

of guilt panged her. *The last thing I should be doing is sizing a guy for his looks after all that's happened here lately. Jeez . . .*

He looked over at her, eyes hidden now. "Could you put your seat belt on, Ms. Ryan?"

Jane rolled her eyes. "The Seaton school is less than five miles away."

He looked back at the road ahead. "It's a state law."

Jane laughed. "Let me guess, you're going to arrest me."

"No, but I'll give you a $500 fine if you want."

She held on the words a moment, looking back at the side of his face. *I guess he's serious,* she realized.

Jane buckled her seat belt.

All business, she presumed. She didn't see a ring on his left hand, not that she'd really looked that consciously.

Would you get off it?

She returned her mind to the current predicament—a complete calamity. She could never even imagine such a thing. But one thing she was sure of:

Carlton has nothing to do with any of this.

Steve's radio hissed in a burst of static, then a voice came on, "Unit One, this is Unit Six. Do you copy?"

"Go ahead," Steve said after pushing on the intercom.

"I just pulled up to the school's dormitory. There's a mail truck there."

"Is Spence in it?"

"No, sir. No one in the vehicle. No sign of anyone around the vehicle. He's gotta be inside the building."

Steve thought through some static. "All right, check it

out. Proceed with caution. This might be nothing, but you never know. My ETA's about five minutes, but I don't want you to wait. Find him and detain him. If it gets hairy, pull out and call for backup."

"Roger, Unit One. I'm 10-6 as of right now."

The transmission ended.

Jane scoffed. "You're kidding me. 'If it gets hairy?' This sounds like some cop show."

"It's no show, Ms. Ryan. Do I have to remind you that in the last couple days we've had almost thirty people murdered by the same woman, and last night that same woman's corpse was exhumed from her grave?"

Jane couldn't argue with that. Instead, she thought it best from this point on to just keep quiet and let the police find out for themselves that Carlton was innocent.

I'm certain of it, she thought. *I know he's innocent.*

(III)

Carlton stood naked, every square inch of his body gleaming scarlet from all the blood. He'd done the work so quickly, as if it were second nature. He could feel the Messenger's satisfaction in their shared heart. He felt uplifted.

Behold. The Messenger.

He didn't feel that he was standing in a simple dormitory shower room—he felt as though all that blood on him was actually sunlight and he was standing on the highest mountain peak on Earth.

He looked around at all those bodies and smiled.

All those girls.

The hammer dripped. It felt weightless in his hand.

They're coming now, the voice in his heart told him, but Carlton was not worried. *You've done well. You've sent my message with honor and pride. I thank you, and the Father of the Earth thanks you, the first fallen Light of the Morning . . .*

But you must hurry now. There's still one left alive . . .

No. Alive was no good, not in this case. Alive was insufficient and signified failure. He knew that he mustn't fail the Messenger.

What was a little more blood on him, anyway?

He heard some scuffling somewhere. *I know I got everyone in the shower room. There must be one more hiding in here somewhere.*

Where? Where?

Next, he heard a whimper. Muffled. Then a single sob.

He stalked around the locker room, his bare feet leaving red footprints. He could feel the Messenger right behind him, guiding him. When the Messenger stepped forward with his left foot, Carlton's left foot stepped forward. When the Messenger's right hand tightened around the hammer's haft, Carlton's right hand tightened.

When the Messenger's heart beat, Carlton's heart beat at the exact same time.

Their footfalls took him toward the dorm chaperon's office. A lithe, wiry woman. One of her jobs was to monitor the girls when they took showers after gym class, and he really had to wonder about that. Slate brown hair, short and choppy, her body long, muscle-toned, nearly breastless. A little long in the tooth, pushing fifty probably. She'd been one of the first Carlton had killed, actually. He brought the hammer's beveled end right down into the top of her spine. She hadn't even known he'd entered the office, so intent she was leaning over her paperwork at the desk. She'd convulsed on the floor for a few moments, shuddering, then died.

But there was someone else in the office. The Messenger *sensed* it, and since the Messenger's senses were now blended into his, Carlton sensed it.

He could smell the sweat pouring out of her skin. He could smell her blood racing through her veins. He could smell her terror.

"There you are . . ."

He saw the tip of her bare foot edging just a half inch out of the shadow under the assistant's desk.

Sopping wet, like a dog just in from the rain. Hair drenched from the shower. She was wearing a white terry robe. Carlton reached under the table, grabbed her hair, and then proceeded to drag her screaming into the showers.

Chapter Seven

(I)

"Jesus Christ, Chief!" the voice erupted over the radio.

Steve keyed the intercom unit in the car. "What! What's wrong?"

A pause. "This is *not* looking good . . ."

"What the hell is wrong!" Steve blared. "Where are you? Are you in the building yet?"

"I'm . . ." A burst of static. "I'm heading up the stairs to the second floor, where the dorm rooms are. There was nobody downstairs in the reception area, but I didn't check around. I thought I heard something coming from upstairs."

"What did you hear?"

"Not sure. A shriek maybe."

"Have you seen anyone in the building yet?

"No, sir, nobody, but . . . but . . . my God, Chief,

there's footprints running up and down the hall floor."

"Footprints?"

Another burst of static. "Blood. It's got to be blood."

"Get up there! Find out what's going on!" Steve rekeyed the mike. "All units, this is Unit One. Respond Code 3 to the Seaton School for Girls on Fourth and Westmore! Suspect is a white male, approximately 180 pounds, brown hair, in a postal uniform. Consider him dangerous."

Jane sat back in her seat, aghast. "Bloody footprints? Is that what he said?"

"That's what he said." And Steve floored it.

The school was just around the next bend, sitting at the edge of the woods that front the bay. Several police sirens were already screeching in the distance. Jane felt the inertia shove her back when Steve fishtailed around the fountain at the center of the court. The car shuddered, its brakes shrieked. Jane whipped forward and back when the car finally stopped.

Steve popped off his seat belt, drew his gun from the shoulder holster.

Jane was staggered. Something very serious was happening here and she was sitting in the middle of it. Could Carlton really have exhumed Marlene's body? *And the footprints?* Could those really have been Carlton's bloody footprints that the cop on the radio was talking about? Finally, she just said, "This is impossible for me to believe—"

Through the open window they heard a long, loud, terror-driven scream.

"Believe it," Steve said and jumped out to join his men.

Jane felt as though his urgency was dragging her behind him on a towline. Other patrol cars raced into the front court. Uniformed police officers were jolting out of their cars and rushing toward the dormitory's entrance from all points; Jane couldn't sort her thoughts for all the noise: sirens, radio squawk, shoes tramping pavement.

Just inside, though, there was dead silence.

"Careful," Steve ordered, holding his pistol upward, finger off the trigger. "Is that blood there?"

A uniform confirmed it. So did Jane's eyes. A line of what could only be blood led from the chair, behind the desk. Now every set of eyes followed the smearlike line; it tracked back to an office.

Two cops stood at each side of the door. One opened the knob, while a third officer three-pointed into the room.

A second of silence, then they heard: "Oh, my God . . ."

Everyone poured into the room, and when Jane saw what they were looking at, she almost fainted.

A nun hung from the farthest wall. Jane could only tell that she was a nun by the wimple around her face, and the veil—the rest of the woman hung naked, white skin badged with crimson smudges. Her head leaned to one side, her mouth agape. Her arms spread out as if crucified, from nails driven into her palms. A puddle of blood ten feet wide shined below her feet.

Jane put her face in her hands.

111

"Who was the first on the scene?" someone asked.

"Jackson."

"Well then where the hell is he?" someone else answered.

"He's upstairs," Steve said. "Said something about the showers."

The trampling shifted now, out of the office and a stampede up the steps. Again, Jane felt as if in tow. The first cop up the stairs stopped at the landing, holding up a hand.

"Watch it," Steve warned.

They all saw it, a leather mail pouch sitting on the floor, its top flap hanging open.

"Don't touch it," someone said. "It could be a bomb."

"It's no bomb . . ." The cop leaned over, picked up the pouch. Steve stepped over and looked in. The pouch was full of knives, awls, nails, and other similar implements. A dozen razor-sharp edges glinted upward.

They proceeded down the hall. Jane didn't want to go, she didn't want to see what else might have happened here—but she had to. *They think it was Carlton,* she kept fretting. But she knew the worst fret of all.

Maybe it really was.

There were no maybes about it when they all piled onto the landing.

Oh, my God, no, Jane thought.

Carlton had hanged himself in the main dorm hall, from the head of one of the sprinkler nozzles in the ceiling. He looked as though his entire naked body had been immersed in blood. His face had turned nearly black from the noose around his neck, his hands limp, blood dripping from his fingertips.

"Holy shit," someone whispered.

"That's him, isn't it?" Steve asked.

"Yes," Jane choked.

She stared at her friend's dead face. Pressure from the ligature bloated his face; his eyes were puffed but open. Jane would never have thought that that could happen. He seemed to be grinning.

"Somebody cut him down," Steve solemnly ordered.

No one was enthusiastic to do the job, but eventually two cops stepped forward, one wincing as he wrapped his arms about Carlton's waist, the other cutting the rope with a knife. They laid the body on the floor, but both cops, now, were peering.

"What is that?" one asked.

The cop who'd done the cutting knelt down, seemed to be looking at the cut end of the rope. "Hey, Chief. This isn't rope."

Steve bulled forward, impatient. "What do you mean it's not rope? What is it, then? Wire of some kind?"

The kneeling cop was turning pale. He gulped. "I think . . . I think it's . . . intestines."

Jane could see it, could see that the thin, stretched material couldn't possibly be rope. *Intestines? Is that what he said? If they really are intestines, then . . . whose are they?*

Steve shook his head. "This is crazy," he said under his breath, then louder: "Jackson! Where are you?"

"In here," came the eventual reply.

The troupe rushed into the nearest door. Now Jane remembered the previous radio transmission. There were indeed footprints in blood leading straight to the spot where Carlton had committed suicide. Jane followed the others into the room . . .

A shower room, like the one Jane remembered from her own college dorm, years ago. A long room walled by pretty pink-and-white tile work, ten shower nozzles. Lockers and benches up front, a multistalled bathroom off to the left. Total silence pervaded the entire area save for a single drip.

But that wasn't the first thing Jane noticed, not by any means. It was impossible *not* to notice the shower's most recent adornment.

Half a dozen teenaged girls hung in a line on the rear shower wall, crucified as the nun had been. Naked, arms outstretched, masonry nails driven through their palms and wrists into the tiles. All of their heads were bloodied from multiple hammer blows. A towel clogged the center drain, leaving an inch-deep pool of blood stretched below them.

No one said a word. Jane just stared, shocked numb.

More tires could be heard screeching outside, more sirens wailed. Ambulances were arriving one after another. A crowd was forming as cordons were drawn.

Jane and Steve exchanged the most somber of glances. Everyone was staring wordlessly at the room's final detail: a bell, drawn in wide smears of blood, on the adjoining wall.

Jane knew it had to be her imagination but when she looked a final time at the line of naked bodies hanging on the wall, something shifted in her vision. If she'd actually seen what she thought she'd seen, then everyone else in the room would've noticed it too. But no one said a word.

I'm not seeing this, I'm not seeing this, she kept pleading with herself. *It's impossible. It's not there.*

For the merest moment, the six dead girls on the wall all opened their eyes at the same time, looked right at Jane, and smiled.

Jane collapsed.

(II)

What's all the commotion? Annabelle wondered.

Sirens blared outside, rising then fading as quickly as they'd come. What was going on?

Annabelle was probably the most petite woman in town, just a shade under five feet tall and a hundred pounds on a "fat" day. She looked like what she was: a classy upscale housewife, elegant facial features, always meticulously manicured, just the right makeup. The shimmering but simple sherbert-green sundress seemed incandescent from its fine material, and had cost $300 at the International Mall, plus another $100 for designer sandals with sparkles across their straps. Her body was well-pronounced in its curves, her breasts erect, and when she walked down the street in the sun, her straight cinnamon hair radiated. In all, Annabelle was the ultimate Florida housewife, and in her wake many men turned their heads, only to bite a lip in envy of her husband.

More sirens quickly rose, then faded again.

She'd just walked through the automatic doors of the new west branch post office, relishing the cool air, when the sound of screaming vehicles startled her. She turned in a rush, saw several police cars accelerating down Rosamilia Avenue. *Must be a big car wreck, or a fire*, she guessed.

"Lord, can you believe all that noise?" came another woman's voice. Mrs. Baxter, one of Danelleton's most infamous gossips, was weighing a package at the self-serve counter. She was a squashed little curmudgeon of a woman, stoop shouldered, white hair bunned and netted. "I haven't seen that many police cars all at once since that time last year when Corey Halverson caught his wife cheating on him—remember, with that man who'd come around and cleaned the leaves out of your gutters? Remember him? Turns out he was sowing quite a few oats with some of the local women, and he was an ex-convict to boot! Anyway, poor Corey Halverson caught the two of them together at one of those fleabag motels over in St. Pete Beach, and he got so depressed he climbed to the top of the Danelleton water tower to jump. Must've been twenty police cars there that day. Of course, he didn't jump but he was going to. Do you remember that, Annabelle?"

Annabelle did not. In fact, she rather doubted that anything like that had happened at all; Mrs. Baxter had a knack for fabrication. Outside, though, more police cars sped by. "Whatever it is, it must be serious," she said.

"I saw more cars racing down Main Street when I was on my way here. It looked like they were heading for that Seaton school, and I can tell you, I've heard a story or two about *that* place."

I'm sure you have, Annabelle thought.

"All those teenaged girls in there, no contact with

boys their own age? We can only imagine what goes on in their minds . . ."

Annabelle rolled her eyes. *What a pain in the butt.* She tuned the old woman out as best she could, heading over to the stamp machine and then the drop box. She hoped the old woman would just leave, but then she heard a rustling sound from the corner. *I don't believe it!* Mrs. Baxter was rummaging through the trash can by the self-service counter, opening junk mail that P.O. box customers had thrown out. Annabelle dawdled, pretending to be putting stamps on her own letters, until Mrs. Baxter left.

Annabelle wanted to go home right away and take a nap. She'd sat up late last night with her husband, Mark, watching some ludicrous horror movie, something about colonial settlers finding an evil root in the ground. The movie was so campy and badly done that Mark had been honking with laughter. Annabelle laughed, too, but not quite so hard. She'd wound up having nightmares, waking up half a dozen times, and when morning finally arrived, she felt exhausted. Mark was working today, a construction contractor. *I've got the whole day to myself*, she thought. What a luxury. First a long lazy bubble bath, then a nap before Mark got home. *But there's one thing to do in between . . .*

Annabelle quick-stepped to her P.O. box. *Seven to ten days for delivery,* she reminded herself. Today was the tenth day. *God, I hope it's here . . .*

Annabelle had the P.O. box for just such events as this. A little indulgence wasn't a bad thing; in fact, she felt she deserved it. It wasn't like she was cheating on her husband or anything. She'd never done that, in spite of innumerable opportunities and sometimes, when primal urges collided with moral sensibilities, the former had come very close to winning out.

Sometimes Annabelle just couldn't stand it.

Hence, this confidential mail-order purchase, this clandestine indulgence.

She felt tingly approaching her P.O. box, then a sudden discontent swept through her, leaving her utterly depressed. *Hope for the best but prepare for the worst*, Mark always said.

It's not going to be here, she immediately knew. More disappointment. *I'm going to open this box, look inside, and it'll be empty. The friggin' thing probably hasn't even shipped yet, won't get here for another week. Or maybe they'll never send it. Maybe I just got shafted . . .*

She turned they key, opened the box—

Jesus!

—then jerked her head around again at another salvo of screaming police sirens. *What is going on out there?* she thought.

When the sirens faded, she looked into the P.O. box.

Her heart jumped in her chest—she nearly shrieked in delight. Inside the box sat a package.

She slipped it out. The return address said Erotronica, Inc. *This is it! I finally got it!* Annabelle stuck the package under her arm, like something forbidden, like a cocaine dealer having just made a secret pickup, and she whisked herself away, flip-flopping briskly out the doors and into the parking lot. Her brand-new, ocean-green Mercedes convertible sat in wait.

She couldn't wait to get home.

But—

Oh, damn it! She had to go back. *I left the box door open and my key in the lock!* The package was an excusable distraction, but that didn't abate any frustration. Annabelle was an instant-gratification type of woman. She didn't want to have to wait even an extra minute for what she wanted.

She threw the package into the Mercedes, and her flip-flops snapped right back into the post office. There was her box, door still open, bronze key sticking out of the lock. She reached forward to clack it shut but paused . . .

This time another police car screamed by but Annabelle didn't hear it.

She was looking at the open box. It occurred to her to reach forward and close the door, but, for some reason, that wasn't possible. She couldn't concentrate. Perhaps she'd been in the sun too much today, and she hadn't had breakfast this morning either. That combined with a bad night's sleep from horror-movie nightmares had brought her well under the weather.

Or maybe not. Maybe it was something else.

Annabelle was only thinking in snatches. She felt sick to her stomach, and she smelled something so foul—something like waste and rotten meat and unwashed bums all mixed together. She wanted to throw up, yet another part of her felt keenly excited. Her nipples ached against the shiny fabric of her sundress. She began to tingle between her legs.

She was reaching forward, frowning at the atrocious

smell, but she knew she wasn't doing so to close the box door. She meant to reach inside.

But there's nothing else in there, she thought with the tiny sliver of reason remaining in her mind. *I know it's empty. I put the package in the car. So what am I doing this for?*

A *flap!* startled her. Annabelle froze, then jerked around. It was five o'clock. The front service area was closed now, and someone on the other side had locked those doors and flapped the CLOSED sign around. And the self-serve area remained empty.

What . . . am . . . I . . . doing?

She lowered herself to her knees, looked into the box. It remained empty; in fact nothing could be seen behind it, either, just darkness. Someone must've turned out the lights back there.

She ground her teeth against that stench. She was right—it was coming from the box, flowing out in a disgusting gust. Nevertheless, she put her hand in . . .

She reached into the box.

There's nothing there, there's nothing there! So why am I putting my hand in?

Her hand was all the way in. Slowly, slowly. No, her arm was going in, an inch at a time, halfway up the forearm, then to the elbow. Then—

She was touching something—something warm. It was slimy, too, like that time she'd found the pack of ground sirloin in the back of the refrigerator. She'd opened it, thinking it fresh, but then the smell had hit her just after she'd touched it. Viscid slime. As it turned out, the meat had been in there for weeks. That's what whatever she was touching felt like.

Oh, God, she thought now. What was this?

Thoughts more foul than the smell swarmed in her head. In her mind she saw things, bodies, reveling over her in some stinking grotto, figures hauling her down—into slime—to slake their lusts. She was molested and prodded and licked, she was mounted and humped, her own body mauled in every position. The figures doing this to her were enslimed as if the pores of their skin were sweating mucus. Every detail of these goings-on absolutely repulsed her, yet she felt more aroused than she had in . . . well . . .

Ever.

It couldn't be mouths that suckled every inch of her body—the orifices were too large to be mouths. Yet her nerves detected teeth in them, and great, fat, budded tongues. Not human mouths at any rate. One such mouth sucked her feet, another sucked her stomach, centering on her navel, yet the diameter of the lips were nearly that of a dinner plate. When the mouth slid down lower, the tongue like a flap of flank steak entering her, Annabelle climaxed spontaneously, orgasms detonating. The immense tongue remained within her, and then yet another mouth clamped all the way over her face, then her entire head. Her head was being sucked like a lollipop.

This foul ecstasy never dwindled. The image or dream or hallucination ground on for what seemed hours, these things in rut, these *creatures*, lining up for her. Annabelle had no objection. She was stretched and pulled, splayed and spread, sat up, flipped over, turned upside-down, to be used over and over again . . .

She couldn't see the things at all, there was no light. All she could do was feel them as she shuddered beneath each one, nipples gorged, back arched, legs open, begging, begging for more.

When they were done, Annabelle sighed. Had she worn them all out? They were dragging themselves up, disinterested in her now, now that they'd spent themselves. She could hear them scuffling away through muck and then, for the merest moment, a light flickered—firelight, she guessed—and she saw them.

Tall lean *things*. Ridged in muscles yet emaciated. Knobby joints, hands with fingers a foot long. Their skin did indeed shine with slime, the hue of old, old paraffin. One looked back at her with black orblike eyes; Annabelle shuddered at the long slack-mouthed face, slits for a nose, and horns sprouting from the warped forehead.

Demons, she knew now.

Then the light went out, and there she was, on her knees in the post office, with her arm halfway into the P.O. box.

Her eyes felt pulled open by hooks. She knew what she was doing. She knew what the hot, organic thing was in her hand . . .

Eventually, something wet and just as hot emptied into her palm. Did she hear a moan? The smell was still overpowering. She slowly retracted her arm.

Hand to elbow was covered in slime. Pearl-like globs clung to her palm and fingers. *Oh my God . . . What in God's name is behind there?*

She was about to fall over and vomit, when someone was nudged her.

"Miss? Miss?"

Annabelle dragged her eyes upward. A postal clerk was standing behind her, a concerned look on his face.

"Are you all right?"

Annabelle's head was spinning. She looked at her arm. It was clean, normal.

"Here, let me help you up."

She struggled off her knees, wobbled a bit once she was back on her feet, then leaned against the wall of P.O. boxes and sighed. "I'm sorry. I don't know what happened to me. Dizzy spell, I guess."

"Happens a lot this time of year." The clerk smiled. "Hot and sunny all day, you get dehydrated."

"I'm sure that's it," Annabelle agreed, because there was nothing else she could believe. "And I'm fine now." She told herself, too, that she felt perfectly fine but her hand shook when she closed her box door and withdrew the key.

The clerk raised a brow.

"I'm just a little jittery," she said. "If you want to know the truth, my husband and I sat up late last night and watched a horror movie that wound up giving me terrible nightmares." *Demons,* she remembered. She'd just had some sort of waking dream about demons having sex with her, the day after seeing that movie about demons. *That's all this is . . .* "Then, I guess, something triggered the memory when I got here. Flashback or something."

A long hand the color of old wax opened on her chest. It stank. And it landed against her skin with a wet slap. It was humid, slimy. Annabelle was paralyzed. She wouldn't look up at the thing's face because she'd

123

already seen what their faces looked like. All she could do was convulse as the hand slid down her top, rubbing infernal slime over her breasts.

"You like that, don't you?" the corroded voice bubbled. "I know you do, I feel your precious little tits getting hard, like they did a few minutes ago in the grotto. My brothers and I enjoyed you very much, and later, when you're with us forever, we'll enjoy you every night for the rest of eternity."

Annabelle's teeth chattered.

"I'm one of the Messenger's sons," the voice from Hell burbled on. "He has many, many bastard sons. We help him spread the word in the domain of our lord. My father needs you to spread the word here. You will do it."

The hand was lathering her breasts in slime, the grublike fingertips twisting her nipples. Annabelle couldn't breathe.

"The arrival of the Messenger is at hand—"

She broke from her paralysis, shrieked in a breath, and ran out of the post office.

"Miss? Miss?" The perfectly normal clerk trotted after her. "Are you sure you're all right? Want me to call a doctor?"

The Mercedes whipped out of the lot and squealed away.

The clerk shook his head. "There's sure as hell a lot of screwy people in this town," he muttered and went back inside.

Chapter Eight

(I)

"It's nothing serious," Jane heard a voice saying. The voice seemed to be directed at someone else, though, not her. Tall dark shapes surrounded her. She felt like the time she'd had an impacted tooth removed, that imperceptible moment right before the general anesthetic had put her out, only this time it was in reverse. Her consciousness was slowly trickling back, her eyes fluttering open as her vision went from dark to grainy to sharp.

"Hello, Jane . . ."

The kind face smiled down on her from beneath spectacles and short blond hair. It was Dr. Mitchell, the family physician. Behind him stood Steve, Kevin, and Jennifer, all looking hopefully down at her. She was lying on the couch in the living room.

"It's nothing serious, Jane," the doctor said again.

"You fainted and fell down. You smacked your head on the way, I'm afraid, but there's no sign of concussion. You'll be fine."

Her thoughts ticked backward as she remembered in blocks. The mass slayings at the Seaton School, Carlton committing suicide. It had been too much for her to handle all at once. She winced when she recalled the state of all those bodies, all those poor girls.

Nevertheless, she felt foolish, especially in front of her children. *I have to be strong for my kids, but look at me.* "Thank you, Dr. Mitchell. I'm sorry you had to go to this trouble."

"No trouble, it's my job."

Steve stepped up next to him. "We're just glad you're okay. You gave us a little scare."

When Jane leaned up, she winced again.

"You'll probably have a devil of a headache for a few hours," the doctor said, "but aspirin will take care of that. By morning you'll be as good as new and I don't see any reason why you shouldn't be able to go to work. Just call me if there are any complications."

The doctor closed up his bag and left. Kevin and Jennifer rushed over to Jane's side and knelt beside her. Kevin was holding his fat horned toad, Mel, in his hands.

"Okay, kids, you heard the doctor," Steve said. "Your mom's going to be fine."

"I actually don't feel that bad now," she said, not altogether honestly. "Just a little headachy."

"You sure you're okay, Mom?" Jennifer asked.

"Yeah, Mom. You don't look okay," Kevin added.

I probably look like death warmed over, she feared. Her eyes felt puffy, her hair astray. "Really, I'm perfectly fine, just like Dr. Mitchell said." She stifled another wince when she sat up on the couch and put her arms around Kevin and Jennifer. "What time is it?"

"A little after eight," Steve said.

At first she wondered through the fading dizziness if he meant eight at night or eight in the morning, but then she looked to the bay window and saw the yard darkening. "That late? You kids haven't eaten yet. Let me get up and fix you something."

"Chief Steve got us blue-cheese and bacon burgers at the Food Island," Jennifer said.

"Yeah, Chief Steve's cool," Kevin said.

The name confused her at first but then she thought, *Chief Higgins. That's right, he said his first name was Steve.* She looked at him. "Thanks, Chief Higgins. That was very thoughtful. I hope they weren't too wild for you."

"It was my pleasure, and they were no trouble at all," he said. "We got you one to go for when you're feeling hungry."

"Thank you." She turned to the kids. "Why don't you go watch TV now, okay? Chief Higgins and I need to talk for a few minutes."

"Great!" Kevin said. "*Croc Hunter*'s on!"

Jane kissed her children and watched them scurry off, Kevin cradling the pet toad.

Steve looked down at Jane. "Are you really feeling better or are you just saying that?"

"I'm sort of just saying that," she admitted. "But I really appreciate your taking care of my kids while I was out. You've much more important things to be worrying about right now."

"Forget it." He took off his jacket and sat down on the couch. At first the sight of his gun and shoulder holster alarmed her—she'd never really seen a firearm up close like that—but she shrugged it off. *He's the chief of police, for God's sake. It's his job to be armed.* "I was worried. You really did take a spill."

She brought a hand to the back of her head. "Was I bleeding?"

"No, just a good conk."

Jane spared a smile. "It's a good thing I didn't land on my face. I can see the looks on customers' faces when they see the branch station manager with a broken nose." But the smile broke, when she thought again about what had happened.

"What's wrong?"

She paused. "I just . . . I can't get those images out of my head—you know—about Carlton. You were right about him, but I still can't believe it."

"If we'd only gotten there a little sooner," Steve muttered.

"How could he do that to those poor girls, and that nun? And then to do that to *himself.* How could *anybody* do that?"

"He went out of his mind," Steve said simply. "He was crazy."

"And a few days ago? Marlene Troy went out of her mind too. That's too much of a coincidence."

"It's abnormal psychology, Ms. Ryan. Shared delusions, multiple hysterics—"

"I don't buy any of that," Jane insisted. "It's just *too much* of a coincidence."

"Not really. We've touched on this before, haven't we? Carlton and Marlene knew each other well."

"Of course they did!" she replied, louder. "They worked together for years."

"What I mean is, they knew each other very closely, and very discreetly, in some ways that no one else would've guessed. I already told you—we've known beyond a doubt that they had sexual contact the morning that Marlene Troy murdered her family and then shot all those people at the main branch."

Jane closed her eyes in frustration. She found the sex part impossible to believe, too, but how could she deny it? The autopsy tests and DNA profiles didn't lie. But she still couldn't see the connection that Steve was implying. "All right, so they had sex. They were having an affair. What does that have to do with the rest of it? What, they had sex and that's why they both went crazy at the same time?"

"No—"

"They were secret lovers and they made some insane murder-suicide pact?"

"Not that either, we don't think. Things like that do happen, but there aren't any characteristics for that scenario here."

"So what's the connection?"

"That design. That bell-shaped symbol that keeps popping up."

Jane nodded, still not buying that one, either. She remembered his earlier insinuations. "Oh, yes—*that* business. You believe that Carlton and Marlene were in some sort of satanic cult."

"Or if not a cult, they were involved in some ritual thing together."

Some ritual thing together. Murder rituals. Sacrifice. Jane shook her head. "Have you talked to anyone— *anyone*—any witness at all, any family member or relative, who believes that either of them were capable of that? Have you talked to *anyone* who said that they were anything but upstanding, level headed, and *perfectly sane* individuals?"

"No. All I know is what I see," Steve answered. "And all I know is this: They both were involved in discreet sexual activity and—"

"Yeah? And what?"

"And they both committed mass murder in the same vicinity. I don't now anyone who'd call mass murder the act of *perfectly sane* people."

Jane had no response to that one. What could she say? *There's no way to deny* that.

"And they both left the same design at their crime scenes," Steve continued. "I'm sorry, Ms. Ryan, but you can't deny it. That bell-shaped symbol with the star at the bottom looks pretty creepy, doesn't it?"

"Well, yes," she admitted, all too easily remembering its outline in blood at the Seaton school.

"It looks like something with occult significance."

"All right, I agree. I can't argue with anything you've said," she gave him. "I'm just having trouble with all of it."

"That's understandable, because you knew both of them very well. Denial isn't uncommon in situations like this. I'd want to deny it, too, if they'd been friends of mine. But from my point of view, I can only look at the subject based on the evidence and the facts. Discreet relationship. Occult symbols. Mass murder. That's what I have to base my investigation on. That, and nothing more."

Again, Jane couldn't argue. *He's right. I guess I am in denial.* "It's time for me to start seeing the light here. So . . . okay . . . say they were in a cult. I don't know the exact definition but I assume that a cult is made up of more than two people."

"Right, and that's my biggest fear right now," Steve let on. "Who else out there is in the cult too?"

The question made Jane feel as though a shroud had been pulled over her. *There could be other people, out there right now,* she realized. *Ready to do the same thing. . . .*

(II)

The campanulation.

The bell. With a single star as its striker.

The Morning Star.

Cymbellum Eosphorus, he thought.

Even through the polycarbonate sheets, each a quarter-inch thick, he thought he could smell the paper that the plate had been printed on: something like wood long gone to rot but something organic as well.

Something just traceably awful.

Dhevic knew that the observation was impossible, at least technically. It was simply one page of a very old book. God knew how many hundreds of years ago it had been printed. The page was an intaglio print, and it had been sealed against time and air and human fingers in the polycarb sheets that had been expertly melted along all four edges. Along the bottom, in English and in Italian, were the words PROPERTY OF THE ARCHIVES OF THE HOLY OFFICE.

A monk defrocked from the St. Gall monastery in Maijvo, Hungary, had sold the plate to Dhevic decades ago, insisting that it had been pilfered from the Sixtus V Wing of Vatican Apostolic Library when the current structure was being built in 1590. From there, Dhevic was told, the plate had been preserved by private collectors handed down through the following decades and finally inherited by the Maijvo monk for successfully exorcising the last owner's son of a multiple demonic possession. The monk was eventually excommunicated for, he'd said, "unholy indiscretions," which Dhevic suspected were sexual in nature. It didn't matter. Dhevic couldn't absolutely verify the print's certification . . .

He simply *knew* it was authentic.

Dhevic knew a lot of things.

The engraving was said to have been torn from a nine-hundred-year-old book entitled *Das Grimoire de Praelata,* said to be written by prelates—or antipriests—who were known as satanic visionaries. They'd put themselves into trances to achieve psychic contact with the hierarchs of hell and then transcribed their epistles for worshipers on Earth. The engraving itself was supposedly crafted by an artist with the same interworldly talent.

Dhevic laughed in the lamplight. The single print

could probably be sold to a private collector for a million dollars, yet here he was, in a $40-per-night St. Petersburg motel, eating Dollar Store baked beans cold out of a can.

He knew he'd need more money; his benefactors always came through, if a little late sometimes. This fleabag was all he could afford. He could hear bickering through the door from time to time. Periodic muscle cars and rudely loud motorcycles tearing down the main drag made the night seem like it was exploding. In the next room, a bed frame could be heard thumping against the wall, an impatient female voice complaining, "Hurry up, man! Your half hour's up!"

Yes, in times like these Dhevic could only laugh to himself at this strange plight he'd inherited. When he looked through the room's bent blinds, he saw a Denny's across the street, and a sign in the lit window: BREAKFAST SERVED ALL NIGHT!

God, I wish I could have an omelet, he thought and laughed again. The beans weren't bad, actually, but after so many days?

He smiled and closed the blinds.

He didn't want to put on the television again—it would just be more of the same—but he switched it on regardless. He'd learned long ago, when he'd first started, never to be alarmed, or shocked. There was no point.

It comes with the turf, he thought.

Besides, he'd seen far, far worse.

The bed creaked when he sat on it. The television screen came alive.

The Channel 9 newswoman stood in front of the school, hairspray-stiff blond hair wilting in the humidity. She was clearly on edge as she recited the events.

"... *the second inexplicable tragedy to strike the quiet town of Danelleton in just three days, both involving postal employees* ..."

The screen snapped to a employee-file photograph of ...

"*Longtime postal supervisor Carlton Spence allegedly went on a rampage today at the Seaton School for Christian Girls, murdering a nun, a dorm assistant, and six students before taking his own life when local police arrived at the school's dormitory building* ..."

The shot cut back to the disheartened newswoman, her voice droning. In the background, police and paramedics rushed in and out of the dormitory's pillared entranceway.

"*This shocking second mass murder of the week brings Danelleton's death toll to thirty-eight.* ..."

The words faded out in Dhevic's head. He'd seen it before—and wasn't surprised. He knew full well that it was happening again.

He nodded off on the bed, still fully clothed. His dreams were awful, they often were, because they typically replayed what he'd witnessed in his visions. Horrors stacked upon horrors stacked upon horrors in a place where time did not really exist. Seconds ticked by in twinges of agony, minutes ticked by in screams. Hours ticked by in atrocities designed to exist without purpose, for their own sake.

It was not understandable. Not by humans.

The human mind could not reckon, it could not grasp this timeless war. *We're just too stupid, too simple and unsophisticated,* he thought.

Some things aren't meant to be known . . .

That would have to suffice.

He sat up on the bed, rubbed his eyes. Then he got up, stepping over a cockroach, and went to the bathroom. He washed his face in the stained sink, as if that might wash away the atrocities of his dreams and visions. He felt tainted, contaminated by these truths revealed to so few.

But he never lost his faith.

A click in his head; he glanced up quickly, spied his face in the mirror and saw water dripping off his beard. He looked like Rasputin, sopping wet as when his body was pulled from the West Dniva River. The familiar yet always strange noise creaked in his head, like a bad hinge, then a quiet bonelike *snap!*

He could see them out there.

Dhevic sighed. He was a tall man but not physically strong. He had no weapons. But he needed the vehicle that his benefactors provided. *If I call the police, the truck will be gone or stripped by the time they get here. . . .*

And it's a damn nice truck!

He had but one recourse. Confront them.

I'm a recipient augur, not a tough guy . . . He toweled off his face, put on his black jacket, and opened the motel room door.

Punks was the only word to describe them. Dhevic knew their plight: abused, terrifying domestic environments as infants and children, poverty, and just plain evil influence. But they were still punks. They were intently clothes-hangering Dhevic's brand-new silver Ford Explorer.

Late teens, Dhevic could see. One black, one white. Buzz cuts and lip rings. Baggy long pants, waistbands of their briefs showing, sneakers untied. Dhevic didn't get the style. Neither wore shirts, and both had an array of tattoos.

"Please. Stop that. Go away. I need that vehicle more than you can know."

Both kids glared up, not even momentarily taken aback by Dhevic's height.

"Fuck off, man. We'll kill ya," the black one said.

The white one pulled a small pistol.

"Let's kill the fucker anyway . . ."

They laughed, White Kid keeping the gun on Dhevic, Black Kid clothes-hangering the Explorer's door. "Fuck this shit, man," the black said, arrogantly eyeing Dhevic. "Gimme the keys."

Dhevic could smell what they were both thinking: Now that he'd seen them, they'd *have* to kill him, to prevent their description from being given to the police. *They'll put me in the truck at gunpoint, make me drive, then kill me on some back road.*

"Keys, man," White Kid insisted. "Now."

"No," Dhevic said. "Just go away."

The punks exchanged incredulous glances. "Man, what is *wrong* with people? Can you believe it?"

"Fuckin' A can't."

"Hey, buddy? Hey, beard?" White Punk aimed the pistol straight at Dhevic's face. "You listenin' to me, motherFUCKer? You gimme those keys right now or I cap your ass."

Dhevic stood there perfectly still, eyes wide. "Look," was all he said.

White Kid was staring back now, right into Dhevic's eyes.

"Do you see?" Dhevic asked him quietly. "Look closely . . ."

The kid's expression collapsed. The gun lowered and he fell to his knees. But he could not take his gaze off Dhevic's eyes.

"Do you see her?" Dhevic asked. He stepped closer, wielding his stare like a weapon itself. "I can. She's waving to you, isn't she? Here, I'll show you more."

"No!" the kid shouted. Tears poured down his face. "Don't make me see any more!" He slid the pistol to Dhevic's feet. A trembling hand reached into his pocket and threw Dhevic a wad of cash. Then he brought his face to his hands and cried outright.

"The *fuck* you doin'?" Black Kid yelled.

"I-I-I just saw my mother . . ."

"The *fuck* you just say?"

"He made me see my mother!" White Kid wept.

"What the shit you talkin' about, man? Your mother's dead."

"No," Dhevic corrected. "She's very much alive. Someplace else. Forever."

Hitching sobs and gagging, the white kid literally crawled away on his hands and knees.

Black Kid's gaze whipped back and forth, between Dhevic and his comrade. His expression kept forming and re-forming, the best he could do to mask his fear and confusion. He looked back at Dhevic, who seemed much more formidable now, and his hands patted his pockets in frustration.

"No weapons now?" Dhevic's voice grated. At his feet lay the pistol; he kicked it over to the black kid. "Before you pick it up, though . . . look."

The kid's defiant stare began to tremble. Dhevic stepped forward once, twice, baring his gaze down into his opponent's face. "And what of you? Would you like to see your sister?"

Their stares locked.

"Her name is—what? Jerrica? Erika? Something like that? Look. In my eyes. Look and you'll see her." His voice ground down like gravel rubbing. "Look and see what they're doing to her . . ."

The kid's mouth fell open, lips quivering. It appeared that what he saw was making his eyes quiver, too. "No more, no more," he murmured.

"It was *you* who hooked Erika up with the stoners," Dhevic said. He said it because he knew it. He knew nothing but everything. "It was part of some deal, wasn't it? Some kind of gang initiation. Well, that's what she's doing now. She'll die soon, too, and be in the same place as your friend's mother—but that doesn't matter. Look. Look."

"No. God. Please."

"And now Twanna," Dhevic said. "Your first girlfriend, right? Right now, she *is* in the same place as your friend's mother. You indoctrinated her . . . very effectively. Look. Look at her now . . ."

138

The kid fell to his knees and vomited. Like the other kid, he began to sob from the impact of the catastrophic vision.

"Those things eating her are called dentatapeds, a species of cacodemon from the Lower Orders. They eat her alive and regurgitate her every night, and then start again the next night. It's part of the entertainment for the Court of Grand Duke de Rais. The entire court rapes her first, of course. Twanna is immortal now. This is how she will spend eternity. Here, let me show you your brother—"

"NO!" The kid teetered on his knees like a svelte tree in high wind. Eyes bugging, he snatched the gun up from the pavement and put it to his head.

"Don't do that," Dhevic said very calmly. "What you have to understand is that you still have a chance, and so does your friend. Keep it all in mind, along with everything you've seen tonight." Then Dhevic gave the kid a selfless smile. "Who knows what the future holds?"

The kid dropped the gun, stood up in his shock. Like the other one, he fumbled in his pocket and threw some cash toward Dhevic. "Please. No more."

"Go. Go find your friend and tell him this: 'O send out your light and your truth. Let them lead me.'"

The kid sobbed as he staggered away.

Dhevic sighed in relief. *This is wearing me out,* he thought with a laugh. He looked up and down the motel front; no one had seen the bizarre confrontation. He quickly pocketed the pistol, then scooped the cash off the ground.

This is a fair shake of cash! he thought.

Then he thought: *Yep. God works in mysterious ways.*

He stuffed the money in his jacket pocket and walked across the main drag, to treat himself to an omelet at Denny's.

Chapter Nine

(I)

The night turned sedate, the moon hanging large and low. A comfortable breeze flowed off the bay to knock down some of the mugginess. Crickets could be heard, their chorus making the evening seem to throb. Jane felt tranquilized.

But still at odds with so many things, so much she didn't understand.

She sat out on the back porch, protected from mosquitoes. She let herself be lost in her thoughts, however confusing they may have been. The night breeze sifted through the screens, lifted her hair. She was trying to feel as good as she could under the circumstances.

She'd already checked on the kids; both Kevin and Jennifer were sound asleep, relieved that her fainting spell hadn't been serious. She'd checked all the outside doors, made sure they were locked. When her thoughts turned to the calamities of the past few days, she blocked them out.

All but one. What Steve had been saying earlier, just before he'd left: *Who else out there is in the cult too?*

Could it really be a *cult?* It made too much sense when Steve had been discussing it, but now? The day done, the kids asleep, the doors locked? *I just don't think I can believe it,* she thought. Not in an area like this. Not in Danelleton. There were no satanic cults, no ritual murderers in league with one another, like some integrated but very discreet cell of terrorists.

I should just go to bed, she told herself, but when she began to do that, a laziness kept her in the porch chair. It was too tranquil right now, too peaceful and serene. She loved the night breeze against her face, and the feel of the weatherproof carpet against her toes. *I could just fall asleep right out here,* she realized, and then a stiffer breeze blew in, rustling the backyard trees. It billowed her nightgown, slipped coolly down her warm skin. It felt—again—serene. It made her feel like the night.

What she didn't know was that the night was coming for her.

(II)

The night was his blood. He took it and lived on it. Technically, this would be called simple subcorporeal channeling. Not so technically: walking-around time for a disembodied spirit.

The Messenger liked to slip about at night. He liked

to see people, to see what they were doing. He liked, too, to get right behind them and puppet them, ooze into their minds until they were essentially one.

He glided on shadows. He stomped through brushes and brambles but made no sound. Now he was moving around the house, like a shadow himself, like a shadow moving in car lights.

What is in here? he wondered.

He stopped and looked into a window, saw a sleeping child, a young boy. The Messenger wanted to slip into the boy's head and spoil his dreams, make him wake screaming.

But not tonight . . .

I must control myself.

In the next window, a girl lay asleep, older than the boy. This roused the Messenger. She would be sweet to terrify, to corrupt, to destroy. Innocence was the problem, though, one of the Messenger's few barriers. He could not machinate her. He knew that if he genuinely exerted himself, he could send her dreaming visions into a tumult, he could drop them right off the precipice into the most foul canyon of the netherworld. He could pollute her dreams to the extent that she would never forget them, never recover. She'd be tainted for life.

Yes, it would be sweet.

But not tonight.

The Messenger smelled something better, just around the corner.

His blood surged from the smell. He was smelling sweet dreams that lay ripe for ruin. He smelled a woman, a robust woman.

In the back. Trees shivered in wind. Moonlight lay flat on new-mown grass. The Messenger's steps left blackened footprints from which tendrils of noxious smoke rose.

He was looking through a screen.

At her. At Jane. *Oh, yes. Much fodder there. So much meat for my gullet.*

Bare tan legs sprawled off the slatted chair. The Messenger wanted to lick them all the way up to her fresh sex, his black tongue leaving a sheen of putrid slime. Her breasts gently rose and fell beneath the semitransparent nightgown. The Messenger wanted to knead them and suck them out. Then he would mount her in the hot muck of his domain and just *have* her, spend himself in her, and then give her to his mascots.

Maybe that will happen sometime, he hoped. Who could tell? He hoped that life in this place would bring her down—to eternal life in *his* place. Then he would have her for his whimsy. Until then, he'd have to be patient, for she wasn't soiled enough.

He *could* machinate her, though. The temptation was overwhelming. His hideous hand reached through the screen, like smoke, and swept through her head. He was killing her dreams at once, showing her the delicious horrors of his own abode—an anticipation, perhaps. An *invitation*. Would she accept?

Probably not. Her heart was still strong, her resolve still too pure.

I can do this, *though,* he thought, chuckling.

She quivered in the chair, the nightmares he'd bidden infecting her like a virus. When he ran his bodiless hand down her breasts, he felt nothing, but when he placed it over her *own* hand, they fused together. Now he moved her hand to her breasts and felt the warm, moist skin himself, plucked a nipple hard enough to make her flinch in her sleep. He moved her hand down to her hips next, pulled up the hem of the night-gown, then plied her sex, fingers smoothing over the downy private hair.

He raised his hand to her throat and watched her hand do the same. He squeezed and her fingers constricted. She began to pant and shiver.

I could make you walk into your son's room and eviscerate yourself while he watched. I could make you walk into your daughter's room and snap her neck. . . .

But not tonight. . . .

Patience was a virtue, and so was prudence.

The Messenger was tired. He knew he must conserve his strength. Besides, there was easier fodder out there. The easy ones were always the most fun.

When he slipped away, the woman named Jane took her hand from her own throat and went lax, gasping. The Messenger was going away now, into some other fissure of the night. But as he passed another window, something caught his orblike eye. A glass box, with some sort of tiny creature in it. A toad.

The Messenger smiled.

The boy's pet, of course.

The Messenger looked at the toad and killed it with one phantasmal sigh, and then he was off, away with the breeze and the cricket trills and the night.

Yes. He was off for easier fodder.

(III)

Annabelle felt afire, her silken cinnamon hair dancing in the moonlight, which poured in from the bedroom window. A shining, naked whirlwind of flesh and sensation and pure, raw desire. Her hands opened flat against her husband's heaving chest; her hips squirmed over his, coltish legs clenching. She was riding him as though he were one of the horses of the apocalypse.

Her husband's name was Mark, a good decent man who focused on his wife as his chief priority. He worked for a defense contractor, the presentation director, and he'd be flying to California in the morning, would be away for a week. Annabelle saw it as her own priority, then, to see that he had a memorable send-off.

The Messenger did too.

And as for Annabelle, she was beginning to understand now, that weird flux that she'd felt in her head for a while: her own conscience melting into someone else's. She wasn't herself anymore—she was *more* than herself. She was two, her desires mingling, her nerves being borrowed, for an ultimate coalescence.

You are part of me, and I am part of you, she heard the words bubble in her ears.

Not her words.

Annabelle smiled.

Her nails were all but digging into Mark's chest, his own hands sliding in sweat over the curves of her rump and back. His face looked contorted as he staved off his release, grinding his teeth so as not to climax too fast. All the while, Annabelle bucked and bucked as the Messenger's shadow form manipulated her from behind. It was too easy.

"Baby, oh God," Mark panted. "You're . . . just . . . the best."

Oh, we know, came the shared thought in response.

Her legs tightened further. Annabelle's desire was cresting in what felt like a wave about to break. Her breasts bobbled, her moans flew around the room. Just another minute and she'd be there . . .

His thrusts trembled; his face looked absolutely pained, eyes crushed shut.

"Oh, baby, I can't hold off any—"

Mark's climax released, and his arms snaked around her back, pulled her chest to his during the last spasms. Then he relaxed in an instant, letting out the longest sigh . . .

"Honey, I'm sorry. I couldn't help it. It's just that you turn me on so much I can't control myself."

Annabelle leaned up, her smile full of warmth and love. Her hand stroked his face. "That's okay, dear. It was wonderful for me, too," she consoled him, and then—

CHUNK!

She rammed the point of the hunting knife straight down into his heart.

"Yeah, wonderful. In a pig's ass," she finished.

She'd placed the oversized Bowie knife under the pillow before they'd started, and had caught him at the perfect moment of distraction. She remained there, straddling him. Now her true ecstacy came to light, before the blooming eyes of her companion. She'd plunged the knife deep; she kept her hands on its handle and could feel it thumping with the final beats of his heart. He'd never even had time to cry out.

Beautiful, the Messenger thought.

A few loops of blood had pumped up, spattering her. Blood dripped off the tingling pinpoints of her nipples. It felt delicious, but what excited her even more was that this was just the beginning.

Eventually she got up, padded absently about the room, bare feet sinking into plush carpet. Had she ever felt this happy?

You did very well. I'm proud of you. Let's go over here now . . .

The seductive force that flowed through her limbs walked her over to the large, framed mirror over the dresser. She could see her dappled skin in the darkness tinged by moonlight. She stared, stared harder, until . . .

I can see you, she thought.

I know, and I can see you.

It took a few moments for her eyes to adjust but soon she could see the figure standing right behind her. No details at all, and scarcely any features save for basic shape.

Tall, wide shouldered, but gaunt somehow. A head larger than the proportion and oddly angled. It reminded Annabelle of a vise.

And something . . . What were they? Two protrusions seemed to curve outward from the forehead, like horns.

Yes, Annabelle. You're all mine. Let me luxuriate in you.

When Annabelle's hands rose, she could see that it was actually the Messenger's hands raising them. He brought them around, then began to caress her, to adore the feel of her flesh and the curves of her breasts with her own hands.

Then he brought the hands lower where they tended to her in the special ways that only she could know.

But the Messenger knew too.

Later, when her bliss was done, she yanked the Bowie knife out of her husband's chest and began to finish the message.

Chapter Ten

(I)

Bacon sizzled, and eggs over easy sputtered in the aromatic pan. Bread was plunged into the toaster, and fresh orange juice was poured.

Please, Jane thought. *Let this be a normal, perfectly dull day*. She milled about the kitchen in a pink terry robe, wearing fluffy bunny slippers that the kids had gotten her for a past Mother's Day. The kids, pajama-clad, busied themselves too, clanking plates out of the cupboard and setting the table. The sun blared through the front window, reinforcing Jane's hope that this would be the start of a regular day with no mishaps, fainting spells, or tragedies. Something didn't feel right, though.

"Are you feeling better today, Mom?" Jennifer asked, arranging the silverware.

Kevin clumsily laid out the patterned place mats. "Yeah, Mom. We were worried yesterday."

"I'm feeling a whole lot better," she replied. "Had a whopper of a headache after Dr. Mitchell left, but I'm great now." She watched a lump of butter melt in a big nonstick pan. "And now that we don't have to worry about that anymore, how do you want your eggs?"

"Scrambled, please," Jennifer requested.

"Sunny-side down!" Kevin jumped in. "I don't want 'em runny! Yuck!"

"Scrambled and sunny-side down," Jane acknowledged. "Coming right up."

Kevin rushed out of the room, assuring her, "Be right back!" while Jennifer sat at the table.

"Oh, wow, I just remembered, Mom. Last night I dreamed I was riding a unicorn through this big sunny field full of flowers."

"Sounds wonderful."

"Did you dream?"

Jane forced herself to think. She knew she dreamed quite a bit but often lost the memory shortly after waking. *Did I?* she wondered over the eggs. She stood still, spatula in hand. Then something—an image, a memory, something very dark—began to bother her. "Yes, honey, I-I think I did dream last night . . ."

"What did you dream about?"

More images formed in the back of her mind, then some memories of sensations. The sensations were exciting yet unpleasant at the same time. Then her stomach began to turn. She stood there, motionless, staring at the hood over the stove.

"Mom?"

"My dreams weren't very good," Jane finally said. Better that than the truth. What she recalled was terrifying. She'd felt smothered. Some other consciousness had been inside of her own mind, prowling about at will. The consciousness seemed entirely bodiless, so how had it been able to touch her? Something or someone had been touching her, erotically at first but then violently. The impact of those two opposite notions made her stomach turn even more. *I dreamed that I was being choked, for God's sake,* she recalled. *I was being caressed and then choked. Someone was trying to strangle me.*

Jane gulped and shivered. Why would she dream such an awful thing anyway? In a sense, though, it was understandable. Awful dreams often followed awful genuine events, and Danelleton had certainly had its share of that lately. But the final realization made her grit her teeth. She remembered who'd been strangling her in the dream.

Myself.

"No, I had a lousy dream, honey. Dreams are weird that way. You can't figure them out. After you think about them, though, they seem pretty silly."

"Well, mine wasn't silly. It was great. I hope I dream about the unicorn again tonight. I could even smell the flowers in the field."

Jane got back to the eggs, or at least she tried to until a slow plodding movement snagged her attention at the corner of her eye. She turned toward the kitchen entrance. It was Kevin.

He looked absolutely morose. He stood there still as a fence post, something in his cupped hands. A second glance showed Jane that he had tears in his eyes.

152

She put the spatula down and rushed to him. "Honey, what's wrong?"

"Oh, no," Jennifer said when she saw what was in her brother's hand. "What happened!"

Jane strained her vision. *What is that?*

Now Kevin's tears bubbled up. "Mel's dead."

That's Mel? Jane thought.

What sat still in Kevin's hands looked like a small hunk of roadkill but as Jane squinted she noticed the horned toad's overall features. But there was something else—wet and glimmery—that seemed connected to the pet's head.

Its innards.

"Somebody killed him, Mom. Somebody killed *Mel.*"

"Well, honey," Jane began. "I'm sure it was just some kind of accident."

"No!" the boy insisted. "Somebody did it to him!"

"Kevin, are you sure you didn't step on him?" Jennifer looked at the mess and made an appropriate face. "It looks like his guts came out. You must've stepped on him or dropped something on him."

"No, I didn't!" Kevin pouted. Now the tears were flowing freely. "He was inside the terrarium—I couldn't have *stepped* on him! And nothing could've fallen on him either. The lid was on! Somebody must've snuck into my room and squashed him in their hand!"

"Kevin, you're letting your imagination get away from you," Jane told him. "No one snuck into the house. The doors are locked. Mel just—" She didn't know what to say to console him. "He just had an accident, or maybe he got sick, some . . . toad disease."

"Yeah, and he upchucked his guts," Jennifer added.

"No!" Kevin was almost shouting now. "I know it was somebody who did this—they did it on purpose!"

"Kevin, who would do a sick thing like that?" Jennifer asked.

"A sick person, that's who! There's sick people all over the place. Like Marlene and Carlton—they were sick in the head but nobody knew. Like the guy who killed Dad!"

Oh, jeez, Jane thought. There was no reasoning with him. *Poor kid. Father killed by a psycho. Two mass murders in the same week. Now this. He doesn't know which end is up.* "Kevin, calm down. Nobody did this deliberately. It's impossible."

"Kevin, really," Jennifer said, trying to help. "No one broke into the house just to kill Mel. Mom's right. He must've gotten some disease in his stomach."

"Somebody *killed* him!" the boy shrieked, then stormed out.

Jane sighed. So much for a perfectly normal day.

Breakfast was shot, most of it being dumped down the disposal. Jane grabbed a spade from the garage and helped Kevin bury the toad in the backyard near the rose bushes. A small Tupperware container sufficed for a coffin; when they were done, Kevin placed a makeshift cross in the earth, made from popsicle sticks. By now the boy's anguish had simmered down to quiet sobbing. Later, she drove to work, making starting time by just a few minutes. Already the day was in the wrong gear, and it had just started. The twisted images of her nightmare—the erotic fused with the revolting—haunted her for the first hour of her shift. *Where did that all come from?* she kept wondering. She didn't like getting off on the wrong foot—it would taint the rest of her shift—but what could she do? Her little west branch post office was now doubletiming until the main branch could be reopened. *Get your mind back on your job, Jane,* she told herself. *You wanted to be station manager—well, now you are. Don't screw it up.*

Her office door stood open a few inches; she could hear several carriers talking in front of the coffeemaker, but it was disconcerting talk. *More of the same,* she thought. They were rehashing the murders, speculating about Marlene and Carlton, and the like. *When something bad happens in a town, people can't stop talking about it. But never when something good happens.* A sad trust. She was just about to start working on the routing reports when a rapping caught her attention.

"Good morning, Ms. Ryan. May I come in?"

Steve could be seen in the gap in the door. *God, I wish he'd stop calling me Ms. Ryan,* she thought. It sounded stilted. "Have a seat," she offered. Seeing him made her instantly feel better . . .

She wondered about that.

"I hope I'm not bothering you," he said and took the chair next to her desk. His blond hair looked damp—he'd probably just gotten out of the shower. Today he wore no jacket and no gun holster, just slacks and a light short sleeve shirt, but when he sat down and crossed his legs, his ankle holster could be seen. *He's a good-looking man, no two ways about that,* Jane thought.

"I know you're busy. I was in the area so I thought I'd stop by to see how you're feeling."

Jane relaxed. "I'm good, thank you, and thank you again for all your help yesterday. Would you like some coffee? I'll warn you though—post office coffee is *bad* coffee."

"The only thing worse is police coffee, and I've already had my morning cup, thanks."

Jane was slightly taken aback. *He stopped by just to see how I was doing. How sweet.* "I'm actually trying to give up coffee. Sometimes it works, sometimes it doesn't." When the phone rang, she frowned. It was Kevin.

"Yes, I know, honey," she said into the phone. The boy was still distressed about the horned toad. "But you've got to understand that these things happen sometimes. Like we talked about this morning. Sometimes pets get sick, sometimes accidents happen. I know you're still upset but you'll feel better soon, just wait and see. Mind your sister now, okay? I'll try to be home early tonight. You and Jennifer can make pizza like you did last time. How's that sound? 'Bye, honey. I love you." Then she hung up, flustered.

Steve could sense her unease. "What was that about pets?"

"Oh, my son's pet toad died this morning—"

"Aw no, not Mel. He showed it to me yesterday when I brought him and Jennifer back to the house. What happened?"

"We're not sure. It just died; it looked squashed. Kevin's still really upset about it; he loved that little toad. My husband gave it to him."

"Divorced, huh?"

Jane's eyes flicked down. "No, my husband was murdered a few years ago."

"Jesus, I'm sorry," Steve said, totally taken off guard.

"Some nut escaped from a psych ward," she said, not even really hearing the words.

"I'm really sorry to hear it." Steve tried to shift through his discomfort. "It must be tough, you know, running the post office and raising two kids on your own."

"Not really. Jennifer's really good about keeping an eye on Kevin. She's very mature for her age."

"Yeah, they're both great kids."

"Do you have children?"

Steve chuckled. "Me? Nope. No wife, either."

"How come you're not married?" she asked but immediately regretted it. The tone was too personal.

"I was a couple times," he lazily answered, "but it just never worked out. Divorce lawyers love me. Got no one to blame but myself."

"Why do you say that?"

"It's like the old cliché, like on some cop show you'd see on TV. I wound up being married more to my job than to my wives. They couldn't hack it—can't say that I blame them. It actually happens all the time with cops, part of the territory."

It was sad the way he'd compartmentalized it. And Jane felt guilty at the secret pang of interest in knowing now that he wasn't married. "I guess we all have our territory," she said. Now, though, she noticed a different discomfort about him. It wasn't the tragic topic of her husband's murder, nor was it his failed domestic life.

"Something else on your mind?" she asked.

"Yeah, I guess, er—well, no."

"Chief Higgins, you're really giving yourself away. What's wrong?"

"The first thing that's wrong is you calling me Chief Higgins. Call me Steve."

"Sure, but only if you lose the 'Ms. Ryan' and call me Jane."

"Deal." He scratched his nose. "Well, there is something. You don't need to know all the details, but—"

"Why not?" she almost snapped back. "Why don't I need to know the details? I've got two employees who just went on double murder sprees, and a whole lot of other employees dead as victims, but I don't have a right to know whatever it is you're hiding?"

"The rest doesn't really have anything to do with your employees," he said.

"What, more stuff about cults? More stuff about that bell-shaped symbol found at both murder scenes?"

He sighed, was about to say something, but then—

His pager went off.

Jane smiled. "You're right, it's like the old cliché, like something on a cop show."

"Tell me about it." He just shook his head. "Can't sit down, can't talk, can't even blink without this thing going off. Most days I don't even have time to eat. We'll talk later, okay?"

"Okay." Jane had to repress herself. More and more, even within the last few minutes, her attraction to him was growing. "And if you don't have time to eat, feel free to come to the house tonight after work. Kevin and Jennifer make excellent pizza."

Steve stood up, grabbed his keys, and smiled again. "I just might take you up on that. See ya."

I wonder, she thought when he left. Had she put him on the spot? *Probably doesn't even have time to think about it.* But at least she'd opened the invitation and perhaps broken some professional ice. *Sometimes I amaze myself . . .*

After a while, she left her office to scout about the station. She made a round through the processing area, speaking briefly to the handlers and making sure everything was running properly. Delivery-point-sequence machines clattered in their factorylike racket, launching letters automatically into separate piles. More busy staff nodded and smiled when they passed her, pushing hoppers full of mail sacks. In the open loading dock bays, their contents were rolled off ramps by more staff, only to be refilled with outgoing mail to the central processing and distribution centers in Jacksonville and Miami. *A typical day at the post office,* Jane thought. It was second nature to her. It seemed strange that other people's mail was such a large part of her life. The average person could never realize all that the job entails, along with the astonishing fact that the U.S. Postal Service delivered more mail in one month than the rest of the world delivered in a year.

She turned down an aisle and immediately soured. Martin Parkins was the senior handler, which was sort of a polite way of saying he was practically unpromoteable. Stoop shouldered, overweight, around fifty. He'd dyed his hair almost jet black, which didn't work at all with the aged face. Big callused hands jacked letters into two-foot trays.

Martin regularly made his disgruntlement known; Jane simply put up with it. Whenever he was up for a level promotion he wound up blowing the interview with his bad attitude, to the extent that Jane didn't know what to do with him. She'd written him up in the past several times but as a federal employee, it was nearly impossible to fire him. She couldn't even fire him for drinking. Each time he was reprimanded, he'd simply enter a alcohol-abuse program for seven days, get out, and start all over again. This time, though, Jane thought she might try a new approach.

Martin glanced up at Jane's approach; the anger-wrought wrinkles in his face reminded her of a mud slide.

"Hello, Martin," she said.

Martin didn't answer directly but grunted something under his breath. He focused his attention back down on his station, hauling out more two-foot trays.

"Look, Martin. I know you and I have never particularly liked each other—"

"Oh, we haven't?" he said back very quickly. "Gee, all this time I thought I was your best friend. You know, since you suspended me last year, and filled my P.E.R. with a bunch of crap and reprimands."

"You were coming to work with alcohol on your breath every other day, Martin. The reason your personnel evaluation report is full of reprimands is because you weren't doing your job properly, and it just made your attitude worse. That was all your own doing and you know it."

Martin still didn't respond. Instead he ignored her, loading up more trays.

"And believe it or not, Martin," she went on, "now that Carlton's gone, you're the senior staff member. You've got more time in grade than anyone."

Martin snorted under his breath. "Uh-huh. And I guess that means you're going to promote me, right?"

"That's right, Martin."

The older man's eyes narrowed. For the sparsest moment, she thought she saw a flash of happiness in his eyes, but the flash faded, overwhelmed by all that angst.

"I'm promoting you to DPS foreman, and giving you a one-level raise," Jane said. Then she thought, *Now, let's just see . . .*

Martin hesitated, then looked back down at his work. "I don't want it," he said, more to the trays than to her.

"Come on, Martin. Don't be obstinate. You've wanted a promotion for five years and now I'm handing you one."

"I don't want *nothin'* from you. I just want to do my job, get my paycheck, and mind my own business."

"You're being juvenile. You're letting a grudge against me affect your professional life. That's not going to do you or me any good at all."

Finally the man's eyes snapped up at Jane. "Listen, *Ms.* Ryan. I don't bother no one, and I don't want no one to bother me. You act like you're doing poor Martin a big favor, but the truth is you ain't got no one else in this joint qualified to take Carlton's position."

"Don't flatter yourself. There are plenty of other employees qualified to take the job."

"Fine. Give it to one of them."

I was so hoping this wouldn't happen . . . but I knew it would, she thought. "Suit yourself, Martin."

He grumbled something further. Jane walked away.

Chapter Eleven

(I)

Martin Parkins felt as though his head would explode. His blood simmered; his temples felt like pins had been driven into them. Where did she get off patronizing him like that? She was playing games with him! *Yeah, she's hot shit now that she's station manager. Offers me a pissant raise when she knows damn well I should get Carlton's job.*

He closed his eyes, gritting at his rage. He placed his head down on the table and took deep breaths. His hands were shaking, his eyelids fluttering. Martin was mad all the time, perpetually pissed-off at the world and the people who'd given him the shaft, and he was *tired* of the shaft. He'd been close to the breaking point for years; today, though, was the worst.

When Jane Ryan walked away from his station, his eyes followed her out with the wildest thoughts: that

163

tight rump in those tight regulation post-office shorts. Her shirt was tight too—probably deliberately. It made her breasts look like they might break out of it. *The tease,* he thought. *Likes to tease old Martin, really get his goat. Wears that shit too tight on purpose.*

When she'd fully left, he smiled. *One of these days I'll tune that bitch up but good. I'll punch her ticket like it's never been punched.*

She was good looking, though. The hot shits always were. Always thought they were a little bit better than everyone else just because they'd happened to be born attractive, and because they had a little more education. Truth was, Jane Ryan was no better than anyone, just luckier. And all Martin was getting was more of the shaft.

He finished the last of his two-foot trays, each containing exactly 460 sorted letters, and decided to take a break. He worked hard too. The only difference was he got no credit. If Ryan had given him that psycho Carlton's job, he'd make a lot more money and would finally have the respect he deserved. The bitch had played him, offered him the shit job, instead, knowing that he had too much pride to take it, and now she was probably writing that up in his eval report too.

Oh, yeah. One of these days, she'll get hers.

He slipped out when most of the processors were cutting out for lunch. Martin didn't want lunch. He went into the bathroom, took the back stall, and sat down. He slipped out his flask and took a slug. Kessler's whiskey. Smooth as silk. A couple more hits and he started to feel better—

—feel better, that is, in the strangest way.

All he could think about was Jane Ryan, and those thoughts were getting pretty low-down. He wasn't mad anymore; he was thrilled. He began to feel very much in control. He couldn't put his finger on the way he felt—it was impossible for him to articulate—but it seemed as though a feeling of security had suddenly overwhelmed him. Like a guardian angel had come down upon him.

A few more hits on the Kessler's and he knew. It wasn't just Jane Ryan. It was damn near everyone. The people out there *needed* guys like Martin to tear down, so that they could feel better themselves. It built them up to trod on low-key mind-his-own-business guys like Martin. Ryan was no different. They were all having a laugh . . .

Well, the next laugh's gonna be on me . . .

He put the flask away, left the stall, and got ready to go back to work. He felt great. In his mind he saw all the ways he could start getting back at all these phony schmucks, starting with Ryan. Yes, he could do a job on her, all right. Just wait for a time she leaves work a little late, wait for her in the parking lot, put a gun in her ribs, and drive her out of there. Take her down the coast a ways, tie her up and have some fun with her for a few hours, and then drop her snooty ass in one of the sinkholes. Then he could start on the rest of them.

Yes, he heard.

A voice.

But not his own voice, really.

It was some other guy's voice.

And in not much more time, he'd get to know the other guy really well, and he'd understand it all.

(II)

Dusk began to pinken the horizon; sunset was always a spectacular event in Florida, even more so in a pretty town like Danelleton. Darkening orange bloomed through the masses of palm trees. A familiar warm breeze flowed over the landscape. Night was coming.

The houses weren't all the same but they were all nice: newly painted, well-kept, a suburban utopia. The sun set lower over one house in particular—Annabelle's house, a long hacienda-style ranch with tile shingles and an arched entrance. A van pulled up in the driveway, whose side panel read STRAUSS HEATING AND AIR-CONDITIONING, ALWAYS ON CALL. The tall repairman with wavy hair and goatee got out with tools and clipboard, enthusiastic for the late call. Erik used to worked all days, mostly commercial units in St. Pete, and it had been hotter than hell. But these late ones, at a private residence, were a lot easier to get into, plus he'd often get a tip.

Sometimes Erik even got lucky. In Florida? All the women? There was nothing better than a residential call by a housewife whose husband was out of town, and a good-looking guy like Erik? More than once he'd gotten tipped twice.

I can only hope, he thought, strolling up the driveway.

Then the hope was dashed. *So much for that idea* . . . Another van was parked up in the drive, not

the home owner's, another service truck, PARAVISION CA-
BLE TV. Then:

What the fuck?

A third van read WALTON FURNITURE REPAIR.

"Great," Erik said to himself. "Two other repairmen in
there, too. No nookie for me tonight." But that was
okay. Erik was aware of his blessings. He never took
them for granted.

He walked up to the front door, then smiled at the
probability. *Yeah, probably some husband and wife in
their sixties, with a house full of grandkids. Still might
get a good tip.*

Before he knocked, something snagged his eye: the
odd door knocker on the center stile. *Fucked up,* he
thought. It was an oval of tarnished bronze depicting a
morose half-formed face. Just two eyes, no mouth, no
other features.

The term *bad omen* was not familiar to him.

When he knocked, and the door opened, though,
Erik was hard-pressed not to do a rebel yell . . .

A woman answered, big smile and big bright eyes.
She'd have been a knockout in a friggin' potato sack,
but in the see-through black nightgown?

Holy shit. The motherlode, Erik thought.

"Hi," she said. "Come on in. I really appreciate you
coming at this hour. It's not easy to get air-conditioning
service after five."

Short, petite. Shining shoulder-length hair like dark
amber. The nightgown's hem was way, way high—
maybe just an inch below her crotch. And if the wind
blew? It would be Muff Town; Erik wasn't sure but he

could almost swear that she was pantiless. She was braless, too, and he didn't have to wonder about that one. Compact little breasts right there with big dark nipples showing through the shadowy see-through top.

"No, uh, no problem, ma'am. We make house calls around the clock."

She giggled and let him in. "A lot of them say that but try actually getting one this late. Seriously, I'm really grateful for you coming. When the air-conditioning is out, this place turns into a oven, even at night. My name's Annabelle, by the way."

"Erik. Nice to meet you."

When they shook hands, Erik found hers hot and moist. And there was a little mist of perspiration just above her cleavage, and down the front of her legs, too. Erotic.

Like she'd just been getting it on maybe.

Still awestruck by that body in the revealing gown, he followed her through the foyer into the kitchen. Nice place, just like the outside, which was par for the course in Danelleton. But again he considered the probability. First of all, he knew there were two other repairman in the joint right now. Second, Annabelle was more than likely married to some rich codger who needed the arm candy, and Erik would be meeting him in a moment.

"Yeah, you're the first repairman I've dealt with today who actually came when he said he would."

All right, this is too funny. Third time she'd mentioned "coming," that and the fuck-me nightgown, like a bad joke in a T&A flick. Was she doing it on purpose or was she just naive? Didn't matter. Erik could have some fun with it too, because he knew this couldn't amount to anything. "Looks like you've got your share of repairmen here."

Now she was leading him down a hallway. It was a little dark but somehow that only accentuated her body in the gown. The sheer material looked like smoke floating around her.

"Oh, yes. The TV man's here too."

"Cable problems, huh?"

"Yes. Something was wrong with the channels, so he had to feed a new line into my box."

Erik had to frown because if he didn't frown, he'd bust out laughing. "Uh, yeah," was all he said.

"And then I had to call the furniture man too—"

Annabelle turned with a smile that was impossible not to describe as wanton. Her breasts stuck out in the veil-like top. "I needed him to fix the knobs on my chest."

Then she quickly turned, leading him down the hall. Erik just shook his head.

"I've got this nice blond-wood chest in the living room. So he fixed the knobs and also the drawers."

Some sweat was accumulating on Erik's brow. Just the look of her, and the deliberate words and the way she'd spoken them—it was all beginning to really get Erik going. But he knew the scoop now. This was too much, a joke. She was just another bored housewife playing with the tough-guy repairman. Hubby would be waiting with a flashlight at the a/c unit, and the fun would be over. That was all right. *Just wait'll the guys hear about this at the shop.* With lines like this one was dishing out? *Bet they don't even believe it.*

"I even had the landscapers here earlier," she said.

Erik couldn't, knew he shouldn't—he didn't need a sexual harassment complaint. But—*Jesus!*—she was harassing him, wasn't she? He couldn't resist his response. "Let me guess. You had some bushes that needed trimming?"

"No!" she laughed. "They tilled my garden!"

You gotta be shitting me, lady.

The end of the hall opened into the garage, and through there, another door took them outside into the backyard. Darkness and pleasant night sounds waited for them.

"Sorry, the porch light's out," she said, leading him to the unit.

"I've got a flashlight," Erik said and snapped it on. The strong beam roved once across her bosom, then she turned. "So what exactly seems to be the problem?" he asked her. "You getting any function at all?"

"The unit functions *too* well, if you want to know the truth. It's on all the time; it's overresponsive, I think. And every time I touch the little control button inside, it overreacts. I guess my thermostat's too sensitive."

"Oh, I can fix your thermostat, no problem. But let me take a look at your inductors." Erik smiled in the dark, threw the flashlight beam down into the unit's grill. Annabelle stood to the side, hands on knees and bent over.

The unit kicked on, sounded fine. *There's nothing wrong with this,* he knew. "Yeah, it's not out here," he said playing along. "I'll have to go inside, check that inflow switch, part of the primary front end. That's inside, can't do that out here."

"You sound like a man who knows the job."

"No brag, just fact, ma'am. I've had a lot of experience. It might also be your system's receiving nodes, too."

"Um-hmm," she said.

Erik stepped closer beside her, where she remained leaning over. A side glance showed him her bare breasts in the *V* of her top.

"But you said you have to go inside?" she asked.

"Yeah, your control unit. That's where the switch is. It's all integrated, ma'am. That's what you've got to understand. We're talking about a problem with the overall mechanical nomenclature of your system's front end."

"Okay." She whirled around and led him back into the garage. *Yeah, this is something, ain't it?* Erik thought. Now was the moment of truth, though. If this was all tease—which he was sure it was—then he'd know in a minute. They were going back into the house.

"When was the last time your unit went on the fritz?"

"Oh, it's on the fritz all the time," she said.

He kept the flashlight on to light their way back. A sudden breeze swept the backyard; it pressed her gown right to her skin, highlighting the lines of her breasts.

"But I don't remember the last time it's been serviced by a pro," she finished.

Another shake of his head. It was time for a test. "Well, when we go inside, let me ask your husband, see if he remembers the last time a repairman came out. Maybe a service record was left with the receipt. I can see what was done."

"No luck there," Annabelle told him. "My husband's out of town, and I don't know where he might keep any records like that."

Okay, Erik thought. *This is starting to get very interesting.* But what about the two other repair guys in the house? Erik was thinking a way around that when Annabelle stopped halfway back to the outside door.

What's she stopping for? Erik thought. *What, she wants to do it right here in the yard?* It was fine by him.

She looked up to the moon, held out her arms. "It's such a beautiful night, isn't it?"

He stepped closer. "Sure."

"I guess you're in a hurry, got another call tonight, huh?"

"Nope, this is the last one. I'm in no hurry at all."

"Then come on! Let's have a beer!" She grabbed his hand and tugged him out toward the other end of the yard.

"Beer sounds great to me," he said, off guard. The yard grew darker the farther they got from the house. "Where, uh, where are we going?"

"The kiosk!"

Kiosk? Erik could only see darkness. But he could smell something, too, something good, but before he could ask—

"It's where I have my quiet time. There's a cooler full of beer and a barbecue."

"Ah, I knew I smelled something cooking. Smells great, by the way."

"I'm cooking a brisket. It'll be done in a few hours. You gotta slow cook it all day."

All right. That made sense. She was cooking a

brisket in her backyard barbecue and she had a cooler of beer back there. Perfectly normal.

Erik strained his eyes. It was very dark, but in a few more steps the wooden kiosk came into view. His vision was adjusting now. The kiosk looked like a lattice-work of crystal in the moonlight. Several high palm trees surrounded it, their leaves gently flittering in the breeze.

"Have a seat!" She released his hand and popped open a cooler, withdrew two beers from ice. Erik sat down on the picnic table bench. The cold beer refreshed him. "Nice little place back here," he observed. "Kinda dark, though."

Annabelle remained standing, reveling in the gentle breeze. "I could light the tiki torches but that would draw mosquitoes."

Erik wanted to get laid. What he *didn't* was to get was West Nile. "Then let's pass on the tiki torches."

She seemed lost in thought, looking up to the sky. Erik was looking at her back. She raised her hands as if in some secret, exuberant prayer. Then—unless Erik's eyes were deceiving him—her hands came back down very slowly. She was caressing herself.

Then she flipped off the straps of her nightgown. The gown slipped down her body like dark fluid, pooling around her ankles.

To hell with the beer. Erik stood up, walked toward her just as she turned. Stark naked now, she smiled in the dark.

"Guess it's time to get down to business, right?" Erik said.

"Yeah," she sighed, and then they were in a clinch.

They kissed ravenously. She pressed right against him, standing on tiptoes. Erik's hands prowled up and down her sleek back, played with her buttocks. When he squeezed both cheeks hard, grinding her pubis to his thigh, she moaned out loud. Her own hand began to play too, up front. It slithered over the denim of his jeans.

Hidey-HO! he thought, sucking her tongue. This was going to be his best service call in a *long* time.

He could feel her nipples hardening against his shirt. Her fingers began to unfasten his belt, and then—

She stopped and stepped back, big smile on her face.

Erik's shoulders dropped. "You're not just teasing me, are you? Please tell me that ain't so."

"It ain't so," she mocked his voice. "We have to check something first."

"What?" He was getting annoyed. "There's nothing wrong with your a/c."

"Not *that,* silly. The brisket!"

The fuckin' brisket. Jesus. Lady, you've been all over me tonight. I don't give a fuck about the fucking brisket.

"It'll just take a second. I haven't checked it since before the sun went down. Get your flashlight."

Erik had plenty of doubts now. At least he got a good feel. She must just be some nutcase housewife who got off on teasing men. *It's a good thing I'm a nice guy,* he thought. *You come on to some guys like that and then don't put out, you'll wind up getting it the hard way.* But, no, that wasn't Erik's style.

He'd set his tool bag down at the edge of the kiosk and he thought he'd set the flashlight down right next to it. He fumbled there now in the dark. When he looked to the side, though, he noticed something white. *What the fuck is that?* He squinted, then reached over. Picked it up.

It was a white cowboy hat.

"What's with the hat?" he asked impatiently. "Your husband's?"

She was staring off again, distracted, only half-listening. "Oh. No. It's the furniture guy's. He must've . . . left it out here earlier."

The furniture guy? So she had him back here earlier, it seemed. And the cable guy, too, he presumed. Erik thought about that a second, then shrugged. Sloppy seconds didn't bother him. *Hell, I got a rubber in my wallet.* But—

He set the hat down on the picnic table. The furniture truck was still in the driveway, and so was the cable truck. "So those guys were back here earlier, and now they're back in the house working?"

A pause. "Um-hmm. They were . . . just finishing up when you came. They've probably even left by now. So . . . you don't have to worry about anyone . . . interrupting us."

Erik guessed he bought the answer. The situation was easy to calculate. When the husband's out of town on business, Wifey packs in as much strange as she can. *Nothing wrong with that.*

"But . . ." Erik looked back at the cowboy hat. "That looks like a pretty expensive hat. What, the guy just left it here?"

"Forget about the hat," she said and faced him. Her nakedness radiated in the dark. She was almost glowing. "He'll come back for it tomorrow."

Erik nodded, then he noticed something else in the grainy darkness. Something right next to the hat on the picnic table. It was a hacksaw.

"What's with the saw?"

"Uh . . ." She smiled. "The landscapers, silly. I told you, I had landscapers here."

"Yeah, I know. To till your garden."

She giggled. "They were cutting some dead branches off the trees."

Erik chewed on that one. It made sense but still . . . cowboy hats, hacksaw, a brisket on the barbecue, and a whack-job naked housewife. The night was getting weird fast.

Her mood switched; suddenly she was flighty again. "Now quit fooling around and get your flashlight. Check my brisket! Otherwise I'll have to light the torches and if I light the torches I have to put my nightgown back on."

Erik got the flashlight.

The bright beam bared down. A trace of smoke leaked out from under the barbecue's lid. It smelled great, like pork roast or prime rib. Erik was looking down at the barbecue, but . . .

. . . if he'd actually looked up and shone the flashlight past the kiosk, he would've seen two bodies.

He opened the lid—

He didn't have time to turn, to run, to shout. He didn't have time to react. He didn't even have time to feel the impact of the shock.

WHACK!

The bend of the crowbar hit him right at the top of the spine. The vertebrae shattered at once. Erik was quadriplegic by the time he had collapsed fully to the kiosk's floor.

He was still alive, though. Brain cells still firing, eyes still seeing, thoughts still flowing. He simply couldn't move. He lay paralyzed, staring up.

"Did you see?"

Her voice fluttered down. She was standing above him, one foot on either side, hands on hips. She grinned down at him. "Did you see what was in the barbecue?"

Erik, understandably, could only think now in unsorted fragments. His heart was slamming for all that had happened in the past few seconds, his horror and terror and fear all colliding. But, yes, yes.

He had seen.

When he'd opened the barbecue lid, two human heads looked back at him from the grill. The porklike waft of aroma had floated up amid steam. It was only a split-second glance but a split second was sufficient. The heads were roasting, crackling a little. One victim had a shaved head and goatee, the other broader, hair singeing off, clean shaven.

Annabelle was now kneeling at Erik's side, breasts swaying, glee in her smile, as she briskly began to saw Erik's head off with the hacksaw. Erik died shortly thereafter.

It took a few minutes, the grisly rip of each thrust of the blade resounding upward as all the blood pumped out of Erik's body. When the head was detached, Annabelle put it on the grill with the others and closed the lid.

* * *

Annabelle wasn't going to eat the heads, by the way. She was a vegetarian. It simply occurred to her that cooking them would be appropriate. It had the right ring to it: cooking heads. She could see the tabloid headline now: PSYCHO HOUSEWIFE COOKS HEADS!

It was just the kind of message she wanted to leave, and she knew that the Messenger was pleased.

He walked her back into the house, actually more drifting than walking. She felt wistful and dreamy, the naked night-nymph wandering aimlessly down silent hallways. She killed the furniture man in the cowboy hat and the cable technician exactly the same way she'd killed Erik. By the time night had fallen, it was safe. No one would see what was going on in the backyard. The four landscapers she'd killed in the house, each in a separate room, cutting their throats during sex.

She couldn't wait for the police to find the bodies, (especially the heads!). She couldn't wait for the message to be spread. She could feel the Messenger close against her from behind, lovingly walking her along, touching her with her own hands.

She left the light on in the bathroom. She wanted to see him behind her in the dark, and after a moment, staring into the mirror's dark veins, she did.

Did I do good?

Yes.

She took two of her dead husband's razor blades out of the dispenser. She smiled dreamily at the corroded face behind her.

Now?

Now, my dear.

Messenger

Her master's messages were done, and now it was time for Annabelle to be done, too. It was time for her to go to a new and exciting place where she could serve the Messenger and his colleagues directly.

Thank you.

Annabelle gashed her wrist, then painted the master's symbol on the mirror. Then she closed her eyes and grinned and very gently and slowly slid each razor deep into the sides of her throat, severing the major arteries to the brain. She leaned back, held her hands up as if to solicit the stars as the blood pumped in soft jets to either side, like crimson angel wings.

Chapter Twelve

(I)

Jane poured the pizza sauce liberally into the center of the uncooked crust, then handed Kevin the rubber spatula. "Try to spread it as evenly as you can, honey," she said. "You don't want too much in one place and not enough someplace else."

"I know, Mom."

When he was done, Jennifer grated a lump of fresh mozzarella over the pizza. While she did this, Kevin's eyes lost their luster and he wandered to the table and sat down. He looked dejected.

"But, Mom," Jennifer was saying. "You know, you are sort of, aren't you?"

Oh, Lord, Jane thought. "What, honey?"

"Aren't you sort of, like, dating him?"

"Steve? Of course not, honey." *Of all the questions!*

she thought. Kids were so precocious. It was something Jennifer had been edging at lately. "He's just a
friend, so I invited him over for dinner, that's all. I don't
even know him that well."

"Yeah, but you like him, don't you?"

"Just do the cheese, honey."

"I think he's cool. I think you should date him."

Jane frowned. "And when you're done with the
cheese, you can start on the pepperoni. I'll start chopping up the onions and peppers." She glanced over her
shoulder, looked at Kevin, who was still sitting sullenly
at the table, chin in hand.

"I wonder when he's gonna snap out of it," Jennifer
whispered.

"He's upset, honey. He loved that little toad."

"Sure, Mom. I loved Mel too, but it's not the end of
the world. How long is he gonna mope like that?"

"It takes time to get over things. And it will take
Kevin longer because he's younger than you are."

Such things were difficult to explain. Failing at it, she
knew, was just another element of motherhood. "Make
sure the oven's on," she said, trying to change the subject. "It needs to be preheated. And grab that bottle of
oregano." They'd busied themselves a few minutes
more, Jane chopping the onions and peppers, when
the doorbell rang.

"That's him!" Jennifer exclaimed.

"It might not be, honey. I'm not even sure if he's
coming. He might be too busy—he's a policeman."
Jane hoped that it was him, though, but—*With my
luck, it'll be the people from The Watchtower.* She set

down the knife and was about to go to the door, but her daughter was already racing for it.

"I'll get it!" Jennifer said, and scurried away.

Jane rolled her eyes. Never a dull moment. Then Steve walked in with a big smile and a white cardboard box

"Hi, everybody. Boy, something sure smells good in here."

What's in the box? Jane thought. *It looks like something from a Chinese carryout. I told him we were making pizza!*

Everybody said their hellos, save for Kevin, who remained gloomy. Then Steve placed the box on the table in front of him.

"How are you today, Kevin?"

Kevin shrugged, saying nothing.

"Kevin!" Jane complained. "Where are you manners? Say hello to Chief Higgins."

"Hi, Chief Higgins," he droned. Slowly, though, his eyes drifted to the box. "What's in there?"

"Well, I'm not sure, Kevin," Steve said, "but I think it's for you."

"For me?"

"Yeah. Why don't you go ahead and look inside."

Curiosity dragged Kevin out of the funk. He picked up the box and carefully opened the lid.

Then his face lit up. "Wow! Look, Mom!"

A baby horned toad meandered about in the bottom of the box.

"It looks just like Mel, only smaller!"

"He's only a few weeks old," Steve said.

"Steve," Jane said, "you shouldn't have. That was sweet of you."

Kevin was bubbling over with excitement. "Wow, thanks, Chief Higgins!" Then, to Jane: "Mom, I'll eat later, okay? I'm not hungry right now. I'm gonna go play with him."

"All right, honey."

"I'm gonna name him Mel, Junior!"

Kevin cradled the box in his hands and tromped to the next room.

"That really did the trick," Jennifer said.

It sure did, Jane thought. *What a nice guy. After all he's had to do today, he took time out to do that.* "That was very nice, Steve. Kevin was really getting down in the dumps."

"It was nothing," Steve told her. "The PetSmart was on the way anyhow."

"Let me pay you for the toad."

"Forget it. Let's eat some pizza; I'm starving."

Dinner was a smashing success. They all traded talk back and forth while they ate. Steve spent a lot of time asking Jennifer about school, her favorite subjects and future plans. Jane could tell that her daughter liked him a lot. The cop side of Steve always seemed very businesslike and by the book, but tonight he'd left that all behind. *Don't get your hopes up too high,* Jane warned herself. This didn't really qualify as a first date; she didn't even know if he *wanted* to date. *Take it a step at a time. Even if this never happens again, we all had a nice time.*

"I'll never order out again," Steve said, pushing his plate away. "That was the best pizza I've ever had."

"Jennifer did it all," Jane said. "It's her recipe."

"Jen, you should go into business for yourself. You'd make a fortune."

"Thank you, Chief Higgins."

"It's Steve."

"Thank you, Chief Steve."

Everybody had a laugh, then Jennifer rushed up. "I'll clear the table and do the dishes, Mom. Why don't you and Chief Steve go watch TV? There's *Simpson* reruns on. And, you know, you can go back into the den and watch it."

Jane blushed outright. *Jennifer, you're impossible.*

Steve smiled to himself, but played it off as innocent, knowing that Jane had been put on the stop in a big way. "That sounds like a perfect idea to me. It's my favorite show."

He followed her out of the kitchen. "Sorry," she whispered. "I don't know what to say."

"It's fine," he laughed. "Kids are kids."

They stopped in the family room to quickly check on Kevin. He was totally preoccupied with the new toad, cautiously letting it roam the couch.

"Kevin, make sure Mel Junior doesn't make a mistake."

"You mean poop on the couch?"

"Why mince words?" Steve said.

Yeah, kids are kids, she thought. They left him be and went to the den. Jane tried to act nonchalant but there were some serious butterflies in her stomach. Nothing was going to happen, of course, and there were no expectations. It was simply the awkward situation.

She felt relieved, though, when they were inside and she closed the door.

More small talk as they sat on the couch. "Are you really a *Simpsons* fan?"

"To be honest, I haven't seen it in years 'cuz I'm always at work. Put on whatever you like, just so long as it's not a cop show."

The casualness about him put her even more at ease. They continued chatting, nothing heavy at all, just each talking in little bits about themselves, their likes and dislikes, where they'd been and where they'd like to go someday. He made it so nice and easy. Her nervousness flew away without her even realizing it; it was as though she hadn't been nervous at all. When he took her hand and held it, it seemed like they'd known each other a long time.

Next, their eyes were finding each other's. If anything, it was more deliberate for her than for him. They were sitting closer, and soon the small talk wasn't making it anymore, their faces closer as they spoke, their words growing softer. It was all too natural when they began to kiss.

The kisses were light, gentle. He seemed very delicate and caring. *God, I can't believe how fast this happened,* Jane thought, *but it's just . . . so . . . nice . . .*

She hadn't even thought about things like this for so long; she felt like an eighteen-year-old on prom night. With her job, the house, the bills, and the kids, sometimes she'd wondered if she'd ever have time again for a romance, and that's what she knew now: that that's what she wanted. She was almost afraid to ask herself how much she wanted tonight . . .

They started to embrace, then. They started to kiss harder.

A distant voice floated into the room:

"Dhevic, an expert in the field . . ."

Must be some dumbass documentary, Jane thought. They hadn't even been paying attention to it. Jane and Steve kept kissing.

". . . an alarming proliferation of what we think of as cult-motivated activity," came another voice now, in a slight European accent.

The words shattered Jane's concentration. *Did some guy on TV just say—*

Steve pulled back from the kiss, not alarmed but clearly diverted. He looked at the television with interest. *Damn it,* Jane thought. *What is that?*

"Sorry, but this sounds like it might be important," Steve said, sitting up on the edge of the couch seat.

Jane went lax, trying not to sigh out loud. She frowned at the television screen and saw a tall man in a dark suit. A camera was following him from behind as he seemed to be leading it through a well-decorated house. Long dark hair threaded with some gray hung over his shoulders. His footsteps echoed on the floorboards.

"From East Coast to West Coast, from north to south." The European accent again. "America is *steeped* in a history of demonological activity. This house right here, Suit Manor, proves a prime example."

Tacky as it was—like some overdone cable show about haunted houses or UFOs—it wasn't a documentary. It was the local news station, which often ran features like this toward the end of the hour. The scene cut to a dusty floor, where multiple human outlines lay. The outlines seemed to be formed from old, dried blood.

"The Suits were recluse millionaires, twin brothers. They invited a plethora of guests to what they referred to as a 'celebration of the vernal equinox.' An orgy ensued, which quickly transformed. The Suits murdered eleven people in the effort to incarnate the demon Baalzephon . . ."

Jane couldn't have been more perturbed. What business did this schlock have on the local news? She crossed her arms, smirking. Steve seemed intent on the program.

She still hadn't seen the face of the long-haired man on TV; the camera kept following him from behind. Now the clatter of his footfalls on the wood floors changed over to crunching: he was walking through a forest. *Let me guess,* Jane thought. *Now it's a haunted forest. Jeez.* Eventually he emerged into a clearing and Jane saw what the area really was. A graveyard. But clearly it was nowhere in Florida.

"Prospect Hill, Rhode Island," came the voice-over as the camera panned across old granite tombstones. "The summer of 1987. Jacobi Mather, a direct descendent of the pre-Revolutionary witch hunter *Cotton* Mather, on this very ground, held a Black Mass on the Feast of Sahmain, and allegedly summoned the Morning Star himself, the Lord of the Air and the Deceiver of Souls—also known as Lucifer."

Even Jane gasped at the program's next cut, and

Steve hitched up an inch on the couch. Now the camera was roving across a very familiar sight: a school. The voice-over continued, *"The quiet town of Danelleton, in Central Florida. The time—a few days ago . . ."*

Jane leaned closer, next to Steve. "Wait a minute. That looks just like—"

"It is," Steve said. "How do you like this stuff? On the local news . . ."

Now the footage showed the long-haired man, still from behind, walking in front of a pillared dormitory building. *"The Seaton School for Christian Girls,"* said the accented monotone. *"Just days ago, demented postal worker Carlton Spence went berserk and murdered a nun, a teacher, and a half-a-dozen religious students. He crucified them, and then, before he took his own life, he left this sign . . ."*

The camera cut to a shocking closeup. On the shower wall, drawn in blood, was the bell-shaped symbol with the star.

Another voice cut in, somebody else overdubbing. *"Here is wisdom. Let he who hath understanding count the number of the beast, for it is the number of a man, and that number is six-hundred, three score, and six . . ."*

The long-haired man was facing the camera now. He looked intense, if a bit wild, with the hair and a long gray-streaked beard. A final cut showed the ambulances loading body bags in front of the school.

Steve's eyes were wide. He seemed miles away.

"You," he said. "My God, it's you."

Jane peered at him. "Steve, you *know* this man?"

"Oh, I know him, all right, the evil son of a bitch."

"Who is he?"

"His name's Dhevic." He held his hand out to the television. "And get of load of this crap. They took some footage from one of his old documentaries and spliced it up with a new interview about the murders here. They're putting it on the local news, for God's sake. Yeah, that's just what people need to see. Talk about hokey."

"I don't understand. What's the deal with this man?"

Steve dismissed it with a smirk. "It's a long story; I won't bother you with it."

Now Jane was genuinely flustered. At first she thought he was going to get up and leave, but then she saw that he was reaching for the remote control.

He flicked the TV off.

"What—" she began to say.

He was kissing her again, more intently this time. Jane responded with the same intensity. Something about the TV clip had wound him up—at least she thought that's what it must be. Steve was more intense now, more deliberate and focused on her. Jane felt exhilarated but behind that an unmistakable feeling of alarm wavered. She was almost afraid. But of what?

His arms slipped around her more tightly. Now his kisses were nearly desperate. Jane didn't know what to do. *I can't go to bed with this man. Or . . . I can, but I know I shouldn't.* It wasn't her style. And what would he think of her afterward? These points made sense to her but when they collided with the sudden surge of her desire . . .

She wasn't sure.

One hand was on her side now, and it began to inch upward. Here was her opportunity to say no . . .

A rap sounded on the door. Jane and Steve flinched,

tried to haphazardly right themselves. "Yes?" Jane said in a rush.

Jennifer stuck her head in, smiling. "I just wanted to let you know that we're going to bed now. Good night, Mom. Good night, Chief Steve."

Jane hoped her face wasn't flushed. "Good night, honey."

"Good night, Jen," Steve said.

Jennifer's smile retreated back out, and the door closed with a click.

"Talk about bad timing," Jane said.

Steve laughed. "At least my beeper or cell phone hasn't gone off."

He took her hand again, leaned close. "Look, I'm sorry. I know I'm making this too fast for you. I didn't mean to do that."

That's when Jane knew.

"It's not too fast for me. Let's go to my bedroom."

(II)

Yeah, smooth as fuckin' silk, Martin thought sourly. He took two good hits off the flask in the bathroom, popped a mint strip, and nodded. He was deceiving himself, telling himself that he felt better now than he had yesterday. The booze never really helped anything, though. Sometimes it would make him forget, but later the memories would return and they'd be worse.

His hatred raged.

Martin was disappointed in himself, and he knew that someone else was, too. He wasn't sure who that other person was yet, but he would soon enough.

God, I was all ready. I was ready to do it, and I know it's what I'm supposed to do. But—

Last night Martin had simply chickened out.

That other thing—or other person—that was coming in and out of his heart for the past day began to rage along with Martin's own hatred.

What's wrong with my head?

Yes. Last night. He'd been *right there*. After work, he'd had a couple of shots at Jill's Thrills, his favorite strip joint. The way Martin saw it, the lower in class the better, 'cuz that's what it was really all about. Lot of the chicks in there tricked. Fifty bucks and they'd come in the car with you for a fast one. A hundred and they'd give you an hour in a motel room. Martin had done it before—plenty of times—but he knew something was changing in him now.

Some other thing, or some other person, was directing him, showing him his real purpose. More and more he felt as though he were becoming stronger through this other voice that had found its way into his soul. He felt comforted. He felt as though he had a true meaning for the first time in his life.

He understood now that there were messages to be delivered, and he was to help deliver them.

The girl from the bar was one of his favorites, an urchinlike little stick of a thing named Cinny. She was pale and lean, with inordinately pink nipples. Tattoos looked like branding marks on her white skin, and her eyes were huge and empty. Martin liked the look—it turned him on—that hollow soul-dead cast of resigned desperation. Crack or crystal meth, Martin wasn't sure what her jones was, but she was always happy to come out to the car with him for a few minutes after her dance set. She was fast and effective, her talent—he was sure—honed by sheer experience. When they'd finished, Martin was all ready, all ready to send the message. Under the street he'd stashed his old K-Bar knife from the Marine Corps, and when she was putting her top back on, her face momentarily covered, he knew that was the perfect time. They'd taught him how to do it in the Corps: just ram the knife's tip right into the little hollow below the Adam's apple. It severed the larynx so they couldn't scream.

Now. Now! the other voice was telling him.

But Martin lost his nerve. Cinny pulled her top back on, smiled wanly and said "Thanks. See ya next time," and she was out of the car and scurrying back into the bar.

He'd been thinking too much. *They know me here, they saw me leave with her, they see me leave with dancers all the time. When she didn't come back, they'd know it was me . . .*

Don't you understand? the other voice asked him.

"No!" Martin sobbed.

It doesn't matter. The message is all that matters.

Martin drove off, greedy for the opportunity to redeem himself to his new guide. But, lo, more failure. First, the girl at the massage parlor, a pretty Korean woman. He got so far as to actually grip the knife hidden in the bag he'd brought, but then he remembered that several other guys had been sitting in the waiting room beside the door with the bell on it. *They'd be able to give the police a description maybe . . .*

192

It doesn't matter, the voice inside scolded him.

One more try, this time with the hooker he'd picked up on the main drag. No one had seen him, and no one could've possibly seen her get in the car. Martin was gunned up by now. He *knew* he could do it. Cut her vocal cords and then peel her like a banana. She was even wobbly in the car seat, eyelids drooping, half whacked out on dope. Too easy.

But Martin simply lost his nerve.

He could sense his guide's disappointment. *One more chance, one more chance,* he begged, hitting on his flask as he drove. *Please, give me one more chance and I'll prove to you that I'm worthy. Tell me where to go and I'll do it. Guide me . . .*

Next thing Martin knew, he was parked at a corner behind some hedges. Nice suburban neighborhood. Quiet. Still. A little after midnight and not a sound could be heard. He was getting out, stalking through backyards, before he even realized exactly where the Messenger had taken him.

A back bedroom. A window.

Dark inside but he could see enough.

A man and woman lay naked together, cuddling. Moonlight painted the edges of their bodies like some surreal erotic art. They were having a little quiet time in between rounds, he guessed. The window was open; he couldn't hear exactly what they were saying but they were talking, whispering, pillow talk in the afterglow. Martin's eyes felt pasted to the woman's body like an image in seedy pornography. Her skin and contours looked gritty in the tinseled darkness. He could see the details of her nipples, her navel, and her pubis too, when the pillow talk faltered and she dragged the sheets off her lower body. The dude was all over her again in a heartbeat, licking lines with his tongue from her nipples, down her flat stomach, to her . . .

Martin spent the next half hour, watching in utter silence, engrossed and aroused. He relieved what he could of his own sexual angst right there on the side of the house, almost blowing it, almost gasping aloud, in which case he surely would've been heard and then he would've screwed up again, wouldn't he? He would've disappointed the Messenger yet again. If he charged in there right now, though—easy because the window was open—he might be able to take them both out. The guy looked pretty fit, and Martin himself wasn't fit at all, but he'd have the darkness and the element of surprise on his side, wouldn't he? *Go in there and just go caveman on them. Go for the guy first, get some lower-body stabs with the knife before he knew what hit him, and then start to work on the woman.* But—

No. It's better this way, my son, he was told. *Just . . . wait.*

Martin waited as instructed. It was as though his guide had known what would happen next. Inside, the dude and woman had gone at it like banshees, a real down-and-dirty show. Then they were lying on the bed, talking. They talked for a long time. And then—

Perfect. Here's my best chance of the night, Martin thought.

The guy was leaving. Put on his duds, gave her a long last kiss, and was out of there. In a moment, Martin could hear a car start around front and drive away.

And now the woman was in there all alone. She was sitting naked on the edge of the bed. *What a brick shit house,* Martin thought. She was lying down again, spread-eagled on top of the sheets. Martin drunk up the sight of that body and thought that she'd look even better after he cut her up. The Messenger would like that, the Messenger *expected* it. For a minute, Martin thought she was going to masturbate, the way she was lying there on the sheets with her legs wide open. It looked like she'd actually brought her hands close to her groin . . . but then she rolled over. *Yeah, perfect. She's going back to sleep.* That was great and there was something he'd just noticed—when he could see her face for the first time—that made it all even *more* perfect . . .

I just can't believe it. Nobody gets this lucky. Maybe it was the Messenger himself who'd effected this situation; he'd brought Martin here, hadn't he? He must know. Martin got out the K-Bar. Oh, what he would do to her with it. . . . Now his hatred was all sparked up by the most irresistible lust. Because in those last few minutes when she'd been lying there on her back, Martin had finally been able to see the woman's face oh so clearly.

It was Jane Ryan.

Martin prepared to go in . . .

"Hey, peeping Tom!" a voice rang out like a gunshot from behind.

Martin nearly had a coronary.

"I'm calling the cops, you pervert!"

Martin couldn't move. He'd been seen! Impulse flooded him: the impulse to run away as fast as he could, but—

Be still.

Martin stood and stared.

My son, your redemption is upon you. Take it.

Martin knew what the Messenger meant, because he'd actually said it before, hadn't he? In Martin's head?

The guide had told him, *It doesn't matter. The message is all that matters.*

Martin, as drunk and as unsophisticated as he might have been, understood the implication. The act was all that mattered. It didn't matter that he'd be caught. It didn't matter that he'd be tried and sentenced to death. Death was eternal, and Martin welcomed that new eternity in the domain of the Messenger.

Go in there now, my son. And deliver my message.

Martin trembled. He tried and tried and tried, but he couldn't force himself to go in that window. Inside, the light had switched on; the bitch, no doubt, had heard the neighbor yelling. She'd pulled on a robe, was putting down the phone, and now she was coming to the window, and if Martin stayed even for another few seconds, Jane Ryan would see him.

Martin ran away.

The Messenger had stopped talking to him after that. The memory of last night's unmitigated failure reminded him of his entire life. Nothing ventured, nothing gained. It you spend your whole life never taking a risk, you never really *have* a life because you never get anything, and Martin knew this: without the Messenger, he had *nothing.* For the last day he'd felt absolutely alive. Martin needed that feeling back.

Please come back into my heart, he pleaded.

He had the knife in a sheath in his belt. He was wearing his shirttail out so no one could see it. Martin was going to prove himself to the Messenger. Today. Right here in the post office.

He'd wait until lunch. The carriers, who were mostly men, would all be on the road, and half the clerks and handlers would be gone. He'd go office to office, carving up as many as he could, and then he'd gut himself and let the Messenger send him on to a better place where he would finally be rewarded for something.

And he knew which office he'd be starting at—Jane Ryan's.

"Martin—there you are." The stern tone assailed him the second he stepped out of the bathroom. It was Jane Ryan, in her tight top and postal shorts, frowning at him in the hall. "Are you finished with the two-foot trays and the Jacksonville drop?"

"Yes," Martin said.

"Good. I'll give you one more chance. You can still have the promotion to DPS foreman if you want it."

Martin stood still. The hall was empty; he could do it now, couldn't he? One hard thwack with the K-Bar and he could have her head half off. He'd cut her clothes off right there on the floor while she gargled blood. His rage seethed. *I don't need one more chance from you, you big-tit bitch. I need it from someone else, and I'm gonna get it. Look for me around lunchtime.*

"No, Ms. Ryan, I don't."

"Okay." She turned around, pointed to the foot of her

office door where two small boxes sat. "See those two boxes? It's a maintenance delivery, spare parts for the new collators, pinion replacement rods or something."

"What about them?" Martin asked.

"Take them down to the basement, will you?" Then she turned and walked off to the front service cove.

Martin smiled. *Sure, Ms. Ryan. I'll take 'em down. And then at lunch, I'll take YOU down.*

"Oh, and Martin?" She'd stopped at the door. "Put your shirttail in. It's against post-office policy. They call it a *uniform* for a reason. So that all staff look *uniform.*" Then she was through the door and gone.

Martin didn't put his shirttail in. He was excited already, sexually. *Oh, yeah. This is gonna be sweet . . .*

He picked up the boxes and took them down into the basement. There was no one else down there. It was nice and cool and quiet. He took a hit off the flask and relaxed. No one to bother him here. Martin could think . . .

He could think about what he was going to do for the Messenger.

"How come your shirttail's out?"

Martin jumped. *Who the hell is down here?*

She'd been standing right there all along. Sarah Something—Woolery, Willoughby, something like that. Martin had seen her around, didn't like her. Of course, he didn't like anybody he worked with, or anybody at all for that matter, but this bitch he disliked more than most. She was young, mid-twenties, blond, a looker. Another snooty Florida beach ditz who thought she was better than everyone else just because she'd been born attractive. *Always turning her nose up at me,* Martin reminded himself. He'd like to strangle her. He'd like to whip out his K-Bar right now and start cutting chunks off.

"Then why don't you?" she said.

Martin stared.

"I know about you," she said. "The Messenger told me about you."

"He . . . did?"

"The Messenger told me that you're taking his blessing for granted. You're selfish and afraid. You're not strong enough to make the sacrifice."

Martin was suddenly sweating. "That's not true! I've got everything planned!"

"You're weak. You must prove your strength."

"I will! I'm going to kill her during the lunch break."

Her eyes fluttered. "You're going to kill her now. Don't be weak anymore. Don't put things off. You know that it's a very special time and that some very important messages must be delivered." She stood feet apart, hip cocked. Her work blouse was unbuttoned a few notches, showing cleavage. She licked her lips. Her hands briefly caressed her breasts. "Do it and you can have me."

Martin *didn't* want her. He was jealous now. Who was she to the Messenger? Martin wanted to be the priority but here she was telling him what to do. He didn't like it. Her knew that he had to get back into the good graces of his guide.

"Now's your chance, Martin," she cooed.

"What?"

"She's coming."

"What, down here?"

She nodded slyly, ran her tongue over her lower lip. "Um-hmm."

"Right now?"

"Um-hmm."

This is bullshit. How can she predict something like that? but then the upstairs door clicked open and footsteps were heard coming down.

Sarah quickly picked up some boxes, to appear busy. Jane Ryan stepped in.

"I think that's it for those boxes of replacement parts, Jane," Sarah said. She set the boxes back down. "Martin and I brought them all down."

"Thanks." Jane seemed distracted. "Where is Martin, by the way?"

"Right here," Martin said.

Jane immediately frowned. "Martin, I thought I told you to tuck your shirttail in, and—" She leaned forward, squinting in disbelief. "Is that a flask in your hand?"

Fuck! Martin was caught cold. He was still holding the flask full of whiskey. He wilted. He didn't even bother responding.

"Jesus, Martin!" Sarah exclaimed. "Is that what you've been doing down here?" She turned to Jane. "Jane, I swear, I didn't know he was down here drinking."

"I understand," Jane replied. "It's been an ongoing problem." To Martin, she said, "I've given you every chance in the book but it's just not working out. I've got no choice but to suspend you, pending a termination hearing. Do you understand?"

All Martin understood was that he was being screwed over by another woman. It was always a woman. Treacherous. Back-stabbing. Self-serving. He was seething now. He was shaking. He wanted to reach under his shirt and grab the knife . . .

But he couldn't.

"Go home, Martin," Jane ordered. "I'll let you know when your hearing will be. But you'd make things a lot easier for yourself if you just quit and move on."

Martin couldn't speak. He just kept shaking.

"And I sincerely hope it wasn't you who was peeping in my window last night. . . ."

Martin's mouth opened, then closed.

Jane went back upstairs.

"You're a failure, Martin," Sarah said in the silence. "That was your last chance. Why didn't you do it?"

"You should've grabbed her, you shouldn't have let her leave!" Martin babbled.

"Always an excuse, like your entire life."

Martin was getting damn tired of hearing women talk to him like he was a loser. *Damn* tired.

He pulled out the knife.

"You don't have the nerve."

"Don't I?" he challenged.

"The Messenger has abandoned you. You're not worthy of his grace. You're a waste of his time."

Martin lunged with the blade. Sarah swatted it out of his hand and slapped him in the face.

"You're a disgrace."

Next, Martin was grabbed by the hair and dragged across the basement floor. He was crying like a baby. Eventually she dropped him by the wall, in front of what appeared to be an old service crawlway or storage area.

"Look in there, Martin . . ." Sarah's voice scarcely

sounded human anymore. Something was tainting her features, something atrocious. Her slender fingers looked twice as long as they should be, with long nail-like talons. Her eyes were huge and black.

She pointed to the opening of the crawlway.

When Martin looked in, he screamed so hard his heart stopped. Something in the crawlway—something with long, pale arms—grabbed him by the head and pulled him in.

Chapter Thirteen

(I)

What a day, Jane thought, frustrated at her desk. *And what a night.*

The latter proved much more pleasurable a thought than the former. All of a sudden it seemed that she had a boyfriend, or a lover—or something. *Maybe to him it was just a one-night stand.* That was the way of the world these days, especially in Florida. Everything was a fling. Everything was just about having a good time for the moment. Jane hoped that wasn't the case here, but she knew she was very vulnerable right now. Last night, their lovemaking had been so good, she felt guilty. She felt like she'd somehow cheated on Matt even in death. It had been the best sex of her life.

Don't get your hopes up, she told herself. *Don't be naive.* It would be easy to be naive in this situation.

She hadn't been with another man since the night of Matt's murder. She'd thought about it sometimes, and she thought about what it might be like to date somebody—but the idea always wilted. She wasn't interested. It just seemed too strange and stressful.

But she couldn't turn off last night's memory. Steve had made love to her three times. It was different each time, which made the experience even more exciting. It was almost as if he knew her: He knew exactly how to tend her desires, he knew exactly how she liked to be touched, he knew exactly how she wanted to be taken.

It had been frenetic but gentle, passionate but aggressive. She knew that she shouldn't feel guilty, and she knew that Matt wouldn't want her to. If anything, the sex had been *too* good.

After the second time, Steve had rolled over, exhausted, his arm around her. The memory was so vivid . . .

"I feel like lighting a cigarette, but I don't smoke anymore," he said, laughing at the cliché.

"Neither do I. We're both better off for it."

"I know. I don't want to have cigarette breath. Then you wouldn't want to kiss me."

"I'll always want to kiss you," she whispered, but then bit her lip. It was too soon to come on strong, or to take this for granted.

"That was great," he said, still breathing rather hard.

"Tell me about it. That was my first time in . . . Well, I won't tell you how long."

"Same here."

Jane cuddled up right next to him. She felt too good

now, better than she had in so long. Contentment and joy and the sweetest exhaustion all wrapped up around her. She could feel his heart beating through her chest as they lay there, pressed to one another, arms draped and legs entangled. Then she tightened her embrace as if to retain something . . . and she knew what it was.

The feeling.

The feeling in her heart and soul. It was as if she were hanging on to it, a desperate clasp to prevent that sensation from slipping out of her arms, escaping her. She'd do anything to keep from losing that, but then, a moment later, she knew that she would. Other things began to surface in her mind. *No, no, just drop it. Don't even mention it. You might ruin it all . . .*

But it wouldn't stop hounding her.

Her eyes were wide in the dark when she said, "There's still a whole lot you're not telling me, isn't there? You keep too much to yourself."

"I know."

Just drop it! But she couldn't. Her curiosity was a curse. "Like this business with the bell-shaped symbol, and the stuff you were saying earlier about cults."

"I know."

"And now that guy on the TV show, the bearded man. You should've seen the look on your face when that came on. Steve, you acted like he meant something to you, some bad memory or something. Your reaction was like you *knew* him."

"It is a bad memory, a *really* bad memory. I don't really *know* him. But I sure as hell know who he is."

"Who? What is he to you?"

Steve didn't answer. Suddenly the darkness seemed smothering, the silence in the bedroom clawing at them.

"Whatever this is all about," Jane said, "it's easy to see how much it's bothering you. I can tell. It's eating you up. Why?"

"It's a really bad subject, Jane."

"The recent murders? I know that's a bad subject. The whole town's still in shock. Everything seems different; it doesn't even feel like Danelleton anymore."

"It's not just that," he said, his voice so low it was nearly inaudible. "Are you sure you want to know?"

"Yes."

"All right. I'll tell you. . . ."

He told the strangest story, strange in that it seemed very familiar but it was a different time. "It was just about twenty years ago. There was a disturbance call at a house in the neighborhood, just a few blocks away as a matter of fact. A nice house, new paint, nice yard, a house like most of the houses around here—a house just like yours. It was a ten–twenty-two that came over the radio—it means unknown trouble. You always have to be careful on those because you have no idea what to expect. Could be a cat in a tree or it could be some guy gone nuts holding his wife and kids hostage with a shotgun. You just never know, so you're really on your toes. You've got the snap off your holster so you can draw faster, just in case. The weirdest part was feeling like that in a town like this. A peaceful, quiet little town. Well, it wasn't peaceful and quiet that day. A bunch of us pulled up at the same time, we were all getting out at once, rushing up to the house. Danelleton was a lot smaller back then. It was the kind of place where your biggest crimes were kids toilet-papering the school on Halloween, an occasional drunk driver, nickel-dime stuff like that. But when the ten–twenty-two came through, we all just got a really bad feeling in our guts. Anyway, we surrounded the house, and it was me and my partner who got the order to take the front door. We kicked it open and . . ."

Jane knew that what was about to be described would be traumatic. She even thought of telling him to stop, to forget it, because it was obviously tearing him up, but she *couldn't*. She couldn't let go of it. She just squeezed him tighter and said, "Tell me."

"For some reason, everything turned silent. I don't know why that is, but ask any cop. When you walk into a crime scene like that, it's like you're wearing ear-muffs. You're so focused on what's suddenly in your face that you don't have any outside attention."

"What . . . was in the house?" Jane asked.

"Are you sure you want to know?" he repeated.

"Yes."

Now his voice shifted down even more, to a grating monotone. "Blood," he said. "There was blood all over the place. It was the first thing we saw when we kicked open the door. In the foyer at the bottom of the stairs. It looked like a half-inch of blood on the floor. And then the body, a woman. She was lying on her back, on the stairs, her feet pointing upstairs so all the blood would drain out of her neck into the foyer."

"Out of her . . ." Jane winced as she tried to picture the scene. But she didn't get it. "You mean somebody cut her throat."

"I mean somebody decapitated her. They arranged the body like that so it'd be the first thing we saw when we went in: a headless body . . . and all that blood."

Jane's curiosity just grew more morbid against her will. She didn't want to know but she *had* to know. "Where was the . . ."

"In the kitchen. It was sitting upright on the counter, right next to the phone—again, on purpose. He'd left it there like that deliberately. It looked like the head was looking at us, like it was waiting for us." Steve sighed, an anxious frustration. "Some kind of facial rigor had set in, I guess. The eyes were open. She was smiling at us."

"Good Lord," Jane whispered.

"And then the rest."

"There's more?" she asked, alarmed.

"Jane, that was just the beginning of the day. That was just the *first* house."

"*What?*"

"It was impossible, it was insane. What we walked into that day, each house after that? It was like nothing we could ever imagine. We found two other bodies there, two kids. Butchered. Just like what—"

"Marlene Troy did," Jane finished. "I can't believe this. An identical crime, but twenty years ago?"

"Yeah—well, sort of. See, the wife didn't do it. She was a victim just like the kids. Somebody else did it. They did it and left. When they left, they went to the next house, then they killed everybody there and went to the *next* house. Then the next house and the next house. Like that."

Jane gasped.

"That was the real nightmare. When me and my partner walked out of that first house, everything went crazy. Cops from every department within ten miles were responding because we simply didn't have enough units. City cops, Clearwater, Largo, county sheriff's department were all tearing down the road. Me and my partner were standing on the lawn of the first house and we looked up the street. All those other units, all those other cops, were pulling up in front of every house on the street."

"What happened next?"

"We were both half in shock, I guess. We just turned into robots and went to assist. One house after another, every house on the street, and every occupant of each house—butchered in place. By the time we got to the last house on the street, we'd counted over twenty dead bodies, most of them like the woman in the first house. Turns out that the killer had actually started at the other end of the street. First victim was like most of the others, a housewife. It was her kid who found her body and called the police. He told us who the killer was—"

"Who!" Jane blurted.

"It wasn't hard tracking him down. It was a postal employee walking a delivery route, only he didn't deliver anything—he just killed everybody. He just went from one house to the next—no one survived except for the kid. He's the only one who saw him. This guy took out an entire street. And then . . ."

Jane squeezed his hand.

"We tracked the guy back to the main post office, but . . . too late. When the guy finished killing everyone on his mail route, he went straight back to the post office and murdered every one there too. Just like what Marlene did, only worse. This guy used a meat cleaver, hacked them all up into pieces. . . ."

He paused for a few moments. The darkness seemed to tick around them, with their hearts.

"He wasn't quite finished by the time we arrived. My partner went back to the car to call for backup. I was standing in front, near the clerk stations, and that's when I heard someone in back scream, so I drew my gun and ran. There were bodies lying everywhere, all down the halls, all around in the sorting and handling areas and the loading dock. Chopped down. Hacked up. Couple times I slipped and fell—all the blood on the floor. By then, though, the screaming had stopped. I could tell it had been a woman, and then I saw one. Another employee. She was convulsing on the floor; the guy'd just hacked her head half off in one swipe with the cleaver. It was my first look at him—the first time I'd *ever* seen a murderer, for that matter. Normal looking guy, mid-thirties, I guess, normal build. But when I looked in his eyes, he wasn't normal anymore. It was something worse than insanity looking back at me. That's when I put my sight on him. What you have to understand is that I was so focused, plus in shock, so I wasn't noticing details at first. The guy's shirt was open and there was blood all over him. Hell, I thought it was the blood from all the people he'd killed, but it wasn't. It was *his* blood. The bay door was open and he was standing at the edge of the dock, and then I noticed something else. There was something around his neck. A rope, I figured. It went from his neck to the overhead rail of the bay door. I yelled at him to put his hands up or I'd shoot, something like that. And you know what he did?"

"What?" Jane asked, but she thought she already knew.

"He just grinned at me. For a second his face didn't even look human. It looked all ridged. His head looked warped. His eyes looked as big as cue balls. Then he said, 'Behold the Messenger. The arrival of the Messenger is at hand.' Then he jumped off the edge of the loading dock and hanged himself."

"My God . . ."

"And it wasn't rope he'd done it with. He'd cut his own belly open, Jane. He cut out a length of his own intestines . . . and that's what he used to hang himself with."

Jane lay rigid, trembling. "That's impossible. It's just like Carlton."

"Yeah, just like Carlton. But even that's not all. You asked about that symbol, the bell-shaped design we found written in blood at Marlene's house and at the girls' school. Well, we found it here too. Everywhere. The killer had written on the walls, on the delivery trucks, even on some of the bodies."

"The same symbol," Jane repeated. "Twenty years ago."

"Exactly."

They lay silent for a while. Jane hoped he'd fall asleep, and she tried to herself, but his recital of those events left her wide awake in distress. How must it have been for him? To see all that, all in one day? "My God, Steve. That long ago? You couldn't have been much more than a kid back then."

"I was a greenhorn, a total rookie. I'd just got out of

the academy at the beginning of that summer. I'd been on the force all of two months when this happened."

"And all those people—murdered for no reason."

"Murdered by a *postal* worker, Jane. Like Marlene, like Carlton. Same MO, same details and implications, but it was all two decades ago."

Jane looked for some way to dismiss it as coincidence, but that was impossible. "I guess there's no denying it. There's a direct connection between what Marlene and Carlton did this week, to what this guy did twenty years ago. There's no way that that's *not* the case."

"I agree. Marlene and Carlton worked for the post office, and so did this guy. The bell symbol was found on the crime scenes this week and the crime scenes twenty years ago. Christ, the guy committed suicide the exact same way Carlton did, and Carlton didn't even live here twenty years ago. I checked his records. He lived in North Carolina, for God's sake, so how could he have known about the guy killing himself that way so long ago?"

Jane had no response.

"And to top it all off, Carlton, Marlene, *and* the killer back then even worked at the *same* post office."

Jane's train of thought stopped. "Wait a minute. I thought you said this guy from twenty years ago worked at the *main* post office. Carlton and Marlene worked at *my* post office, the west branch, which is brand-new."

Steve paused, looking at her in the dark. "That's where you're wrong, Jane. The PO you just opened last week? It's the *same* post office from twenty years ago. The same building."

"But . . . I don't understand."

"Jane, twenty years ago, Danelleton was a lot smaller, it was a blossoming little suburban community. The town council members put a lid on those murders as fast as they could, and the first thing they did was close the post office, shut it down for good. They couldn't afford the notoriety. A mass murder like that? Not the kind of thing that's gonna do wonders for real estate values. So they built a new post office, what's now the main branch on the other side of town. Time went by and—believe it or not—everyone forgot about it. Most of the people who lived here then aren't even here anymore. No one on the town council is the same. None of the postal workers are the same. Hell, there aren't even any Danelleton cops who were here back then. I'm the only one. About the only good thing about those murders is how fast people forgot."

Jane could see what he was driving at. "But now Danelleton has grown so large that one post office wasn't enough to handle the influx of new residents."

"Right. Now the town needed an auxiliary post office to handle the extra mail load. They talked about building a second office but they figured why bother? We still got the old place sitting there. It's been closed for twenty years, and no one remembers. So instead of spending a ton of money building a new place, they refurbished the old place."

"*My* post office," Jane muttered.

"Yep. The west branch that you're running is the same place where the murderer worked twenty years ago. And the same week the place gets reopened, two of *your* employees go out and do the same thing. This has been gnawing at me since the thing with Marlene. I'm the only one who knows, the only one who remembers. I just kept thinking, it's impossible. No coincidence like that could ever happen. The chances aren't even one in a million, they're one in a billion."

"You're right. It *is* impossible. It's *uncanny.*"

"And that damned symbol is the link," Steve went on. "I'm not sure *how,* but it's got to be. All that stuff I was saying before, about satanic cults—the stuff you didn't believe. It's got to be true. That's the only way that the connection can exist."

Jane tried to think of a way to deny it. She tried to find a hole in the logic. But couldn't.

"That guy we saw on TV tonight? Yeah, I know who he is. His name's Alexander Dhevic. He claims to be some sort of demonology scholar. Every now and then I'll see him interviewed on those hokey documentaries about the occult. He used to go around the country on these talks shows, spieling about the upsurge of cult activity in recent years. Satanism, these teen groups that practice Black Mass and animal sacrifice, hype like that. But when all this went down twenty years ago, Dhevic was snooping around in Danelleton. So he's *another* link."

"Dhevic," Jane whispered the strange name.

"I don't know his story, but there's something really fishy about the guy. There he was then, and here he still is now. We tried to question him twenty years ago, but he slipped out of town, like *fast.*"

"Why would he do that?"

"Wish I knew. But that's why I figure the symbol is demonic—Dhevic's a so-called demonologist, and that's why I was asking if you thought Carlton and Marlene could've been involved in some kind of cult."

"And maybe Dhevic—"

"Right. Maybe this crackpot Dhevic is more than just a demonologist. Maybe he practices all this crap too."

Jane shivered. Like everything else this week, this was too much information to deal with all at the same time. Murders, past and present. Identical crimes twenty years apart. Symbols and suicides. Links to satanism. Links to Jane's post office. And now this man named Dhevic. *It's just . . . too much,* she thought. She hugged Steve tighter. "It makes the hairs stand up on the back of my neck. It's hard to believe this sort of thing could ever happen here."

"Let's not talk about it anymore," Steve whispered. All that stress in his voice—when he'd been telling what had happened—was gone. He was himself again, which was what Jane wanted, what she needed. He was hugging her back now. "Just forget about it . . ." And then he was kissing her again.

Jane fell back into the oblivion she yearned for. Her desires were surging again, and that's all she cared about. In a moment they were consuming each other with their kisses, their bodies cringing for the touch of the other. Jane's bliss returned and swept her away. This time their lovemaking was even more frenetic than before—they knew each other well now, they knew each other's bodies. Jane simply let herself go, let herself be taken by this man . . .

She had no idea how much time had passed when they were done. *What am I going to do?* she asked herself, exhausted yet again, happily worn out. *I can't be falling in love with this guy, can I? It can't happen that fast.*

A little while later, Steve got up. "I better go now," he said regretfully. "I'd like to stay but—"

Jane didn't want him to go but she knew he had to. It was very difficult for her to say, "I know. It's too soon. Let's not rush this." She was determined not get emotional or make a fuss. *Don't be a pain in the ass, Jane,* she ordered herself. *That's the last thing he needs.* She watched him get dressed, her eyes straying over his lean body. *Oh, God,* came the drifting thought. *No, I cannot let myself screw this up . . .*

She stood up, unabashed by her nakedness. She embraced him and kissed him one last time for the night. She didn't want to let go of him, and she clearly sensed that he felt the same way.

"When can I see you again?" he asked.

"Oh, I don't know, let me think. How about . . . anytime you want."

"Okay, I'll see you then . . ."

He smiled at her in the dark, kissed her hand, and was gone.

She sat on the edge of the bed, hands in her lap. She could still feel him in her, and she liked the feeling. She could still smell him on her. Outside, she heard his car start and drive away. He wasn't even gone five minutes and she couldn't wait to see him again. Was that infatuation, or something more? Jane knew. *Yeah, I guess I'm in love. How do you like that?*

How much time passed while she was sitting on the bed she couldn't be sure. She lay back down, didn't bother getting under the sheets. The window was open, a cool breeze flowing in. It felt so nice the way it ran over her skin. She thought more about Steve, couldn't get the image of his body out of her mind. No, she wished he hadn't left, wished he'd stayed and made love to her one more time, but that was crazy. They'd both worn each other out. She was getting aroused again, though. She couldn't help it. Her nipples began to tingle as though he *were* still here, kissing them, stroking them between his fingers. She brought her hands to her belly, was tempted to slide them down lower and begin to touch herself, but her fatigue was getting the best of her now. *Oh, God, I hope I see him tomorrow* . . . Her hands fell away, and she turned over, to let sleep take her down.

"Hey, peeping Tom!" a voice shot out.

Jane bolted up. Her eyes were used to the dark now; she looked over at the open window. Did a shadow jerk away? *Jesus! Someone's been out there the whole time, watching us!* Probably just a kid, some teenager peeping in windows, but still . . . It was too creepy. She jumped up, switched on the light and pulled on her robe. She quickly called the police emergency number, then wondered what to do. Yes, it was probably just some kid but—

What if it wasn't?

She grabbed the heavy flashlight she kept by the

bed, a makeshift weapon, then ran to the window and looked out.

"I'm calling the cops, you pervert!" the neighbor's voice called again.

She saw somebody running away, could hear the rapid footfalls pounding across the grass. *Thank God he's gone* . . . All the lights flicked on in the next house, and the owner, an amiable retired man, came out in his robe. "How do you like that, huh, Jane? A peeping Tom."

"Yeah, just what we need at this hour," she answered through the screen.

"Well, I wouldn't worry. He took off like a bat out of hell, and I called the cops."

"Me, too. Thanks."

Later, a patrolman came by to take down some information. The night had been ruined now. Jane just said to hell with it and made some coffee, breaking her off-and-on caffeine pledge. The cop, too, told her there was nothing to worry about. Things like this happened every now and then, and they were harmless. They'd keep a cruiser in the area. He even said that another neighbor may have gotten a tag number.

Jane sluffed it off. The cop was treating it like no big deal so she figured she should too. But there was one thing she didn't tell him:

For a sliver of a moment, when she'd seen the shadow move at the window, she thought she'd seen the face too. She didn't tell the cop that it looked a lot like Martin Parkins.

That had been last night. The memory still hovered

over her head as she sat at her office desk. Her time with Steve had calmed her; just thinking of it seemed to make the day's headaches go away. When Sarah Willoughby stuck her head in the opened door, Jane had almost entirely forgotten about the bad business with Martin.

"You wanted to see me, Jane?"

Did I? "Oh, yes. Come in."

Sarah was a nice girl and a reliable worker. Never late, never called in sick, never a problem. She was still young, and still lower on the pay-level ladder, but Jane had every confidence in her.

Sarah entered and took the opposite seat, smiling perkily. "That's too bad about Martin. I was just helping him move those boxes of spare parts down in the basement. I had no idea he was drinking."

"Oh, I know. It was bound to happen. I feel bad about suspending him but at this point, there was nothing left to do. And with that done, I have an opening. You're next in line, Sarah. Martin didn't want to be DPS foreman anyway, which I offered him before I caught him drinking. You don't have as much seniority but your work record is flawless, and I have nothing but confidence in you. I hope you take it. It's also a one-level pay raise, and after ninety days, you go up one more level."

Sarah's pretty eyes bloomed with surprise. "Wow, this is unexpected. Thank you, Jane. I know I can do that job better than anyone, and I know the whole routine. I won't let you down."

"I'm sure you won't, Sarah."

"That's odd, though, isn't it? I mean, Martin had all

those all those years of time-in-grade. He could've turned himself around. Why didn't *he* take the job?"

"Well, I suppose it's because—"

"Because he'd only have it for one day before he got suspended," a familiar voice entered the room. Steve was standing there in the doorway. "Sorry to eavesdrop. I saw the door open."

Jane and Sarah looked up in surprise.

"Sarah, why don't you get your things moved into your new cove," Jane suggested, a polite way to get her out of the office. She was thrilled to see Steve, but she could tell by his tone and expression that he had something serious to talk about. "I'll stop by and talk to you a little later, and give you your new job description files."

"Sure, Jane. And thanks again." Sarah scurried out, a big smile beaming on her attractive face.

But when Steve sat down, he wasn't smiling.

"Hi," Jane said. "I can tell something's wrong. And how did you know I suspended Martin today? Did someone out front tell you?"

"No. I didn't know you suspended him."

"But you just said—"

"Martin Parkins," Steve droned. "His car's right out in the employee lot, the red Escort."

It wasn't a question; Jane was being told. "I guess he's still in the building, clearing out his desk. I had to suspend him because I caught him drinking down in the basement. I'm pretty sure he'll save himself the embarrassment of an appeal hearing and just quit. Anyway, that's why his car's still out there."

Steve nodded. He opened an envelope. "Could you call him in here? I have to show him this."

"What is it?"

"An arrest warrant."

Then Jane knew. She'd forgotten for a moment. "Last night after you left, my neighbor called in a peeping Tom complaint, and the policeman who responded said—"

"That somebody got a tag number," Steve finished. "Another resident at the end of your street saw him burning rubber out of there. Christ, I wished I'd been there when it happened—I could've taken him in right then and there. There's no doubt. He's the guy. Motor Vehicles gave us his street address so I went by there and he wasn't in. I hope he's ready for a big surprise."

"So you're actually going to arrest him?"

Steve looked puzzled. "Why not? Don't you *want* him arrested?"

It seemed harsh, especially right after losing the job he'd had for ten years. But . . . *I guess it'll teach him a lesson, and that's definitely what he needs right now. Maybe a hard knock and a little probation'll show him the light, give him the motivation to get his act together.* "You're right," she agreed. She picked up the phone and asked the front service manager to have Martin come to her office. Then she turned to Steve: "To tell you the truth, it's not very surprising. He's always been sort of a bad apple. Bad attitude, doesn't get along with his coworkers, not to mention several suspensions for drinking on duty."

"You never know with guys like that. What they do

when no one sees them, I mean. He probably peeps in women's windows all the time, just never been caught."

When the phone buzzed, Jane picked it up, listened, then frowned. She hung up. "They just told me Martin's not on the site."

Steve frowned himself, nodding. "He probably saw me walking in or pulling up in the parking lot and put two and two together." He flipped back the blinds and looked out the office window, into the sunny parking lot. "And look at that, his car's still there. I'll have someone from the station come out here and put a lock-block on his tire. He must've left on foot. I gotta get some people out there to look for him." All of a sudden, Steve looked harried. Jane could only imagine the frustration: Last night they'd made love and it had been wonderful; now they were stuck together by this problem with one of her employees. They couldn't be themselves in this scenario. He glanced at his watch and pocketed the arrest warrant. "I have to go and get this guy picked up. But I'll call you later, okay?"

Jane stood up and walked around the desk. She closed the door. She didn't say anything at first, she just kissed him. "I understand," she whispered, hugging him after the kiss. "You have your job to do, so go do it."

"I'm just . . . a little worried about you. I don't want that weirdo coming back here. He could be close to going over the edge—"

"Don't worry about me. I'll be fine."

She kissed him again and showed him out. *The last thing he needs is to be stressed out over me.* She walked him out to the parking lot—he waved sheep-ishly as he drove off. Jane just smiled.

She stood there in the sun for a few moments. It was going to be a hot one. When she looked around, she felt gratified. Her little west branch post office was bustling, customers coming and going, trucks pulling up in the back lot. Everything normal. Everything like clockwork, the way it was supposed to be.

And me and Steve, she thought. *Together.* Still more gratification. The feeling darkened, though, a few mo-ments later, when she realized what she was looking at. The dusty red Escort, Martin's car. It reinforced the uneasy truth. *He's out there somewhere.* Where would he go? What was his state of mind? Was he really close to going over the edge? In this day and age, the situa-tion was almost proverbial: disgruntled postal em-ployee goes psycho, and comes back with a gun. It happened all the time, and it had happened here. The only difference was Marlene was disgruntled. *She was part of a cult, and so was Carlton . . . and no one ever knew until it was too late. And twenty years ago?* Now she was staring at the building. *Another mass murder took place. Right in there. . . .* And the act had been perpetrated by a man, a postal employee, who . . .

Was in a cult.

The worst questions marauded her now. *Is Martin part of that cult, too?* She shivered in a spite of the ris-ing heat, and even in the blazing sunlight, she didn't feel safe.

The clerks up front had said that Martin was no longer on the site, but how could they know for sure?

Maybe he's hiding, Jane thought, her stomach tightening. *Maybe he's still in the building* . . .

(II)

"Jesus. Why can't anything be normal in my life?"

"What's that, Chief?" Stanton asked.

Steve had whispered the comment unconsciously to himself, hadn't even realized he'd said it. Stanton, a sergeant, was his day-shift watch commander: hard, smart, by the book. *I don't need him to hear me talking to myself,* Steve thought. "Nothing," he said. "Just thinking out loud."

The warrant had a full-search provision. Right now they were standing in the middle of the private residence of one Martin D. Parkins.

"Why is it these places always look the way you *think* they're gonna look?" Stanton asked.

"Well, I hate to be judgmental," Steve said, "but it seems to me that Martin Parkins is a shit head. It makes perfect sense to me that a shit head's gonna live in a shit hole." The place was an efficiency just out of town. A lot of the old fleabag strip motels were converted to apartments, and this was one: a total dump. Garbage piled up everywhere, rotten carpet, a dilapidated wall-unit air-conditioner that rattled so loud they turned it off in spite of the heat. Lawn furniture for chairs and a busted futon for a bed. Cockroaches watched them from the sink, antennae fidgeting.

"Piece of shit car, piece of shit apartment, no possessions worth a dime," Stanton said. "But the guy's been with the post office for years? Those guys make decent scratch. What's he do with his money?"

"Strippers, it looks like," Steve answered. On a table by the wall were matchbooks from a multitude of local strip clubs. There was also a Polaroid camera and a stack of photos; Steve picked up the photos. "Correction, strippers and crack whores."

Stanton groaned when he eyed the pictures. "What a high-class guy." The pictures showed a variety of skinny, pallid broken-down women posing naked on the futon. Broken teeth and broken lives. Any cop knew the look.

"I better book these pictures with evidence, have somebody compare them to any Jane Doe morgue shots," Steve said. "This case feels worse every minute."

"Guy like that? Loner? Antisocial? He could be killing hookers and who would know?"

Yeah, Steve thought. He wouldn't be surprised.

"Hey, Chief? The chick at the post office say Parkins is a drinker?" Stanton asked, nosing around the bed now. His expression crumbled at another stack of photos on the floor, next to a pickle-can wastebasket full of soiled Kleenex. Some of the photos looked just as soiled.

The chick at the post office, Steve repeated in his head. He meant Jane. Steve hadn't been able to stop thinking about her . . .

He shook off the distraction. "Yeah, she suspended him for boozing on the job. He'd had several write-ups in the past." A big metal garbage can sat in the corner of the filthy kitchen, the kind most people put out at the end of their driveway. Steve lifted the metal lid and whistled. "What do you think, Stanton? You think Parkins is a drinker?"

Stanton looked in the can and rolled his eyes. It was full of empty whiskey bottles. "He could start his own glass factory. You know, I drank that stuff during my first semester of college, and I never had a hangover. Got *D*s in all my classes, but I *never* had a hangover."

"Let that be a lesson to you. Be smart. Stick to tequila."

They snooped around some more, found more of the same. A footlocker full of porn videos. More Polaroids. More cockroaches. At one point, they heard a loud *clack!* and both turned with guns drawn. It was a rat that had run across the pile of dirty dishes in the sink.

"Let's get out of this dive, Chief. My wife'll kill me; it's making my uniform stink."

"I'll get someone from evidence section to come over and pick up the Polaroids. Parkins won't be coming back," Steve estimated. "He's probably on a Greyhound bus heading north."

"I'm sure you're right," Stanton said. "But just to be safe, put somebody in an unmarked outside to watch the place from the street."

Steve slapped the sergeant on the back. "Great idea. *Perfect* way for you to spend the rest of your shift."

"Thanks."

They were leaving, but Stanton's voice halted Steve at the door. "Hey, Chief. Check it out."

Steve turned. Stanton was holding a scribble sheet he'd found on the kitchen counter. Steve looked at it. "What's this? Doodling?"

The sheet had various phone numbers scribbled on it, plus pen lines, squares and circles, like when someone unconsciously doodles while they're talking on the phone.

"This is really starting to freak me out," Stanton said. "What the hell's going on in this town?"

One of the doodles was a bell with an asterisk star for a striker.

Chapter Fourteen

(I)

I'm not that much of a sucker, am I? Jane thought. She staved off despair deliberately, replacing it with something close to anger. She felt utterly naive. Steve had called her once, at about 6 P.M., told her he had to work late, but he wanted to see her, could he come by around ten? Of course, she'd told him yes, her heart pattering.

She frowned again at the clock radio by the bed— 1 A.M., it informed her in glowing red numerals. Five minutes later than the last time she'd looked.

She glanced at the phone too, about every five minutes, as though that would make it ring. She'd never felt sexier than now, in an aquamarine kimono-style nightie whose chiffon fabric was so sheer it left all but nothing to the imagination.

What a dope, she thought. *Just go to bed. He's not coming . . .*

The television was on, her attention everywhere but on it. The screen fluttered in the dark bedroom, throwing odd shapes of light on the walls.

Through the glum thoughts, she heard a TV host saying: "*. . . shocking multiple murders that have recently stricken the quiet, crime-free town of Danelleton . . .*"

Jane moaned, sprawled anxiously on the bed. *Not this again.* She leaned up. One breast had popped out of the sheer kimono top, but she didn't bother putting it back in. Why? She was feeling around the sheets for the remote when her eyes moved to the screen. Some tabloid show, and there was that guy again, that bearded man that Steve was talking about last night.

Dhevic, she recalled.

"*. . . with us tonight is professor Alexander Dhevic, a leading authority in the subject of satanism in our age.*"

Jane looked on with distaste. How could things ever get back to normal if they kept dragging it up for the public in schlock shows like this?

Dhevic and the stilted host were talking at a long conference desk. "*. . . and much more,*" Dhevic was saying in that edgy accent. "*But the most-interesting aspect of the Danelleton murders, however tragic, are their similarities to a case that occurred in the same town, and at the same post office, twenty years ago . . .*"

No surprise to her; Jane already knew the story, from Steve.

She looked at Dhevic's face closely. He didn't *look* like a charlatan. Where someone like Anton LeVay looked hokey and overstated, Dhevic looked studied, earnest. True, the show itself was hype, but Dhevic's eyes appeared serious, full of belief.

Then:

Of course it does, she caught herself. *So did Uri Geller; that was all part of the act. These people aren't experts in anything—they're actors who make their living using that skill to cause people to believe their crap.*

"If we might break a moment, to let me ask you something," the host said.

"Certainly."

"Just these rumors that you're psychic, professor, and that you've helped police departments find serial killers, and so on. That your ancestors were fortune tellers or— what?—soothsayers for the Egyptian pharaohs." The host eyed some papers on the desk, searching for information. *"Not soothsayers but—"*

"Augurs," Dhevic corrected, not that Jane had ever heard the word. *"And if you believe that, I've got a bridge to sell you!"* The attempt at levity almost didn't come off, for the accent. *"It is malarky, I've read the same articles you're referring to, and there's no truth to them, I assure you. My descendants are European, for goodness sake, as you can probably tell by the way I speak. I've never helped police, I'm not psychic, telekinetic, or able to communicate with the dead and such. Now, I'll admit, I can bend a spoon . . . with my hands."*

The host seemed taken aback, but recovered. *"I see. So actually, you're just—"*

"An out-of-work college professor who happens to have an extensive background in history and a particular

230

interest in the mythological history of the occult, ritualism, and demonology. My only credentials are my books."

He sounded credible to Jane, so credible she was bored. They began talking more about the Danelleton murders past and present, and the suspicions of cult involvement, when Jane turned the set off.

"I don't need to hear *this* again."

But in only moments she wished she'd left it on. The room's darkness and total silence now reminded her how alone she was. *Damn him,* she thought. *And damn me for taking him seriously. I'd like to break a plank over his head. Jeez, I hope he has the balls to call me now, just so I can hang up on him.*

She settled into bed, then lurched up almost shrieking, when the phone rang.

"Hi, sorry it's so late," Steve said. "It was a long day."

Jane *didn't* hang up on him. She faltered and said, "Oh."

"You're mad, I can tell. I'm sorry. You've probably been sitting up all night waiting for me to come by."

"I have not," she smugly assured him. "I fell asleep at ten."

"I miss you. Can I still come over?"

She faltered again. "Steve, do you know what time it is?"

"Yeah, I know. We were looking for Parkins all day and night. I am the chief of police, you know. I couldn't just bug off."

"No, but you could've called."

"I know, I'm sorry."

"Besides, if you're still at the station, it'd probably be

one-thirty by the time you got here. We've both got to be at work early tomorrow."

"Yeah . . . I know. You go back to bed now. I'm sorry I woke you up. But I miss you." A hesitant pause. "Can I call you tomorrow?"

Suddenly, she felt alarmed. "Wait, no!"

"No—what?" He sounded crushed. "No, I can't call you tomorrow?"

"No, I mean—Come over. I'll wait up."

"Great. And I won't be long, either. Actually I won't be any time at all. I'm not at the station now."

"Where are you?"

"Standing at your front door. I'm on my cell phone."

Jane hung up and rushed to the door. So much for breaking a plank over his head. When she pulled the door open, she didn't say anything, she just pulled him inside and they began to kiss. He paused a moment, to look at her in the sheer kimono, but he didn't have much time. She was already getting out of it and alternately pulling his shirt. Jane was on fire and she could tell that he was too. There were no words, just desperate hands all over each other, just hot breaths being shared as they kissed. The kimono dragged along over the carpet, rung around her ankle, as they stumbled into the living room. Jane lay naked on her back, her hands outstretched; he fumbled out of the rest of his clothes, and then for the next half hour they were consumed with one another. They made love from one end of the living room to the other, oblivious to everything around them. At one point, Jane was lying back, her knees pressed to her face while his mouth laved her sex, and after the first climax a stray glance showed her that she hadn't even closed the front door . . . but she didn't care. The night's warm air rushed over them. The steady throbs of peepers and cricket sounds pulsed into the room. Later they both lay sprawled, carpet-burned and exhausted. "You wore me out again," Steve whispered.

"Good," she whispered back. "I love to wear you out."

"Hey, guess what?"

"What?"

"The front door's wide open."

"I know. I don't care and, besides, I'm too exhausted to get up and close it."

"Me, too, but . . ." He struggled to get up. "We still haven't found Parkins, so I ordered a patrol car to drive by your house every half hour."

Jane laughed at the possibility. "He'll see the door open in the middle of the night, rush in here with his gun, and—"

"Yeah, and see his chief buck-naked on the floor. That's one story I *don't* want making the rounds in the locker room."

Her eyes were wide on him, wide on the toned muscles and lines of his lean body. He was shiny with sweat and so was she. She wanted to go again but knew it would be too much. She watched him close the door and put on the chain.

"I never would have thought it," she said.

"What's that?"

"That one day I'd have a naked cop walking around in my living room."

"Yeah, well I *like* walking around naked in your living room. That could be a problem."

"Why?"

"I'll get spoiled. Pretty soon—who knows? I'll be walking around naked in your living room all the time. You won't be able to get rid of me."

"You let me worry about that."

After he'd locked the door, he came back and offered his hand.

"Let me help you up. We should go to bed."

"No," she whispered and pulled him back down. She wrapped herself around him. "Let's sleep here tonight, right here on the floor."

He didn't object, and had fallen asleep at her bosom minutes later. She smiled and began to drift off herself . . .

Her eyes darted open, just at the fringes of sleep. Something moved at the very corner of her vision. Moonlight bathed the wall behind them. She craned her neck, careful not to wake Steve. She squinted and focused, and she saw . . .

A line. A crooked line running from the baseboard across the floor, where its end disappeared into shadow. She blinked, dismissing it as merely some sleep-inspired mirage. She knew it wouldn't be there when she stopped blinking.

But it was.

What is *that?*

Then she heard a skittering. *Rat,* she thought at once. *Please don't tell me I've got rats!* But even if it was a rat, what would that have to do with the crooked line? The sound came from the wall, and rats don't leave slimy trails, do they?

More skittering, and she frowned, slipped out of

Steve's sleeping embrace. He didn't wake up when she'd edged herself away. She stood perfectly still for a moment, stunned by the clarity of her silhouette projected by the flood of moonlight: a perfect razor-sharp black cutout against the wall, every hourglass line of her body, every contour. It could've been an erotic painting, but then the painting moved when she moved. She shook off the digression, then padded naked over to the line on the floor. *What the hell is this line?* she thought, bending over to look at it. Had Kevin drawn on the floor in crayon? *No way,* she felt sure. Kids were known to do things like that, especially when they were distressed, but . . . *I would've seen it. There's no way I wouldn't have noticed this line if it had been there earlier.* She was absolutely certain it wasn't. Then she bent over and touched the line.

It was wet.

Blood? No. She winced when she sniffed her finger. It smelled foul, like something rancid. The line could only be described as dark slime. She was going to close the window and turn on the light, but she heard the skittering again.

Her gaze jerked up, and she stared. Something about the size of a rat moved out of the shadow and back onto the lit part of the floor. It was crawling as an insect would, but it couldn't have been a palmetto bug; they simply didn't get that big. Neither did beetles. It skittered over closer to her, and then all the air went out of her chest when she realized what it was: a horned toad.

It . . . can't . . . be . . .

Her son's horned toad was dead. Jane was sure. She

saw it. She buried it. Yet this thing on the floor was very much a horned toad and it was very much alive. It scrabbled closer, leaving the odd trail behind it. *Don't be ridiculous,* she thought. Of course, it was a different horned toad, a wild one. *Oh, I know.* It suddenly dawned on her. Steve had bought Kevin the new horned toad, and it had simply gotten out of the terrarium. She slipped her kimono back on, paced quickly to Kevin's room, and looked at the small glass tank. She just needed to prove to herself that the new toad had escaped.

But the new toad was in the tank when she looked in.

All right, all right, this is silly, she told herself, padding back to the living room. Kevin's new toad *hadn't* escaped. So what? She was looking at the one on the floor again. *It got in from the outside,* she told herself. *Big deal.* But—

What was that line? That trail it left behind it as it moved across the floor?

She looked closer at the toad. It stank, like something rotten, just like that line of slime. She remembered what had happened to her son's toad: something had squashed it, to the extent that its innards had been disgorged. She leaned over even closer, cringing at the stench.

The horned toad on the floor was dragging its guts behind it, from its mouth. That was the cause of the slime.

"Steve! Look! Look!" she was saying next, heart pounding. She jostled him on the floor until he woke.

"Honey, what is it?"

"Look at the toad on the floor!"

He got up groggily. "Huh?"

Jane was pointing, frantic. When Steve looked at it, he said, "Jane, it's nothing to get upset about. It's just—"

"It's not the one you bought. It's the first one!"

"You said the first one died."

"It did! I buried it!"

Now he was laughing under his breath. "Then this one got into the house somehow. It's a wild one."

"No it's NOT! It's Kevin's first one, the one my husband got him." She pointed again, shaking. "Steve, its insides are hanging out of its mouth! The same thing that happened to Mel! That's the same toad."

Steve's shoulders slumped. "Then its one hell of a hardy toad, to be able to crawl out of its grave after being buried alive, come back in the house, and still be crawling around with its guts hanging out."

"That's impossible!"

Steve put his pants on, got a plastic cup from the kitchen, and scooted the toad into the cup. "Stinks like the dickens, Jesus . . ." He kept a palm over the cup.

"Where are you going with it?" Jane asked.

"I'm gonna put it out in the yard. It's dying."

"No, you don't understand. It was *dead* a few days ago."

Steve paused to pinch the bridge of his nose. "Jane. You're telling me that you believe this toad . . . came back to life?"

"I—" No, of course she wasn't. But what *was* she implying? All of a sudden she realized how ridiculous she must sound. *He's going to think I'm a nut!* "I just mean . . . well, I don't know what I mean. It's just really weird—the situation."

"It's late, you're tired. You probably had a bad dream and got disoriented, that's all. I don't want to just put it in the garbage, it's still alive. And—"

Steve paused again when he lifted his hand and peeked into the cup.

"What?" Jane asked. "It got out."

"No. Er, I don't think so." He showed her the inside of the cup. The stench was worse now. It was *steaming*. The toad didn't appear to be in the cup anymore, replaced by a stinking black liquefaction, as if the creature had rotted down to muck in the minute or so it had been in the cup. It looked like a cup full of waste.

Steve didn't say anything. He went outside, down the driveway, and dropped the cup into the garbage. When he came back, they remained silent. He took her hand and they went to Jane's bed, their moonlight-forged shadows moving crisply across the wall and away.

Neither of them noticed the third, larger shadow that remained on the wall: tall, gaunt, long-limbed. The head of the ink-black silhouette seemed oddly angled, and horned. Then the silhouette spread as its host raised great ten-foot-long wings behind its back, and then it disappeared with a chuckle.

Chapter Fifteen

(I)

The high sun blazed over Jane's west branch post office, sitting in the middle of another perfect Florida day. Wild parrots cackled, not a cloud in the sky, hot but breezy. Customers came and went, careless and content. Everything was normal.

Jane felt anything *but* normal. Last night, Steve had spent the night, but they didn't make love again. It had been late, and the incident with the toad had knocked the rest of their time together off kilter. *I don't know what I was thinking. What* was *I thinking?* She simply felt bewildered, and sitting across from her was Sarah, who looked equally bewildered, but by something else.

"It's just so strange," Sarah said.

"Well, what you have to understand is that Martin is a very strange man. He's always been strange. Very antisocial, a loner. And now, obviously, a peeping Tom," Jane observed.

"So where is he? What happened to him? Nobody's seen him since yesterday morning when you gave him his notice, and he still hasn't come back to get his car. It's been in the lot all night."

"Steve thinks—" she began, but then corrected herself. She wasn't ready to let her employees know that she was involved with the chief of police. "The police think he left town. There's a warrant out for his arrest. It's probably all for the best."

"Sure, but what if he didn't? What if he's still around town, hiding somewhere? Aren't you afraid he might come back to your house, drunk and mad as hell?"

It was a consideration, but one she pushed away. Steve had stepped up patrols on her street, and every cop in town was looking for Martin. She wasn't going to let the prospect bother her. "I know, Sarah, it's a little scary, but you let me worry about Martin. He's a harmless pervert, I'm sure. Let's just both get back to work now."

"Okay. See you later." Sarah walked out of the office, leaving Jane to her thoughts. A few minutes later, one of the front clerks stepped in, Doreen Fletcher, a young, slender brunette in her early twenties, who'd just started a few months ago.

"Jane, sorry to bother you, but there's a man here to see you."

A man? It must've been Steve. "Thanks, Doreen. Just tell him to come in. He knows he doesn't have to knock."

Doreen went back in the hall. "Ms. Ryan's right in there, sir. Just go on in."

"Thank you," came the reply.

That voice, Jane thought. *It's definitely not Steve.* But she was certain she'd heard the voice before.

Then a tall, imposing figure entered the office, and when Jane took one look, she knew. Long dark hair with some streaks of gray, trimmed beard, a dark and tidy but rather out-of-date suit.

Alexander Dhevic, Jane thought.

"Ms. Ryan? Jane Ryan?" he asked. "I apologize if this is inconvenient, but it's essential that I speak with you. My name is—"

"Come in, Professor Dhevic," Jane said.

(II)

Claudette Peterson heard the doorbell from the auxiliary speaker her husband had wired to the back deck. It was easy for him—he was a successful electrical contractor—and they were tired of missing visitors when they were lounging by the pool. Claudette never tanned well, her only disappointment with Florida; she was a flaming redhead with flawless white skin sprayed with freckles. But nature had graced her with a slim, voluptuous body that made bikinis irresistible for her—she simply used copious amounts of sunblock. She groaned in the lounge chair when the doorbell rang, put her margarita down, and went through the house to the door, skin shining from all that oil, her hair tied up in a scarf. Her nipples constricted when she passed from the outside heat to the inside air-conditioning.

"Yes?" she said, opening the door.

It was the mailman. Not the usual one; one she'd never seen.

"I have a telegram for you, Mrs. Peterson," the carrier said. "I need you to sign for it. Right there at the *x*."

"Oh, of course." *A telegram?* Claudette didn't think she'd ever received a telegram in her life—she didn't even know what they looked like. "I hope it's nothing serious," she said, concerned. Telegrams were usually bad news, weren't they? A death notification, a relative in a car accident, or some such crisis. Her husband was safely at work—an office job—and her parents had died years ago. She did have a few relatives spread out over the country, but she was close to none of them.

The mailman handed her a clipboard. "Just sign at the *x*, please."

When she took the clipboard, she frowned. The mailman was staring at her body, feeling her up with his beady eyes. *Great,* was her cynical thought. She was realistic, of course. She could have put a robe on before answering the door, or wrapped a towel around her. *I guess I'm getting what I asked for.* His stare made her distinctly uncomfortable but—*If I don't like it, I shouldn't wear stuff like this around other people.* Her peach-hued bikini couldn't even be called a thong, it was more g-string than anything, the cups of the bra minuscule, and the shiny polyester patch down below stretched so tightly across the triangle of her crotch, very few details of her sex were left unrevealed.

Goosebumps crawled up her back when she returned the clipboard. The mailman was staring directly at her crotch. He was grinning.

"I don't appreciate that," she said.

"Don't dress like a stripper if you don't want to be stared at by men." He couldn't have replied more rudely. "Christ, lady, your pussy looks like you painted it."

Claudette was revolted. The man was almost drooling! "You're not the regular mailman. What's your name? I'm reporting you."

"My name's Martin Parkins, and guess what, bitch? I don't even work for the post office any more. So go ahead and report me."

"Martin Parkins," she repeated. She wouldn't forget, and she was going to call the police, too. Was he impersonating a postal employee? That sounded like a federal offense. But if so . . .

What was this slip of paper in her hand?

"At least read your telegram before you *report* me," the man said.

Claudette looked at the paper. It was no telegram, it was just a sheet of Xerox paper on which had been scrawled: WELCOME TO HELL.

Then Claudette screamed, but only for a second. Martin had shoved her backward into the room and, almost instantly, from behind, a hand clamped over her mouth. Someone else had already gotten in the house! But the hand . . .

What is God's name—she thought.

There was something wrong with the hand. It wasn't normal. It stank, it was covered in slime, and the long thing fingers seemed to have more joints than a normal hand. Her eyes bulged as she was held in place by the second intruder, but then it occurred to her—in sheer horror—that *several* other men must be in the room, because she could feel more hands wrap around her from behind, molesting her. A half dozen more hands at least. Who were these people?

Shock was beginning to dim her vision; she noticed the mailman close the door and lock it, then he walked over and sat down on the couch. He sat intently at the edge of the cushion, staring raptly as Claudette squirmed in the multihanded embrace. "I'm at the end of the line, if you know what I mean," he said, and lit a cigarette. "Sloppy sevenths. I'll watch until it's my turn."

But Claudette was essentially not comprehending now. The room seemed darker than usual. Had the other men closed the drapes? But she also noted weird orange light flickering behind her. And what those awful hands were pinning her down to wasn't the plush heather-green living room carpet.

It felt like mud.

Shapes shifted above her. Long fingers wormed at her crotch and breasts, popping off the bra and tiny bottoms. Someone, or thing, was kissing her now; Claudette was so revolted she almost threw up when a tongue that seemed a foot long pushed through her pressed lips. When she bit the tongue, nothing happened. It was like biting leather. The only reaction from her attacker was a hot chuckle that flowed into her mouth, then the tongue went all the way down her throat until she could feel it wriggling in her stomach. Meanwhile, fingers invaded her sex, and her breasts were kneaded like raw baker's dough. When Claudette began to convulse from suffocation, the impossible black tongue retracted. She heaved in a breath just before she would've died.

"They're called spermatademons—ain't that a hoot? I mean, that's what they call them down there," the mailman rambled on. "I had to be on the other end of that, too, just like you, only with me, it was part of my punishment. Oh, I guess you don't know what I'm talking about, huh?" A bleak laugh. "Let me put it this way: it hurts to sit down. Those boys ain't particular."

One was on her now. The other pinned her shoulders down and spread her legs with hands that gripped like metal bands. Her vision began to clear; when she turned her face away, she saw—

What in God's name?

Claudette wasn't in her living room. She was in a cave whose hewn rock walls oozed and steamed. And she noticed at once the source of the weird flickering orange light. Torches topped by wads of pitch were flickering from various areas, their shafts stuck into rock. It looked medieval.

I'm in hell, she realized through the madness.

"It's this," the mailman said. He pulled something out of his bag that at first she thought was a club. "You got any idea what this is, Mrs. Peterson?"

Claudette could hardly answer. Huge fleshy things were entering her, thrusting in and out like pistons.

But she could hear, and she heard the mailman say this: "It's kind of like a key, I guess. It opens a door that they call a Rive. You're on the other side of that door right now."

Something was changing her. She should be horrified but she wasn't any longer. She was excited, she was eager for each new lover who climbed on top of her. The mailman was still holding that clublike object. It must've weighed twenty pounds: a stout bar of old metal that looked like iron, a ring at one end and a starlike ball at the other end.

"This is a bell striker, Mrs. Peterson," the mailman continued, "and believe me, it ain't from around here. Has special powers is what the Messenger told me. It opens that door I was telling you about. It opens that Rive."

Claudette wasn't really even hearing him anymore. She was climaxing in spastic quakes. Even when she saw the details of the impossible men who were taking her, she wasn't disgusted. Brownish veins could be seen through their semitranslucent white flesh. Primeval, huge-eyed with fang-filled slits for grins, heads misshapen like small boulders. And horns.

So her lovers weren't men at all.

She stole a peek out of the cave and could see more of the void beyond. It looked endless. She saw masses of naked people, some deformed, some missing limbs, others only retaining part of their former humanity after undergoing some process of hybridization. She could also see a lake not too far from the mouth of the cave. The lake was steaming, and it wasn't water that filled it, it looked like blood, bubbling. From the lake things that seemed to have beaks rose up and plodded into the mass of humans, tearing into them, ripping off strips of skin and pecking out eyes with gleeful abandon. Some were actually pulled into the lake, screaming as they were devoured by still more unspeakable things below the surface. All the while, the chasm echoed in a never-ending cacophony of moans, laughs, shrieks, and screams.

Claudette was pretty much insane by now, out of her mind in an erotic frenzy. She didn't care what happened to her. She wished she could be here always. She could see the mailman on the other side of the Rive. He put the bell striker back in his bag, then took off his clothes. Around Claudette, the pallid demons lay exhausted; she'd spent them all and only wanted more. She panted, muck-covered, inflamed, and looked up.

The mailman's naked body looked strange. His stomach was swollen and his skin was covered with blue and black blotches. "I'm dead," he said and kind of chuckled, "but the Messenger keeps me alive to do his business. He has messages that need to be delivered, and I'm helping him. I'm being punished"—he held his hands out, to display his slowly rotting physique—"so this is what I get. I gotta earn back his respect, you know? Now I'm gonna take my turn and when I'm done, I'm gonna slit you open and clean you out like a Thanksgiving turkey. Nothing personal. It's just what I gotta do, okay?"

He began to walk forward, approaching the Rive. Claudette waited anxiously, squirming in anticipation. But then the mailman stopped and yelled, "Damn it!"

He was looking down at his bare groin. His penis, which was already half gone to rot, fell off. It sat curled on the carpet like a lost tidbit.

"So much for me having my turn. Ain't that just my

Edward Lee

luck? I'll tell ya, life, death, either one. They're both a kick in the ass."

The mailman went back to his bag and pulled out a large carving knife.

Chapter Sixteen

(I)

The door exploded, flying to bits out of its steel security frame. Two uniformed police stepped quickly back with the door ram, while several more skirted around them and tactically entered the house, guns drawn and aimed high and low. The house was surrounded by local mobile units, several ambulances, and some county sheriff's department cars.

"What's the name here?" one cop just outside asked. He was watching the windows.

Another cop, surveying the corner of the house, said, "Peterson. No rap sheet, no calls, nothing. Husband's at work so it should only be the wife inside."

"So what's the scoop?

"Neighbor said he thought he heard a scream after seeing a mailman at the door. But there's no mail truck."

"What is all this mailman shit?"

Inside, the first team clearing the living room stopped cold, their faces blanched as they looked down at what lay on the floor.

"Chief Higgins!"

Steve entered and stopped, looking down just as grimly.

The thing on the floor was only vaguely recognizable as a human female. Steve felt instantly sick to his stomach. Had the woman actually been skinned? *Who could do something like that?* The crimson stick figure lay asprawl. Even the face had been cut off, but the scalp had not; the expert cutting job left the shining, perfectly straight red hair intact and carefully lying over the victim's shoulders. An open gash in her abdomen gaped, the cavity within empty. Most revolting of all was the position: almost a lewd pose, legs spread, arms out like a woman in wait of her lover on the living room floor. A grislier thought occurred to him with the image. Last night he'd made love to Jane . . . on the living room floor.

He gritted his teeth, tried to blink the atrocity out of his head, but it wasn't working even when he looked away.

This couldn't possibly be Parkins, he tried to convince himself.

"Aw, Jesus!" another cop said, backing away from the coat closet.

Steve went over and stared. In the closet hung several light jackets, a pool robe, and a few raincoats. But right at the end hung what could only be Mrs. Claudette Peterson's skin, hanging there like a suit of clothes. The only part not intact was the face, which had been cut off the neck and hung through an eyehole off a peg on the hat rack.

"Check it out, Chief," one of his uniforms said. "No big surprise by now, huh?"

Steve practically staggered over to the voice. *What now, what now?* What could be worse?

His gaze fell on the floor of the bedroom, where a pile of organs lay. The other cops were looking away, silent. Then Steve's gaze lifted to the wall, to the blood-fashioned symbol that he was now beginning to see on a regular basis around here—the bell with the star shape for a striker.

(II)

Jane's eyes widened on the drawing: the bell with the star shape for a striker. At first, she was so on edge by Dhevic's sudden appearance at her office that she didn't fully focus on what he was saying. "Have you seen this before?" was the very first thing out of his mouth, and then he held a leather folder that contained what appeared to be several thick polycarbonate sheets. The plasticized material was being used to protect a piece of paper, from what Dhevic described as a very, very old book. He placed the first protective sheet on her desk blotter. "It's an engraving in a tome entitled *Das Grimoire de Praelata*." Then he'd gone on to talk about how these occult visionaries called prelates some thousand years ago had used psychic powers to establish mental contact with particular souls in hell. Some of these prelates were artists and engravers, and here, supposedly, was one of their engravings.

She easily recalled the nature of the source, a so-called expert on the occult, as seen on tabloid shows. However . . .

Something about him, this tall, intense, middle-aged man, seemed genuine.

"Have you, Ms. Ryan?"

"Have I seen this symbol before? Yes, I have."

"I know you have," he said very mysteriously, and she was too uneasy to ask him what he'd meant. Then he went on, "It's a quasi-geometric shape that we call a campanulation. Effectively, it's left at the scene of a ritual murder, written in blood. It's thought to be more of a homage—or simply more powerful—if it is done in the blood of an oblation."

Jane sat listless at the desk, glancing down at the engraving in the old book, then up to him. He'd remained standing, his presence filling the small office. "Oblation?" she asked. "What's that?"

"The blood of a sacrifant—I should say the blood of an innocent person used as the body of a sacrifice. The only more powerful offering is the campanulation left in the blood of an acolyte, one who sacrifices *himself* as a suicidal tribute. Have there been any such suicides that you know of, Ms. Ryan?"

She didn't answer, at least not vocally. But there had been, hadn't there? Marlene. Carlton. Both had killed themselves, leaving the symbol in blood. Theirs *and* their victims.

Dhevic continued, with that floating, accented voice, while pointing to the engraving. "The campanulation. A bell shape. It's a representation of *that* bell, Ms. Ryan. Note the star-shaped clapper."

"I see it," she said.

"Something's happening here, Ms. Ryan. You know that it's not merely coincidental."

"How do I know that?" she asked, not sure what point there'd be in challenging him.

Was he smiling? "You know. You've got ritualized crimes from twenty years ago corresponding to identical crimes today, and the single most pertinent common denominator is—"

"My post office," Jane finished.

"That's correct. And what I must know is this: Do any of your employees belong to any radical religious cults, or conform to odd religious beliefs?"

Jane smirked. "No. The police already asked me the same thing—"

"I'm not surprised."

"—and I told them the same thing. I told them no."

"But you're struggling with that, aren't you?"

Jane paused in a weird silence. She *was* struggling with that. Steve believed it, he simply couldn't make a solid connection. But even Jane couldn't argue with the logic. "I agree. There is some kind of cult connection, there has to be. It'd be illogical at this point to *not* believe that."

"Now we're getting somewhere. Do you mind if I sit down?"

Jane looked up at him. She simply didn't know what to make of the man. Steve had implied that Dhevic might even be part of it, part of the cult connection camouflaging himself with his credentials, but now that Jane had met the man, she didn't buy it. She didn't necessarily like him, but she didn't believe he was a killer. She could see it in his eyes. *I should just call Steve, tell him the guy's here. He'd want to talk to him anyway.* But when the thought left her head, Dhevic was looking at the phone, then glanced back to her with a raised brow.

This is really friggin' creepy. "Please feel free to take a seat, Professor Dhevic."

"Thank you." His suit was a nice cut, she could tell, but it was old, worn. He looked like someone on and off the skids. But he must have money. Those television tabloid shows, the books he'd written? He was an enigma.

Next he asked, "Are you aware of any sort of a peculiar iron object on the premise?"

Jane winced. "What?"

"I know it's an odd question. Something about a foot and a half long, a rod, Ms. Ryan, an iron rod. It has a ring on one end and a—"

"I don't know what you're talking about. Just when I was starting to think you're harmless, you ask me something really nutty like that."

He looked right back at her. "I don't want to make you uncomfortable. I'll leave at once, if you'd prefer. Or feel free to call the police, if you're suspicious of me."

A chill went up her spine. First she'd thought about calling Steve, then Dhevic was looking at the phone. Now he'd mentioned calling the police . . .

Jane just went ahead and said it: "Now I suppose

254

you're going to tell me you're psychic, you can read minds—"

He smiled fully this time. "No, Ms. Ryan. Nothing like that. I'm nothing like that at all."

"I saw you, several times, on television. Documentaries, and—"

"Hokey, overdone tabloid shows about satanism. I'm not very proud of those appearances, but they do serve several purposes. One, any foreknowledge, any at all, is better than none, because it keeps people thinking. It doesn't matter if it's a frivolous documentary on late-night cable. It keeps people aware."

Jane just shook her head. "I still don't know what you're talking about."

"And, two, I need the money. I have benefactors but let's just say that they're sometimes less than timely in delivering my allowance. There's not an office I can go to, there's no cashier or pay clerk. I have no home, no base, I'm constantly on the move in my responsibilities. Think of it this way: I *work* for an establishment, like a traveling salesman, only I'm not selling anything, I'm investigating something."

"Mass murders?" Jane asked.

"In a sense, yes. I'm keeping watch."

Jane just kept looking at him.

"I know this is difficult for you to take in all at once. We don't have time for me to explain it all right now, I'll just have to ask you to trust me."

"Why should I?"

"No reason, not objectively." He remained gazing back at her. "Use your intuition. As I've just said, if you'd prefer that I leave, I'll leave. If you'd like to call your friend the police chief—"

"How do you know he's my friend?" she blurted.

Dhevic smiled. "I'm psychic."

"Bullshit." She reached for the phone, began to dial Steve's cell phone . . .

Dhevic remained unfazed.

Jane hung up. She wasn't sure why, but she knew she wanted to hear what this man had to say, however bizarre. She wanted to give him the—

"The benefit of the doubt is never a mistake, Ms. Ryan."

Jane sighed. "Fine. Just go on with what you were saying."

"I was explaining my television appearances, which are laughable, I admit. But even a laughable warning can be useful to the open-minded."

"I *think* I know what you're saying. Even a *Bugs Bunny* cartoon can be educational, right?"

"Exactly!" He seemed enthused that she'd made the association. "I'm ashamed of that stuff, but it does serve my purpose."

Jane supposed she was beginning to understand. "And what were you saying about—what? An iron something or other?"

"It's a relic, or thought to be by some. Belief is everything. If people *believe* that a relic has supernatural power, then they'll kill for it. The Ark of the Covenant, for example. The nails of Calvary or the Shroud of Turin. A better example. In 1920, construction excavators in Moselle, France, unearthed a pewter tureen that was soon rumored to be the Holy Grail. It was said to heal the sick and effect miracles. People killed for it."

Jane thought she was finally getting the man's point. "Was it really the Holy Grail?"

"It doesn't matter. All that matters is that people *believed* it was, to the extent people were killed in its procurement. The *belief* is the power. Do *I* believe it was the genuine Holy Grail? No. But that doesn't matter."

"So," Jane deduced, remembering what he'd said earlier. "You were asking me about this iron object, a relic. You're telling me that certain people believe that it has some occult power?"

"Yes."

"And the *belief* in that power is the cause of Danelleton's murders? The ones this week and the murders twenty years ago?"

"Yes."

"And the people who seek this object are in a cult?"

"Yes. Exactly. Marlene Troy, Carlton Spence, and others—there will be others, all seduced into what you can think of as a cult of worship. It's like an infection. Indoctrination into the cult is spread from one to another. Because of this relic, Ms. Ryan, this simple and very old piece of iron that I believe is connected to this facility."

She was starting to get confused again, listening to him while continuing to look for red flags, something, anything, to indicate that Dhevic might be a flake. But she just wasn't seeing it.

"What is the object?" Jane finally asked. "What's this relic you're asking me about."

Dhevic's steady accent rolled out in crisp syllables. "It's an iron rod, about a foot-and-a-half long. It has a ring on one end, and a star-shaped ball on the other. The star shape is a luciferic symbol."

"Luciferic," Jane repeated.

"The Morning Star."

Even Jane remembered her old and rather boring mythology classes. "The first nickname for Satan."

"Yes. He has many names, but that was his first. That's what God called him when he threw his once-favorite angel off the twelfth gate of heaven." Dhevic paused, watching her eyes. "Supposedly."

"A star-shaped ball. An iron rod. And a campan—"

"Campanulation. A bell, Ms. Ryan." Dhevic pointed again to the engraving in the old book. "What's inside of a bell?"

"I don't know what it's called. A ringer, I guess, a gong?"

"A striker. The relic I'm inquiring about is said to be the bell striker . . . from *this* bell." His finger remained on the bell in the engraving.

Jane looked at the engraving, then back to him.

"That's what some people *believe*, just as some people *believe* a four-leaf clover will bring them good luck."

"You're losing me again," Jane said.

"God has a Messenger," Dhevic continued. "That messenger is an angel named Gabriel, and Gabriel announces himself with a trumpet, according to the Bible. There are many references to God's messenger. It was Gabriel who was sent to deliver the message to Daniel of the coming of the Seventy Days. He announced the birth of John the Baptist, and he informed Mary that she would give birth to Jesus. Yes, God's messenger. Well . . ." Dhevic's voice lowered. "According to myth, Lucifer has a messenger too, and that messenger's name is Aldezhor."

The strange name seemed to flit about the room, like a moth seeking exit.

"The campanulation—the bell-shaped designs left at the murder scenes—are Aldezhor's emblems. They pay homage to Aldezhor's tool—the bell in that engraving, which is called the *Cymbellum Eosphorus* or the Bell of the Morning Star. You've heard the term hell's bells? This is where it comes from. When it sounds it's time for the Messenger to speak for his master. To put it more simply, Gabriel blows a trumpet, Aldezhor rings a bell."

Jane tried to absorb the information. An occult relic that people were killing for? A talisman? *What does this have to do with me?* she thought.

"Some people believe in guardian angels," Dhevic said. "Well, let me put it this way. Angels have guardians, too, on earth. Think of them as stewards, custodians for the cause. I am one such custodian. My duty is to follow Aldezhor, the Messenger. Ultimately my job is to retrieve the iron striker and return it to its keepers at the Biblioteca Apostolica Vaticana, where it was kept hidden for five hundred years. It's my job. It is not a clergical duty, and it's certainly not a Catholic duty. It's simply my job and I've been doing it for my entire adult life. Do I believe that the striker is genuine? Of course not."

"That's a relief," Jane said. "But your job is to track

down this phony piece of metal that a bunch of satanic kooks think is from hell? Am I getting this right?"

"Essentially, yes."

"Who do you work for? An investigations firm?"

"No. The job was handed down to me."

"By whom?"

"That I can't say. It's a professional confidentiality."

Hmm. Jane's mind turned over question after question. Even the situation seemed incredible, simply the fact of this man being here in her office, discussing this bizarre topic. "Aldezhor. The devil's messenger. A demon that this cult believes in."

"Not a demon," Dhevic corrected. "Worse."

Jane almost laughed. "What could be worse than that?"

"Aldezhor, like Lucifer, is a *fallen* angel. *He* was once God's messenger, and was ejected from heaven along with the Morning Star. The Archangel Gabriel replaced him." Yet another pause. "According to the myth."

"So what's all this have to do with me, my post office, my employees?"

"Proximity. God's message to the world is a message of peace, hope, faith, and love. The devil's message is one of hate, lust, betrayal, and murder. It's almost funny. What could be more ironic than postal employees—who are messengers themselves—being utilized to deliver the word of Lucifer?"

Jane shook her head. "But why *my* post office? Why not a larger processing center in a big city? Why not Miami or Jacksonville?"

"Again, proximity."

"I don't understand."

Dhevic opened his mouth to speak but faltered. Something happened. He looked off and appeared suddenly pained. His eyelids fluttered, and his hands trembled on the desk. *Is he epileptic?* Jane thought, alarmed. *Is he having some kind of fit?*

"Oh, God," he muttered.

"Professor Dhevic? Are you all right? Should I call an ambulance?"

He steadied his hand. When he looked at her again, there were tears in his eyes . . .

"What's wrong!"

Dhevic ground his teeth. "I told some lies to you," he groaned. "And with me, there's always a price to pay for that."

"What? Lies?"

"I'm an augur. Do you know what that is?"

"I don't know what you're talking about!" Jane blurted.

"I'm a *seer,* Ms. Ryan. I see things. The past, the future . . ."

I called this one totally wrong. "You're a crackpot, just like Steve said!" She put her hand on the phone, but his own hand instantly pressed down on top of it.

"Listen to me," he croaked. "I have visions. It's in my blood, my heritage. I have these moments that I call inklings. I know that they are channeled to me from . . . somewhere else. Always for a reason, a reason that empowers my calling. It's not a job, Ms. Ryan. It's a calling. I lied so you'd believe me. My calling was handed down to me through my blood, my ancestors, my heritage."

"Let go of my hand," Jane said very slowly. "I'm calling the police."

"Not yet! Listen!" He looked sick again, his head rowing back and forth. He looked like he might pass out at any moment. "I'm an augur, and augurs aren't allowed to lie. It's a violation of our oath. If we lie, we're punished. I'm being punished right now."

"If you don't let go of my hand, I'll start screaming—"

"When I told you I didn't believe that the striker was genuine, that was a lie too. It *is* genuine. And it's manipulating people *now*, *your* people. *Here.* I *know* it's here, and I know it's *been* here for the last twenty years. You've got to let me look for it. You've got to let me find it, otherwise many many more people will die . . ."

Another bout of trembling allowed Jane to finally snatch the phone away. She stood, backed up to the wall, and dialed Steve's number.

But her finger stopped before hitting the last digit.

Her eyes were locked on Dhevic's. He stood up slowly and looked down. His eyes seemed bottomless.

"Aldezhor is terrifying to look at," he whispered. "He's indescribable."

"You're insane," Jane whispered back, unable to tug herself out of whatever hold he'd put on her.

"Demons serve him, the most unspeakable things . . ."

"Leave . . . me . . . alone . . ."

"I told you, I'm a seer. I can see heaven and I can see hell. They both exist, they very much exist."

Jane opened her mouth to scream for help but a final look into those huge empty eyes paralyzed her.

She could see someone there, deep beyond his gaze . . .

"He's waiting for you," Dhevic said. "Your husband? Matt?"

Jane dropped the phone.

"Can you see him? You can see him, can't you? He's waiting for you—in heaven . . ."

I can, she realized. *It's him.*

Matt was smiling at her, standing in an aura of tranquil bluish white.

When Dhevic blinked, the vision snapped.

"But someone else is waiting for you too. He will manipulate you through your fears, your weaknesses, and your dreams. Don't fall to his seduction, Ms. Ryan. Aldezhor. The Messenger."

Jane screamed at the image—that *thing* looking back at her in Dhevic's gaze. Then the image whited out. When the scream had ripped out of her throat, she teetered against the wall. "Jane? Jane?" Several employees had rushed into the room to help her.

Dhevic was gone.

Chapter Seventeen

(I)

Jane felt sick to death driving out of the west branch lot. *Dhevic, Dhevic, Dhevic,* the name kept pounding in her mind. And those things he'd said? Those things he'd shown her?

She didn't know what to think now, or what to believe.

All she knew was this: *I have to tell Steve . . .*

The nausea began to abate once she got out on the main road, opened the car windows, and let the air blow on her face. Yes, she needed to talk to Steve, but what would she say? And what would *he* say in response? *I can't go in there and tell him that Dhevic is an augur, for God's sake! A bell from hell? A fallen angel named Aldezhor? I can't tell him that! I can't tell him Dhevic showed me visions of heaven and hell! He'll think I'm nuts!*

But what *had* she seen, really? She rolled over every conceivable explanation. Hypnosis, the power of suggestion under stress, simple gullibility in the face of a very good liar and actor. *But why? Why would Dhevic go to all that trouble?* He'd known that she was involved with Steve, and he'd known her dead husband's name, but that could all be explained logically. He could've seen her and Steve together. He could've read her husband's obituary a long time ago. Not too difficult. But again it made no sense. What purpose could Dhevic have in wanting her to believe this?

Unless it's true, was the only answer she could come up with.

She cleared her mind of the whole mess, took deep breaths, and drove straight to the Danelleton police station. *I'll figure out what I'm going to say when I say it,* she decided. She parked in the visitor's lot and was taking long strides into the clean red-brick building. Cops milled about at the booking desk, several nodded or said hello. Then a sergeant was politely directing her to the proper hallway. A wave of relief swept her when she saw the sign on the door: CHIEF STEVEN HIGGINS. The door was ajar. She raised her hand to knock but paused. Movement caught her eye, and something else . . .

A scent.

Perfume? she thought.

She put her eye to the gap in the door and looked in.

Steve was standing behind his desk, his jacket off, his shoulder holster and gun draped over the chair. There was someone standing next to him, and at first Jane was too shocked for the image to register. Every excuse flowed through her mind: *Don't freak out, don't jump to conclusions. It's a civilian employee, a clerk, a secretary or someone. Maybe it's a police officer in plainclothes. Maybe it's someone from the town council or the mayor's office . . .*

It was someone, all right.

A woman. A statuesque blonde in a beige pinstripe business woman's suit, long toned legs, high heels, a short skirt.

They seemed to be whispering. Then Steve put his arms around the woman. She returned the gesture and they embraced. It was a long, even intimate embrace. Jane thought she was feeling sick earlier, when she'd seen Dhevic. Now, in an instant, she felt ten times more nauseated.

The last thing she saw was Steve kissing the woman.

Jane's heart felt wrenched out of her chest. Part of her wanted to storm into the office and start yelling but . . .

No. That's not me. She would've loved to put him on the spot, ruin everything for him with this other woman, wreck his day just as he'd wrecked hers. Throw a tirade right there in his office, a real Jerry Springer-type fracas. But then she thought a minute more and realized how useless that would be.

I've been had, that's all, she thought. *It happens all the time. Men do this to women every day—I should've seen it coming. Instead I set myself up. Just turn around and walk away.*

Jane looked back inside. Steve and the blonde were still embracing.

She turned around and walked away.

(II)

"Sometimes you make me feel like I'm just some big muscular moron," Dan said.

Sarah smirked. "Dan, I hate to tell you this, but you *are* a big muscular moron." She stood aside, arms crossed, watching his biceps bulge as he lifted one box of letters after another off the collator rack and slid them into the take-away shelves.

"Thanks, thanks a lot," he said.

"Dan, there's nothing wrong with being a big muscular moron." Now she actually had to chuckle.

"Yeah, and look at you. I guess your beach bunny days are over, now that you're the big boss around here."

"I'm not the boss, Jane is. I'm just the new DPS manager. True, I'm *your* boss. I'm the boss of everyone who works in the DPS station. But that's not really the point, is it?"

Dan was big, a weight lifter. Blond hair, dark tan, rugged—the perfect Florida mold. He wiped sweat off his brow with a brawny arm, then laughed, a laugh of defeat. "Yeah, there she is, little Miss DPS Manager, arms crossed, tapping her foot, watching the big dumb moron load letter boxes. Supervising, right? Making sure the job gets done right. Making sure the big muscular moron doesn't screw up. Well, let me tell you something. I do my job. I don't screw up. And if you don't want to date me anymore, that's fine." His pecs and biceps flexed again when he lifted the next box. It was a little overdramatic; he didn't *have* to flex them so tightly, but he just wanted her to see. He knew the kind of guy she went for, and he was it. "Plenty of girls in this town who'd be happy to date a guy like me."

"Dan, Dan, what is this *date* business all of a sudden? We never *dated*. We *can't* date—it's against post-office policy for employees of the same office to be romantically involved."

He shook his head in more frustration. "Look, all I know is I walk in here and ask you what time we're getting together tonight, and you pull this stuff. We've been going out for almost a year. To me, that's *dating*."

"No, Dan, that's two friends fooling around. We were the same pay level and had the same time in grade. All that's changed now."

"Yeah, since your big promotion. All of a sudden Sarah the Party Animal becomes Sarah the Responsible Manager. Gimme a break. You're such a hypocrite, it's almost funny. Christ, I can't believe how much you've changed in the last two days."

"Oh, poor little Danny Boy getting a little insecure. Big tough Danny Boy doesn't like the idea that a woman two years younger than him is now his supervisor."

"That's got nothing to do with it. Some people are for real, some people aren't. You aren't."

"Poor little Danny Boy's masculinity is being shattered. The big strong muscleman can't hack being a subordinate to a hundred-and-twenty-pound woman—"

"Shut up. You're being stupid."

Dan loaded more boxes, in silence. Sarah just smiled. Yes, she had changed a lot in the last two days. She'd been blessed. The Messenger had shown her just how "for real" she truly was. He'd given her strength when before there'd only been weakness and vulnerability. *Thank you,* she thought dreamily.

She could feel him behind her—the Messenger—right up close next to her, his ethereal hands roving her body, stimulating her for what was to come. His desires merged with hers, a perfect state of sharing. She could never be *this* close to anyone else.

"Yeah, yeah, that's just fuckin' grand," Dan complained out of his silence. "You can't date me anymore since you got your big, high-falutin' promotion. Jesus Christ, Sarah, you spent the night with me last night. We made love . . ."

Sarah couldn't resist. "You call that *making love?* Don't make me laugh, Dan. I hate to tell you this, but I get more action from a cucumber."

Dan grit his teeth, bit away the anger. "What the hell are you talking about? You came like Halley's comet."

Again, Sarah couldn't resist. "Yeah, it took you seventy-five years to get me off." She stood back and watched, watched his anger boil up, watched his face redden. Dan was the kind of guy who had nothing beyond his macho image. His identity existed in his physical body, and in the cliché that women desired him because of it.

Sarah always hated that cliché; it offended her. But before her indoctrination by the Messenger, she'd been victimized by it herself, for her entire adult life. Now she had changed. Now she was different. Now she was strong.

Dan made her sick. His muscles, his tan, his good looks? It challenged her. He thought he was superior to women?

It was time for her to—

Do something about that, the Messenger whispered into her mind.

"I will," she said.

Dan looked up from another box. "You will, what?"

"Nothing, Danny Boy. Just keep flexing those muscles. Just keep thinking that you're God's gift to women. You gotta have something to keep that pea brain going."

He faced her, standing upright. "You really are trying me, aren't you?"

"What are you gonna do, Dan? Hmm?"

"I'm gonna do my job—I'm gonna do it well, like I always do—then I'm gonna go home and chalk this one up to experience. I don't know what your mind game is, Sarah, and I don't want to know. You're just a high-horse bitch who thinks she's better than everyone because she just got a pissant one-level raise. So why don't you go powder your fuckin' nose or something? I've got work to do."

The Messenger caressed her; Sarah sighed. Now her master was walking her forward toward Dan, outstretching her arms.

"What the *hell* is wrong with you?" Dan said, but he had no time to say anything more because Sarah hopped up on the table, wrapped her legs around him, and yanked his face to hers. She kissed him as if famished. Bewildered, he kept trying to pull away but her arms just kept getting tighter, and soon he was lost in her again. He just gave up and kissed her back.

Sarah and the Messenger *loved* to play with people.

"I don't get it," he said between kisses. "You're nuts. First you're giving me a ton of shit, and then . . . this . . ."

Sarah's hand slid up and down over his groin, feeling him through his post-office shorts. When she felt him aroused she said, "What did you just say? You've got work to do?"

"Yeah," he replied, sucking her neck.

"Well, why don't you do it, instead of slacking?"

Dan pulled back, glaring at her.

"Instead of coming on to me, you should be sorting the letter mail."

"Coming on to you!" he almost shouted. "You came on to *me!*"

"Come on, Dan. I ought to write you up for this. Sexually harassing your supervisor—"

Enraged, he tried to push away again, but her legs wouldn't unwrap. When he grabbed her knees and tried to pull her legs apart, they didn't budge. Dan was a very strong man, so this puzzled him.

"You're just trying to set me up, you bitch," he breathed. "You're crazy. *I'm* gonna file a complaint about *you.*"

Sarah chuckled. "Don't bother; it won't be taken seriously. I was going to fire you anyway—"

"For what?"

"Dan, you know what your job is. Everyday when you're done sorting the letter mail, you're supposed to maintain the central collation machine, and I know for a fact you haven't done that *all week.*"

"Bullshit!"

"We've gotten a lot of complaints this week about

letters getting torn by the machine. That means it's not calibrated right, doesn't it?"

Anger was bulging the veins in his forehead. "Yeah, that's what it means, but that hasn't happened. I clean the collator every day!"

Finally her legs unlocked, and she released him. She could feel the Messenger behind her, reveling in every moment of this. Turning the big muscular moron on and off, on and off.

When he pulled away, he stalked over to the collator, a long bulky machine nearly the size of a sedan. He flicked on the power switch—

"Come here!" he yelled at her. At the stack tray at the end of the machine, letters were filing out, untorn, perfectly stacked.

"There's nothing wrong with this!" he said. "You're just trying to make up crap about me, phony negligence charges. This machine's in perfect working order! I know it is, because *I* maintain it!"

The dreamy smile never left Sarah's face. She sauntered over and lifted the service hatch on the collator's midsection. When she did this, the racket from the machine trebled. Inside, gears hitched and revolved. Sharp-edged ratchets, with tines like rakes, snapped back and forth.

"Tell me those ratchets are aligned," she said.

Temper cresting, Dan looked inside, then glared back at her. "There's nothing wrong with them! What's your problem?"

"The lead ratchet. Look. It's out of line. Anyone can see that—at least anyone who knows their job."

Dan looked back in.

Sarah was not a strong woman, but the Messenger loaned her some great strength. One hand latched to the back of Dan's head by the hair, the other clamped his neck. Then she shoved him down.

The resistance he offered would have been considerable in any other circumstance. In *this* circumstance, however, Dan's strength against hers was akin to that of a palsied old man. He didn't make a sound when she shoved his face into the ratchet's teeth.

The machine made a sound, though, the sound of the ratchets suddenly working against Dan's face. Sarah's arms held him down as firmly as steel rods. His body shuddered. His massive legs kicked futily, and blood flew out of the machine like spaghetti sauce kicked out of a blender. When he fell still, Sarah pulled him out and let him turn over on the floor.

"Poor big muscular moron Danny Boy," she whispered down to her now-faceless subordinate. The rest of the DPS shift was gone now. She dragged him by the boots to the door in the corner.

The door to the basement.

Chapter Eighteen

(I)

Get over it, Jane told herself. *You're a big girl. Stop acting like a jilted teeny-bopper.* It was easier said than done, though. Since her visit to the police station, she tried to keep her mind blank. Tried but failed. It had been a bad day overall—the Martin Parkins problem, Dhevic showing up, and next, Steve with another woman. No, blanking her mind was a cop-out. Jane knew she had to face the reality, she just didn't want to right now.

At the end of her shift, she drove home in a gray daze. Paranoia kept forcing her eyes to the rearview mirror, afraid that she would see Martin's Ford Escort behind her, but then she would continuously remind herself that the police had towed the car away to the impound lot. Kevin and Jennifer knew something was wrong; they could tell the minute she got home, but Jane smiled it off with a fake smile that hurt.

A quiet dinner with the kids, then they were off to watch television. When the phone rang at about 7 P.M., Jane lurched, nearly dropping the plate she was putting in the dishwasher. Part of her hoped it was Steve . . . but why? *I know what he's all about now,* she told herself. *I don't want to talk to him, not ever again. Besides, he wouldn't have the audacity to call.* Had he seen her looking in through his office door? Had the desk sergeant told him she'd been in only to walk out a few seconds later? It didn't matter.

But the call mystified her. It wasn't Steve, it was the maintenance supervisor from the post office. More strangeness. He told her that Dan Winston, one of the DPS operators, hadn't clocked out, and his car was still in the lot.

What's going on? "He probably just forgot, and went out with a friend after work," she suggested. "But thanks for calling. I'll talk to him tomorrow."

Then the phone rang again.

"Hi."

It was Steve.

Don't yell, don't explode. There's no point in any of that. The advice made good sense, but then Jane snapped. She yelled. She exploded.

"You've got balls calling me! What kind of an idiot do you think I am! I've got better things to do than be jerked around by you! Don't ever call me again!"

Steve sounded alarmed. Obviously, he *hadn't* been told that she was at his office earlier. "Jane, what are you—"

"Don't give me that crap! I came to see you today at your office!"

"Yeah? Why didn't you come in?"

Jane's temples pounded. "Oh, I came in. Your door was opened a crack. I was about to knock, but then I looked in. Can you guess what I saw?"

"What?"

"Jesus! You kill me. I saw you making out with that woman! That blonde!"

"You saw me . . . Oh, you mean Ginny? She's my—"

"Your new girlfriend, obviously!"

"She's my sister—"

"Oh, yeah, your *sister!* Is it a common practice in your family to stick your tongue down your *sister's throat?*"

"Jane, you're really overreacting here, you're jumping to a very wrong conclusion."

Jane couldn't think through the wall of anger. She wasn't stupid, and she wasn't going to be lied to. *I'm not going to let this guy make a sucker out of me,* she thought, and then she said, "Don't *ever* call me again! *Ever!*"

Tears were welling in her eyes when she slammed the phone down. She hitched through a few sobs, dried her eyes with a paper towel, and tried to compose herself. *God, I hope the kids didn't hear all that,* she fretted, but when she peeked into the living room she saw them contentedly sitting on the couch, engrossed in the Discovery Channel. She slipped out through the other side of the kitchen and down the hall toward her bedroom. Emotions assaulted her; she felt naive and juvenile. She felt heartbroken. *What did I expect?* she scolded herself. *I only met the guy a week ago, and now I'm acting like I just got dumped out of a ten-year relationship. Grow up, Jane.* But rationalizations didn't help. It wasn't black or white—it was all gray. Did it matter she hadn't known him long? *I was falling in love with him,* she realized, tears returning. *And now it's over.* One way or another, this was going to hurt.

Numb, she stripped off her clothes and shuffled to the shower. She hoped the cool spray would relax her but instead it did the opposite. All the tension of the day dumped on her, and suddenly she felt bogged down, exhausted. She turned the water up harder, colder, until it stung like pinpricks but she just grew more groggy. Her eyes were drooping when she got out and dried off. Did she hear a tick? She covered up with a towel and looked out the bathroom window, *Stop being paranoid! Martin Parkins is* not *outside! He's out of the state by now . . .*

She slipped into her nightgown. Her heart was thudding; she couldn't get Steve out of her mind, couldn't erase the image of him kissing the blonde.

Later, after she put the kids to bed, she tried to watch some television but it was useless trying to concentrate. It was still early but she turned in anyway. *I'll feel better tomorrow,* she thought. In bed, she flicked off the light and darkness came down on her like a wall falling.

With all her fatigue, it should've been easy to fall asleep. Instead she tossed and turned, entwined herself in the sheets. Her mind wouldn't let go of the day. In half-dreams, she kept relaxing in the impression that passionate hands were on her—Steve's—rousing her, but then she'd flinch awake when she realized they were someone else's. Large hands, callused and clammy, enslimed. Each time she'd bring her own hands to her skin, revolted by the certainty that she'd find slime, there was nothing. The dream deepened later, though she couldn't be sure how much later. She could barely move, trapped under squirming weight. Were two men molesting her in the dream? One hand on her breast felt smaller than the hand on the other, and less slimy. Grainy darkness swirled around her; she was being mauled. When the form of a face moved close to hers, she reached to the side, to her nightstand, and grabbed the pen she kept there to jot down phone messages, and then she jammed it into her attacker's eye. There was no sound, no scream. The face hovered closer, and now she could see it in the moonlight: It was Martin Parkins. He was smiling at her, the pen sticking out of his eye. He simply got up and walked away, disappeared into the room's murk.

Then she awoke with a gasp, the room safe and empty, of course. A glance to the clock showed her that only a minute had lapsed.

God . . .

When she finally did fall fully asleep, her dreams were ugly and demented. The hands were on her again, and so was a mouth. No, not Steve's mouth by any means, and not Martin's. Jagged teeth clicked against hers. Jane squirmed, masturbating against her will. Atrocious, soup-thick breath gusted against her face, and the tongued slipping around inside of her mouth was very long, very thin . . .

And forked.

Messenger

Next morning, the sun shone through wisps of snow-white clouds. Around back of the Danelleton police station, cops were changing their shifts in the motor pool, exchanging blotter reports and gossip. Things seemed to be getting back to the normal if not boring pace everyone was used to.

Out front, a mail truck pulled up. The postal worker got out and entered the building, work boots snapping on the clean pavement. Several cops smiled and waved. One may have whistled.

Inside, the desk sergeant barely looked up from his paperwork. One eye spied the package that was placed down on the desk.

"Express Mail, great," he said. "Must be those DNA results we ordered from McCrone Labs in Chicago. The chief's been waiting on this. Do I need to sign for it?"

The postal worker smiled and gave a nod, then handed him the receipt board. The slip was signed, and a copy was torn off for the sergeant.

"Thanks," he said.

"You're quite welcome. Have a great day." And the worker left the building. The sergeant opened the package, then slowed. *No return address?* he noticed. The FROM square on the mailing label was blank. *On an Express Mail? That's weird.* Then he fully opened the package and found a sheet of white Xerox paper sitting on top of some packing tissue.

This ain't good, no, this ain't good at all, he thought. *I better get the chief . . .* On the sheet of paper some-

279

one had crudely sketched a bell with a star for a striker. The sergeant had seen others like it before, from the murders.

He picked up the phone to call Chief Higgins but paused. The box felt fairly heavy and was about the size of a VCR. He pulled out the packing tissue, looked inside, and—

(III)

Oh, my generous Messenger, thank you for this blessing, Sarah thought, walking briskly back to the mail truck. Yes, the Messenger was *full* of blessings to bestow. Sarah felt electrified to be of such importance. The LLV waited for her, no more mail in it—she'd delivered the Messenger's package, so she was done for now. She got into the truck, restarted it, and was casually pulling away when the entirety of the police station entrance exploded. Sarah scarcely flinched at the howitzer-loud sound, and barely glanced at her handiwork. Shattered glass rained down in bits; it sounded like rain on the LLV's metal roof. Flames billowed from the blown-out windows, and shouts and screams could be heard. The two-step ammonium-nitrate explosive device had been relatively easy to make; she got the directions off the Internet. Even the primer and contact trigger and incendiary material were a cinch.

Sarah smiled as she drove off. In the background, chaos ensued. Cops from the motor pool tried to enter the building but were staved off by flames. Several men, blackened and smoking, crawled out only to die on the front pavement.

It's beautiful, she heard the Messenger congratulate her.

Another cop ran out screaming, full flames wafting off his back and head.

Yes. Beautiful.

Sarah sighed, and rejoiced in the Messenger's caress as she drove away.

Chapter Nineteen

(I)

The television screen throbbed with action: the Danelleton police station almost completely burning down. Fire trucks encircled the building's front, their hoses shooting plumes of water into the conflagration. Ambulances screeched off, sirens wailing, only to be replaced by more.

The blond newscaster looked absolutely shell-shocked, her hand around the microphone shaking.

"—in yet another inexplicable tragic crime said to have been committed by a Danelleton postal employee. Witnesses claim that Danelleton native Sarah Willoughby delivered a mail bomb to police headquarters at approximately nine o'clock this morning."

The screen cut to a bright portrait photo of Sarah: the pretty girl-next-door face, shining blond hair, beaming white smile. The greatest anomaly was its obviousness: This was anything but the face of a bomber and murderer.

The newscaster spoke over the picture. *"Three Danelleton officers were killed, and four injured in the blast. Ms. Willoughby, an employee in good standing, was recently promoted by branch station manager Jane Ryan."*

The scene cut again, to a sunny suburban street lined with nice houses on well-kept lots. Several police cars were parked, doors open and lights turning, askew on the street. Also parked there was a standard white mail truck. The camera roved from the vehicles up to the nearest house, where several uniformed police, along with Chief Steve Higgins, were marching away from the front door, hauling a delirious and handcuffed Sarah Willoughby. She squirmed and kicked, the police holding her up so that her feet wouldn't touch the ground. The camera zoomed chillingly to Sarah's twisted face; she was screaming and grinning at the same time. She looked insane. The whites of her eyes had hemorrhaged red. The next cut showed the police propping Sarah up while an EMT injected her with a sedative, after which she was strapped down on a gurney and driven away in an ambulance.

"Ms. Willoughby was apprehended shortly thereafter by police officers under the charge of Chief Steve Higgins. She was later checked into the psychiatric wing of the Pinellas County Detention Center, for evaluation and treatment."

"This is just beyond belief," someone said.

Jane and several employees sat stunned around the

TV in her office. It was like watching news footage of a bombing in the Middle East but then the worse reality set in. Every detail was familiar. This was a place they'd all seen before, and these were *people* they'd seen before. This was not the Middle East. It was their hometown.

"It's the craziest thing I've ever seen in my life," someone else muttered. "I can't believe what I'm seeing with my own eyes. Christ, I was *at* that police station a few days ago to pay a parking fine. Look at the place now . . ."

On the TV, the police station was a blown-out blackened hulk. The newscaster continued her grim report. *"—and county fire investigators suspect the use of an incendiary bomb, a device specifically designed to burn fast and do as much fire-damage as possible before firefighters can arrive."*

Closer shots of the blackened building.

"And we're supposed to believe that Sarah—little tiny bubbly *Sarah*—did *that?* Killed all those people and did all that damage?"

"She was so nice," someone else said. "But in that footage? She looked demented, totally out of her mind—"

Yeah, Jane thought. *Out of her mind. A satanic cult member.* Her face was drawn and pale. It was everyone's consensus. This could not be happening here . . . but it was. "It's got to be a mistake," she muttered lamely.

"It's no mistake."

The additional voice in the room startled them. Jane turned, saw Steve standing grim-faced in the doorway.

Everyone got back to their duties when Jane asked them to, leaving her and Steve alone. But Jane couldn't have felt more uncomfortable either way. *Don't even mention the bit with the blonde,* she told herself. *You're not involved with him anymore, you're not even friends. This is strictly professional, so act the part.* "I think I should go see her—Sarah, I mean. I need to talk to her."

Steve had helped himself to some coffee and sat down. "That's not advisable, Jane. She's delirious. She's stark-raving mad."

"I don't care. I've got to see her, find out why she did this. I've known her for years. She'll sure as hell talk to me before she'll talk to some psych-ward goon, and she's not going to talk to the police. I need you to get me a visitor's pass."

"No way. Jane, she's in the *psych ward* of the county prison. That place is a freak show."

Jane wasn't sure what was compelling her. Perhaps it was just the need to feel like she was doing something rather than sitting around and watching it all happen. *Maybe if I'd been closer to Marlene and Carlton, and kept a closer eye on Martin—maybe none of this would've happened.* She looked right at Steve and in her most stolid voice said, "If I ever meant anything to you, you'll do this for me."

"Jane, you *do* mean something to me. You mean a lot."

"Yeah, I saw how much yesterday, when you were making out with your *sister.*"

Steve shook his head. "You're being paranoid, Jane. I wasn't making out, for God's sake. It was a hug and a peck on the cheek. And she *is* my sister. I haven't seen her in a year; she lives with her husband and two boys in Bellingham, Washington. Why is that so hard to believe?"

Jane supposed it *wasn't* that hard to believe, really. Nevertheless, she didn't.

"Would you please just get me into the detention center to talk to Sarah? You should want me to anyway. You'll want information, right? I know her better than anyone there or in your department. I'd be to your advantage too."

"I can't do it," he insisted. "It's too dangerous. And let's not talk about that now, let's talk about our relationship—"

"Steve, there is no relationship—"

"Let's at least talk about it . . ." He reached across the desk, touched her hand, which she instantly pulled away.

"There's nothing to talk about," she said again.

Steve sighed in frustration. "All right, look, I'll get you a cred pass so you can see Sarah. I'll pick you up tonight and take you there myself. And on the way, we'll talk about our relationship."

Jane felt tugged by opposing horses, about to be pulled apart. "Steve, even if there was a relationship between the two of us, we've both got a lot more to worry about, don't we? Good Lord, people are getting killed, and several of my employees are responsible. Not to mention one of my DPS handlers didn't show up for work today, and I've *still* got no idea what happened to Martin."

Steve was suddenly reminded of something. "Oh,

jeez. With the explosion at the station and all, I completely forgot."

"Forgot what?"

"We found Martin Parkins, Jane. We found his body this morning in the woods behind Bowen Field."

"His *body?* You mean he's—"

"He's dead, murdered. Someone jammed a pen in his eye and drove it straight through to his brain."

Pen, Jane thought. *In the eye . . .*

"That's horrible," she said stonily.

"All too often, horrible things happen to horrible people," Steve said. "What goes around comes around. It may have been a prostitute who did it. At his apartment we found Polaroids of a lot of local prostitutes. We took the pictures into the county sheriff's department and they told us that a few of the girls have been reported missing. Could be that he was killing some of these girls, and it could be that—"

Jane made the morbid conclusion on her own. "That last night he picked one up, tried something violent, but she defended herself."

"Exactly. It's impossible to say for sure but it's starting to look like that."

Jane felt bad for Martin's tragedy; it didn't matter that she'd never liked him. But in the back of her mind, the coincidence heckled her. *That weird dream I had last night . . .* She'd dreamed that Martin had been molesting her and—*and I stuck a pen in his eye . . .*

"So what about Sarah Willoughby?" Steve asked.

The comment snapped her train of thought. "Well, I just asked if you could get me in to see her, and you said you would."

"I'll get you in." He put his hand on her shoulder. "I'll be back around seven when I'm off duty, to pick you up."

Steve drove in his unmarked police car, the scanner turned way down. Jane rode next to him, in silence. She didn't know about this at all, yet it was her own doing. *Don't complain, Jane. You're the one who asked.* She simply felt compelled to see Sarah, to talk to her. Maybe she could get some answers that no one else was getting: about her state of mind, about her connection to Marlene, Carlton, and Martin—who were all dead now—and about the cult or whatever it was.

She had to take Steve into consideration, too, which only made the situation more stressful. *He had an awful day, too,* she reminded herself. *His station house was bombed and he lost several men.*

"Looks like all we've got right now," he said ironically, "is each other."

In a sense, he was right. One tragic puzzle after another was falling on them both. And neither of them knew what was going on. Only guesses, only speculations that weren't doing either of them any good.

"The woman you saw me with is my sister; her name's Ginny," Steve said, breaking into her concerns. "Believe me. I'll prove it."

Jane felt bushwhacked. "How?"

"She's in town for another week. I'll take you to meet her. We'll go out to dinner, the three of us. I told her all about you—she wants to meet you anyway."

She didn't know what to say. Could it be true? *It has to be. Something like that would be too easy to verify.*

She took his hand. "I'd like that. I'm sorry I overreacted. I guess the past week—"

"The past week has been too much for both of us. We never saw it coming; how could we? Things will be fine."

Suddenly Jane felt content and wonderful. She'd simply overreacted to a landslide of stresses and hadn't managed herself well once she'd become involved with him. His hand over hers tightened.

Oh, Jesus . . . Then she remembered the reason she'd come to see him at his office in the first place. "I forgot to tell you. That man . . . He came to see me yesterday."

"What man?"

"Alexander Dhevic."

His expression turned stern. "Christ, Jane! I told you that guy was a flake! He's dangerous! You should've told me. If that guy ever comes to your office again, you call me right away. The guy's a nut. He's either playing the murders up for his next book or documentary, or he's part of it himself."

"It's just what he said, and maybe even the way he said it—"

"He's an actor, Jane. He's a con man. Don't listen to him, don't let him get to you—"

"He said the murders were demonic too. He had a picture of the bell; it was an engraving from a very old book—"

"And let me guess, he told you it was the symbol for some demon."

"Yes. Aldezhor, the Messenger of hell. I mean, come on, Steve, the devil's equivalent of the Archangel

Gabriel. A demon *messenger,* working through *post-office* employees? What are post-office employees?"

"Messengers, I know. He laid the same bunch of jive on us twenty years ago. It's a crock of shit. He's trying to make himself famous as some renowned expert on the occult. Any time there's a series of bizarre murders in the country, he acts like he knows all about it so he can get big fees on these tabloid shows."

Jane couldn't believe what she said next. "I think he's psychic or something—"

"He's a shaman! He's a fake! Guys like Dhevic know how to get under people's skin—it's their profession. Don't fall for his crap!"

She knew he was right, but the details of Dhevic's visit kept pecking at her. She recalled what he'd said, just before he left: *He will manipulate you through your fears, your weaknesses, and your dreams.* "He said something about dreams, that this demon—er, actually a fallen angel—exploits people through their dreams."

"So does Freddy Krueger, but I don't believe in him either—"

"No, no, you don't understand. At my office, you told me that Martin was killed by someone stabbing him in the eye with a pen. Well, last night . . ."

Steve was getting testy. "Last night, what?"

"Last night I dreamed that Martin was trying to rape me, but . . . I defended myself by . . . sticking a pen in his eye."

"It's a coincidence, Jane! Forget about all this!"

She squeezed her memory harder, to remember

more of the nightmare. There'd been two men with her, hadn't there? Martin.

And someone else.

Someone else with features so hideous it made her sick to think of them. And Dehvic had told her that Aldezhor was hideous to look at.

"Then another thing," she went on. "He knew about Matt, my husband. He mentioned him—it was almost like he showed me a vision—"

"Come on! Dhevic's *playing* you!"

"How could he know about my husband?"

"Research, Jane. That's what these guys do to make their living. They make people believe that they know things they couldn't possibly know. Then you'll think he's clairvoyant or psychic or whatever."

"Okay, but why? Why would this man, a perfect stranger to me, and someone I could do nothing for, go to all that trouble?"

Steve paused. "Well . . . I don't know. Did he ask you for anything? Money? Information about the murders? Did he ask to interview you for a book or show?"

"No, nothing like that," she said. "But he did ask me for access to the post office."

Steve gave her a puzzled look. "What the hell for?"

"I'm not sure. He said he wanted to look for something, something about the bell."

Steve winced at the wheel. "Look, I dealt with his guy Dhevic twenty years ago. He was a flake then, and he's a flake now. Just steer clear of him. Don't listen to him. Next time you see him, call me immediately."

Before she could say more, Steve was slowing down

for a turn. Had an hour passed since they'd been driving? The sun was going down.

"Here we are," he said. "Inside, the cons call this place the Concrete Ramada."

They were driving down a service road lined with high fences that were fronted and topped by heaping coils of razor wire. In the security lights, the wire was pretty; it shimmered like Christmas tinsel. Beyond, she could see the multistoried detention center, a hulk of beige cement and slitlike windows. Steve showed his badge at a security gate, then pulled in. When he parked in the visitor's lot, he squeezed her hand and said, "Let's go."

Inside, Steve processed them both, checked in his gun, and got floor passes for them both. An elevator took them to the top floor, but as they were going up each preceding level, Jane could hear a roar like a football game but then she realized it was merely the vocal chaos of the general population. It was an ugly sound. She was relieved by the silence when the door slid open on the top floor. A stark sign told them: CELL-BLOCK 6D—PSYCH EVAL & DETENTION.

Eventually a stocky detention officer took them down a clean, antiseptic-scented hallway. White metal doors lined the hall, and when he stopped at one, a buzzer blared and someone snapped inside the door.

"Just so you know, this one's probably never even going to be arraigned," the officer told them.

"Why?" Steve asked.

"She psychotic."

"CDS induced?"

"Not like I've ever seen. She's delirious, hallucinatory, and doing a lot of word salad, but her blood screen was negative for drugs. She's also very violent, so be careful. We got her on a hundred mg's of Loxapine, enough to mellow out Attila the Hun, and she's *still* trying to bite her way out of the straitjacket."

"I'll be careful," Jane said.

"I'm going in with you," Steve told her.

"No. If she's in a straitjacket, she can't hurt me. She knows me, she'll talk to me. Just let me do this on my own. If there's a problem—"

"Hit the buzzer on the wall," the detention officer said. "Stay near the buzzer."

Jane walked into the cell. It was just like the movies: shiny white padding lined the walls and floor. Sunlight came down from a single high window.

The door slunked shut behind her.

The sight of Sarah as a violent psychiatric patient was just like the movies too. She sat huddled in one corner, white utility pants, barefoot. Her once-pretty blond hair looked a wreck, and her arms were wrapped around herself in a canvas straitjacket, whose shoulders she was chewing on. When Jane walked in, Sarah snapped her gaze up and grinned. She was cross-eyed.

"Sarah, for God's sake, what happened?" Jane said right out.

"Not for *God's* sake."

"Then for whose?"

"The Messenger's sake."

The Messenger, Jane thought. "You mean Aldezhor?"

Sarah's eyes raged. "Don't *ever* say his name! Never! His name is a holy thing! We are not worthy to speak it! It's a secret that must never pass our lips!"

"I'm sorry, Sarah. I didn't know that."

"If you speak his name again, I'll tear my way out of this thing and suck your brains out of your ears!"

"I won't speak it again, I promise." Jane's heart stepped up at each outburst; her adrenaline surged. "But I'd like to ask you something, Sarah. You set off a bomb at the police station today. You killed several people. Why?"

"Fodder," Sarah replied. "Meat for the grist of my lord's mill. But I've done my part. We all have."

"You've done your part for *what?*"

"For him. For the Messenger, and the sending of his wondrous message. He walks the earth through us. We are *his* messengers."

Jane stared at the macabre figure that was once her employee and friend.

"He's back," Sarah said. "We're bringing him back," and then her face turned maroon as she struggled in the straitjacket. There was a creaking sound along with several ugly *cracks!* and that's when Jane realized that Sarah was breaking her own bones . . .

"Stop it!" Jane yelled.

Sarah was manipulating her fractured arms now, shucking herself out of the jacket. She didn't react at all to the imponderable pain—all she did was grin, never taking her eyes off of Jane.

Fear paralyzed Jane. Her brain screamed at her to lunge for the alarm but she couldn't. Sarah's insane glare held her in a dizzy rigor. *When she gets out of that, she's going to kill you,* Jane realized, but still she couldn't move. Then Sarah rose to her feet, shrugged out of the straitjacket. She stood bare-chested, her breasts heaving, laved in sweat and blotched by scuff-marks. Her arms flopped at her sides as if multijointed now, shards of bones sticking out of the skin, blood running. Her hand flexed, then she squeezed her eyes shut and raised an arm, tentaclelike, and—

"Stop it!" Jane shouted.

With thumb and index finger, Sarah broke off one of her front teeth and then—

"Stop!"

—used the jagged edge to cut herself. On the flat of her abdomen, she calmly etched the shape of a bell and a star-shaped striker.

"Behold the Messenger, Jane," croaked the voice that was anyone's but hers. "The arrival of the Messenger is at hand . . ."

Next, Sarah slowly inserted an index finger into her left eye socket, pushing, pushing, until the thin bowl-shaped bone snapped. The finger burrowed into the brain.

Sarah grinned one last time, then toppled over dead.

Chapter Twenty

(I)

Steve tucked her into bed, only the bedside lamp on. He held Jane's hand as he sat beside her, the long day weighing on them both.

Jane shook slightly beneath the sheets. She was tired of seeing death.

"You look really pale, Jane. Should I call Dr. Mitchell?"

"No," she said. "I'll be all right. This is just too much. I can't handle seeing my employees kill themselves."

"I know." He looked at her more deeply. "I probably should call the doctor. You might be in shock or something."

"No." She gripped his hand tighter. "I want you to stay but, but—"

"But what? Jane, I *want* to stay."

"I don't think that's a good idea."

He put his chin in his hand. "Jane, I swear to God, the woman you saw me with yesterday is my sister. You'll meet her soon, I told you."

Jane felt that she believed it now, but there was still too much to reckon. "I'm so confused, Steve. I—"

"I love you, Jane."

The words stalled her, like a small car colliding with a large brick wall. *I love you too,* she thought, but she just couldn't say it now.

"Let's talk soon, okay?" he asked. "I want this to work—I want it more than anything. So many awful things have been happening lately, we can't focus. But once this is all over . . ."

"Yes," she said. "I want things to work too. And they will."

He seemed relieved, and by the look in his eyes, Jane knew he was sincere.

"I'll look in on the kids, make sure they're tucked in, then I'll take off. I'll call you tomorrow. And if you need anything, call me on my cell or beep me, no matter what time."

Jane nodded, squeezed his hand a final time, then let go. He kissed her on the cheek and left.

Yes, Jane thought after he left. *I love you . . .*

(II)

Sergeant Stanton looked ghoulish in the dashboard lights. When he lit a cigarette, the flickering orange flame gave him a corpselike hue.

Steve sipped a cold cup of coffee next to him. "That's damn good work. How'd you get a line on him?"

"Credit card, or I should say a check card. We extracted his bank records—Jesus, Chief, the guy almost never has anything in his checking account—but he used it a week ago—with thirty-five bucks in his account—to get gas at a Citgo station on St. Pete Beach. Stands to reason that if he's on the road, he's staying in a motel, but there aren't any receipts from the card. Either that, or he's got cash on him."

"Or he's sleeping in his vehicle," Steve suggested.

"Guess so. But at least we know we can track him when he uses the card. That's the good news. The bad news is the county magistrate won't give us a warrant to haul him in for questioning. No evidence for probable cause."

"Goddamn Constitution." Steve gazed absently out into the night. *You're out there somewhere, Dhevic. I'll find you* . . .

The radio crackled. Steve answered it and was instructed by the dispatcher to call an extension on his cell phone.

"Who you calling?" Stanton asked.

"State police."

"Why?"

"I don't know, but it can't be good . . ."

(III)

The voice fluttered around her head, like great black birds circling.

"Behold the Messenger . . ."

Dhevic's voice?

Now Sarah's: "The arrival of the Messenger is at hand . . ."

Jane opened her eyes but saw nothing, just a land-scape of ink black. She tried to get up from whatever she lay—it felt like a trench of carved stone—but she couldn't. She couldn't move at all.

"Hail, Aldezhor . . ."

A dream, Jane thought desperately. She felt hosed down in warm water but then realized it was her own sweat. *It's just a dream. Wake up . . .*

The darker voice returned, "He will manipulate you through your fears, your weaknesses—"

Jane stared blindly into black.

"—and your dreams."

A sound then, like a guillotine falling, and suddenly she could see. A vista of fire and rock snapped before her eyes.

Chaos.

The heat took her breath away. She lay, indeed, in a stone pit, coffin-shaped. When she finally sat up, more intense heat wafted against her face. She looked down at her nightgown-clad body and saw that she was ema-ciated from dehydration and malnourishment, arms and legs like sticks. Her once-full breasts hung as thin flaps of skin beneath her drenched gown, her stomach sucked in, her ribs showing. She had almost no strength yet she willed herself to stand up and look out at the impossible hellscape.

Black smoke rose in noxious billows, some stream-ing from abyssal crevices, some pouring off of distant piles of bodies. Fire crackled eternally, and in the air, before a luminous scarlet sky, great beaked things flew leisurely in and out of dirt-colored clouds. Wind rose and fell, deafening her, but was it really wind or just an endless gust of screaming?

Figures ambled up a stone rise. Tall, gaunt, with lopsided bald heads and arms and legs as long as a normal man's height. Their bodies were the color of curdled milk, and they were coming for her.

Eventually the realization smacked home . . .

I'm in hell . . .

Jane began to run. She slipped into a crevice and found herself running through a torch-lit labyrinth of black rock. Around each corner, a new horror appeared, heralded by screams. Jane stopped in her tracks at the appearance of two small figures . . .

Jennifer and Kevin stood before her, but . . .

My God . . .

Her children, too, were emaciated, their faces little more than pallid skin stretched over their skulls, hollow-eyed. They grinned at her, showing nail-like fangs. Tiny horns sprouted from their heads.

"Hi, Mom!" Jennifer said. "What's for lunch?"

"Here's what I'm eating," Kevin announced, and off his shoulder he plucked his rotten but still-alive horned toad. He stuffed it into his mouth and began to munch, rot showing behind his grin.

Jane ran.

But not for long. Along the next wall of the labyrinth, Carlton was carving the skin off of a squirming girl's chest and abdomen. The girl had been crudely crucified, her hands nailed to the rock by iron pitons.

"Hi, Jane," Carlton said over his shoulder. He yanked

a sheet of skin off the girl as though he were tearing down wallpaper.

Jane screamed when she turned.

Horned versions of Marlene Troy and her dead husband, Matt, welcomed her with open arms. They were living corpses, naked, grinning at her.

Matt rushed to her, embraced her. His stench nearly knocked Jane unconscious.

"Sweetheart," he whispered in glee. Jane tried to squirm away but couldn't. She could feel his dead erection rise. "You're not really fucking that cop, are you?"

Jane screamed.

His embraced tightened, then a bony hand came to her throat. Suddenly his grin switched to a drooling glare of hatred. "Do you give him head like you used to give me? Hmm? I'll bet you do, you little tramp. Well let me show you something," and then his other hand rose. He was holding Steve's severed head.

"How's *this* for some good head?"

Jane broke away, her screams pinwheeling behind her. Next came a rock cove in which a woman was being raped by the thin pale things she'd seen earlier. The things were mangling the woman, but instead of screams of terror the woman shrieked in joy. That's when Jane noticed who it was . . .

Sarah's horns reared when she craned her neck to look up at Jane. Her suitors were taking turns with her; demonic sperm shone on her skin. The wounds she'd carved on her chest in the psychiatric cell seemed to be glowing now: the bell and star-shaped striker.

"Remember what I told you?" Sarah slurred.

"This is a dream! This is just a dream!" Jane yelled.

"That's right, Jane, a dream of what awaits you. The Messenger likes you, he admires you. He's keeping an eye on you, Jane."

"And so am I," another voice guttered.

Martin Parkins staggered forward from the other direction, his postal uniform hanging in rotten shreds. The pen remained stuck in his eye, and he torqued it upward, unseating the eyeball from the socket. "Yeah, bitch, I'm keeping an eye on you too," he said. He held the eyeball up to look at her.

It's just a dream, just a dream! Jane kept screaming.

"Oh, God, that feels so good," Sarah cooed. Jane made the mistake of looking down, to see one of the pallid figures kneeling intently. It was drawing its foot-long index finger in and out of Sarah's brain, through the hole she'd made through her eye socket in the psych cell.

"Run! Run!" another voice was suddenly bellowing at her. A large figure, dressed in black this time. The bearded face loomed—Dhevic—with the largest horns of all jutting from his forehead. He was pointing toward another crevice—a crevice that was slowly grinding closed, like a great stone door. Dhevic shoved her away, and bellowed "Run! Hurry! Go and see it!"

Jane was nearly mindless now. Her feet stomped through steaming hot muck to the crevice. One of the pallid creatures was right behind her, pawing at her with its monstrous hand, when Jane sucked in her gut and squeezed through the crevice. She made it all the way through only to see that the follower had not. The crevice ground closed on the thing, which had only squeezed through to the waist. Bones crunched, and from its doglike mouth came a hail of gelatinous vomit.

Jane staggered backward, leaned against a high flat rock. *Just a dream, just a dream* . . . but then she inched her face to the rock's edge and peered out.

More scalding hot air blasted her face; it singed her eyebrows off, reddened her cheeks. She knew she must pull away from the pain but for whatever reason she was too intent . . .

. . . on seeing what was out there.

She was looking down into a valley, and in the valley sat a church. The church was black, and vast stained-glass windows were set into its outer walls. Light throbbed from within, brightening the stained-glass scenes that depicted all manner of demonic orgy and mutilation. Jane's eyes dragged up the face of the church, to its looming black steeple, and the inverted cross erected there.

Just a dream, just a dream, she kept thinking, suffocating in the blast of heat. Behind her, the crevice was reopening. Jane could see greedy waxlike faces in the gap—but she didn't care. She'd either wake up or she'd die.

Her heart was missing beats. Her eyes remained wide on the church steeple. Just beneath the cross was a bell-tower.

The bell began to ring.

Chapter Twenty-one

(I)

"I don't know why I'm here," Jane said in the open door.

"I do," Dhevic said. "Please come in."

"I—" She stepped back, hesitant. It was broad daylight, yes, the sun on her back, normal traffic coursing back and forth on the main road behind her. It was a normal day, so what was she afraid of?

"I apologize," Dhevic said in his crisp accent. "What I told you earlier, about my . . ."

"Benefactors," Jane finished.

"They sometimes forget about me. The least expensive motels in the worst parts of town are generally a necessity. It's clean, though. I've sprayed it for bugs and caught all the rodents with traps."

How delightful, Jane thought, and walked in. She repocketed the slip of paper he'd given her with the motel address.

Several bags of groceries sat on the small desk; Dhevic had obviously just returned from shopping. Through the front window, Jane could see a new silver Ford SUV parked there.

"I knew you'd come," he said.

"Oh, sure. I forgot, you're psychic. You're an . . . augur."

Dhevic only smiled in response. "I understand your sarcasm, but still . . . you're here, aren't you?"

"Yes. There were more murders yesterday. Another one of my employees—"

"Another *messenger*," Dhevic corrected. "Yes, I know about that."

"How much do you know?"

Dhevic made two cups of instant coffee from a portable burner he'd plugged into the wall. There were stains on the wall that appeared to be handprints, and a hole, too. Jane didn't want to think that it might be a bullet hole.

"Did you dream last night?" he asked, and handed her a cup.

"Yeah, I dreamed. Of a black church, with a bell tower. And the bell was ringing."

"The *Cymbellum Eosphorus*? Do you believe in it now?"

"The dream was just stress related, Professor Dhevic," Jane snapped. "I had the dream based on the power of suggestion, because of what you told me in my office. But *you* believe in it, right? You said so the other day."

Dhevic didn't respond, at least not vocally. Jane tried to keep focused on his face. "The other day, you said something about this demon—"

"Not a demon, a fallen angel," Dhevic corrected. "Aldezhor, Lucifer's messenger; Hell's equivalent of the Archangel Gabriel—"

"Fine. So then there's this cult," she clarified, "and the members of this cult believe in Aldezhor?"

"They are his heralds. They proclaim his prophesy. They are his messengers."

Jane frowned. "Is that a yes?"

"Yes. There is . . . a cult."

"They believe this myth, and they act on it, as though it were true?"

Dhevic looked at her, but said nothing.

"They kill because they believe they're—what?—paying homage to Aldezhor? Making sacrifices for him?"

Dhevic nodded. "It's more complicated than that, but, yes. You can think of it that way."

"Are drugs involved?"

"No drugs."

"Hypnosis? Brainwashing?"

"No. Only the power of faith played against weakness and innocence. Almost anyone can become an acolyte of Aldezhor."

"Martin Parkins is an exception, I suppose, but my other employees—Carlton Spence, Marlene Troy, and Sarah Willoughby—were all level-headed, conscientious employees and quality people in general. None of them was the type to join a cult. How did they get mixed up in it? How did they get recruited?"

"No recruitment," Dhevic explained. "They were seduced. They were *taken*. You can think of it as something akin to demonic possession—"

"Oh, come on."

"They were machinated."

The strange word stretched a pause across the room. "What's that mean?" Jane asked, exasperated.

"Aldezhor gets people to do his bidding by tricking them, by praying on their fears and obsessions, making them believe they're true. He amalgamates lies with truth, so that he is believed. Keep in mind, his ultimate purpose. Aldezhor is the mouthpiece of Satan, the greatest liar in history. All of his messages, therefore, are lies."

"What's that got to do with—"

"Machination—it's an occult term, related, as I've said, to possession. Aldezhor is an incubus; when he becomes discarnated—when he machinates—his sexual persona emanates. He possesses his victims through a process called discarnate machination. He walks behind the possessant almost as though the possessed is a life-sized marionette. He controls everything, a puppeteer, sees everything, feels everything. You can see him in smoke, rain, and in mirrors. Sometimes, when the auras are correct, you can see him standing right behind the possessed."

Auras. Great. "And you believe this?" she asked. "Tell me. The other day you went into a trance, or something like that. And you said you believed it."

Dhevic's voice seemed to resonate. "It wasn't a trance. It was the side-effect of a vision. I have visions. It's my heritage; it's been passed down to me from my ancestors over centuries."

The air stilled. Jane tried to contemplate a way to deal with it. *Visions? Machination?* She didn't know of such things. But was it possible for her to believe in them?

She thought harder. She remembered what she'd seen in Dhevic's eyes two days ago. And she remembered what she'd seen last night at the psychiatric wing . . .

"Say it *is* true," she began. "What do you want? Why did you come here? The police think the only reason you're here is to exploit the situation for these tabloid shows."

"Then the police are wrong, and that's regrettable."

"So answer the question. Why are you here?"

"To recover the icon," Dhevic said. "The icon is the nimbus of Aldezhor's power to become incarnate. The recent sacrificial murders have all been perpetrated by your employees—*postal* employees, through the force of the icon—"

"The icon?"

Dhevic opened his leather folder and removed the polycarbonate sheet he'd shown her in her office. "You know what the icon is," he said.

"The—" She tried to remember the pronunciation of the word. "Campanulation? The bell?"

"No." He pointed down. "The striker."

Jane looked at the engraving again. At first she was bothered that the church in the engraving was identical to the church in her dream but, again, the power of suggestion. She'd seen the engraving in her office already, and her subconscious mind remembered that and inserted it into the dream. *The striker,* she thought. She squinted. The ball of the striker was star-shaped. *It stands for the Morning Star—Lucifer.* "So this striker, this icon—"

"Is what's called a power relic," Dhevic finished. "Think of it this way: the striker is the object of your cult's worship, like a crucifix in a Catholic church."

Jane tried to sort her thoughts. "And you're here because . . ."

"I'm here for the icon. I'm here to retrieve it, to confiscate it—and return it to a secure location."

More silence.

"I don't believe for a minute that a *striker* from a bell in hell—"

"The *Cymbellum Eosphorus,*" Dhevic intoned.

"—is in my town, causing people to become possessed."

The man nodded. "I understand. I'm not asking you to believe it. Just help me retrieve it. I believe it's hidden somewhere in the west branch post office."

She thought further. *Okay. There's some hokey piece of iron that people believe is part of this bell. I can deal with that. Dhevic thinks it's in my branch. If it is, the logical thing to do is let him get it, and maybe all of this will end.*

"You want me to let you into my post office to look for this thing, is that it?"

"Yes," Dhevic said.

"Well, I don't know if I can do that," she told him. "People will ask questions, and the police already want to bring you in for questioning. I'm probably breaking some law by not telling them that I know where you're staying."

"I've committed no crimes."

Jane peered at him. Everything was opposites. Whenever she looked at him she couldn't believe he was anything but benevolent, if a bit bizarre.

"Tell *me* how to find the icon. If I find it, I'll bring it to you."

"It's a very dangerous object. It's very powerful—"

"It's only powerful if you believe in it. I don't believe in it. I just want this to stop. I'll go along with whatever charade I have to to end it."

"Is this a charade?" he asked in a softer voice. "Look at me. I want to show you something."

Jane grit her teeth. "No."

"You'll believe . . . if you look at me."

"No! You're hypnotizing me—"

"Very well." The man was smiling gently. "The icon will be hidden in some dark place, below ground, a basement, a crawlspace or a conduit—"

"Of course. How creepy," she mocked.

"Because its owner *exists* in dark, low places."

"Fine." She thought about it and thought about it. *Maybe I should let him go with me, find this thing, and be done with it.* She kept feeling like she could trust him, without knowing why. "I have to go to the bathroom," she said, distracted.

"Right over there," he told her and pointed.

She got up hesitantly and looked around at the dilapidated accommodation. "I mean—there aren't, like, roaches and rats in there, are there?"

Another smile. "No. I evicted them all personally. I

told them that if they expected to stay, they'd have to split the cost of the room with me."

Jane spared a laugh and went in. Actually, Dhevic had cleaned the bathroom quite well—that or the housekeeping staff, but Jane doubted that this motel even *had* a housekeeping staff. She sighed and looked at herself in the mirror over the sink. Her eyes had dark circles; she was tired, worn out. *All the more reason to get this over with,* she thought.

She stiffened at a skittering sound. *Roach, probably.* The things made her hair stand on end. *Forget about going to the bathroom and just leave,* she suggested, but a morbid curiosity seized her.

The skittering came from the bathtub behind her. She pulled back the shower curtain and, indeed, saw a large palmetto bug roving around near the tub mat.

But that's not why Jane nearly had a heart attack.

Lying on top of that rubber tub mat was a slim naked woman with her throat cut. Jane's feet felt nailed to the floor. The woman was young, with long flowing mocha hair, her mouth agape in death.

At the end of the tub sat a pile of clothes. Jane recognized the colors at once: the light-blue shirt and the slate-blue shorts. A post-office uniform. And that's when she knew who she was looking at; it was Doreen Fletcher, one of her newest employees.

Carved on Doreen's chest was the likeness of a bell with a star-shaped striker.

Jane sucked in her scream. She popped open the narrow bathroom window, crawled out, and ran.

There was no time to think. Her biggest fear was that her heart might begin to fibrillate from the shock of

what she'd seen. *The car, the car,* she thought mani-
cally. What if Dhevic was waiting for her? Fortunately,
she'd parked toward the end of the motel, in front of
the office. When she peered around the corner, her car
remained, and there was no sign of Dhevic.

She took a chance, jumped in, drove away with her
foot to the floor.

Police, police, police, came the next staccato bursts
of thought. *Steve, I've got to find Steve.* She could pull
over right now and call him but she didn't want to
stop. It would only take a few moments before Dhevic
realized that she was gone—and what she'd seen—
and he would be after her. She pulled off the main
road onto a side street, cutting across town. There was
a county sheriff's station just up the road. *I'll be safe
there. I can call him from there—*

But the rest of her thoughts severed.

Hands were on her from behind.

Rough hands first cupped her breasts, then slid up to
her throat. Now she truly believed her heart would stop.

Dhevic's right behind me, in the back seat . . .

But as the hands tightened, her terrified eyes shot to
the rearview mirror, and that's where she saw the face.

Not Dhevic's face at all.

It was the face of Aldezhor . . .

Suddenly ghosts of the fallen angel's hands were
covering her own on the wheel. She heard a chuckle
and a whisper, felt the faintest kiss at the side her neck,
then a foul hot tongue licked her skin.

She heard words not in her ears but in her head.

*You will not foil me. And you will not challenge my
servants.*

Messenger

The hands were forcing Jane's to steer to the side—
The arrival of the Messenger is at hand . . .

Jane's car thudded over the curb, plowed down into a ravine, and collided with a yard-wide oak tree.

Chapter Twenty-two

(I)

Jane awoke in a fog, the most obscene nightmares tittering at the fringes of her memory. Had she awakened to the sound of a bell?

She raised a hand to her throbbing head, felt a fat bandage there. When her vision cleared she noticed with some shock that she was in a hospital room.

What happened? Her memory was a blank.

"Hi, Jane."

She looked aside and saw the smiling Dr. Mitchell peering back at her through his circular spectacles. He was holding a clipboard.

Steve stood worriedly bedside him, holding Jane's hand.

"Don't worry, you're going to be okay," Steve said.

"What happened?"

"In clinical terms," Dr. Mitchell answered, "you have a

minor orbital concussion and sequent but extraneous abrasions . . ."

"In not so clinical terms?" Jane asked.

"You dumped your car into a ravine off of Craker Avenue, banged your head pretty hard. One of my patrol units spotted you and called an ambulance. Jane, what were you doing out there?"

She felt bewildered. "I—I don't remember."

"A retrograde amnesic effect, Jane," Dr. Mitchell said. "It should pass in twenty-four hours, and so should the blurry vision and grogginess. If symptoms persist, though, call me."

"I think you should stay the night," Steve said.

"No, I don't feel that bad, just a little light-headed." She winced in frustration. "I just . . . wish I could remember what *happened.* Is my car—"

"Totaled, I'm afraid," Steve said. "We towed it into town. And the kids are fine; I posted a female officer at your house to look after them. Christ, Jane, I was worried."

"Well I still am. . . . What the hell was I doing so far away from the post office?"

After Dr. Mitchell had released her, Steve took Jane home to his house. She wanted to talk about what happened, but the frustration just kept overwhelming her. *Why can't I remember anything?* "This is just so aggravating . . ."

"You heard the doctor," Steve said. "That smack on the head gave you a temporary loss of short-term memory. But you gotta do what they say, get some rest, take it easy for a few days."

Sure, she thought. *Take it easy. Gimme a break.* She couldn't remember *anything.* But in a moment, her eyes widened as a single memory popped into her mind. "Steve . . . I think—"

Steve brought her some coffee to the kitchen table. "What? You remember something?"

"Dhevic," she whispered. "That's where I was."

"Dhevic? Where is he?" Steve stood poised at the information. "How did you get there?"

"He . . . left his address the day he came to my office."

"We've been trying to find out where he is all week, but— Why did you go there? I told you the guy's *dangerous!*"

"I had to talk to him. There were so many things he's said, things that were too uncanny. There was no one else to ask, Steve. But when I got there . . ." Jane closed her eyes, struggled to remember.

The next flash of memory slapped her in the face. Her new employee, Doreen, lying naked and dead in Dhevic's bathtub. "My God, Steve, I remember now. You were right—"

"What?" He was leaning over, intent. "What do you remember?"

"There . . . there was a dead body in his bathtub, one of the girls who works for me. Her throat was slashed and . . . she had that bell-shaped symbol cut into her chest—"

"Jesus Christ!" Steve exploded. "I told you he's the guy behind all this! You're lucky he didn't murder you too!"

"I got out through the bathroom window before he could get to me . . ."

"Where's he staying?"

Jane gave Steve the slip of paper; he snatched the phone. "Dispatch, this is Chief Higgins. We finally got an eyewitness for capital murder against Alexander Dhevic. Send all units ten-six to the Palms Motel on thirty-fourth Street. Arrest Dhevic on sight, multiple homicide. And put out a state-wide all-points." He paused to ask Jane: "Any idea what he's driving?"

She'd seen that, too, hadn't she? The big SUV right in front of his motel-room door. "A Ford Explorer. It was silver. I know the make and model because I almost bought one once."

Steve piped the vehicle description to the dispatcher, and he hung up. Then he hugged Jane. "I'm sure he's not dumb enough to be anywhere near the motel now, but at least we can take him in when we find him."

"Where do you think he'd go from there?"

It was almost as if the woods conspired against him. Dhevic's footsteps crunched through heavy thicket; fallen branches snapped like firecrackers. He knew he had to be very careful now; he'd avoided the main road and came in through the other side of town, on foot. *They'll be looking for me,* he realized.

He wasn't terribly worried though. He knew that his Lord and Master would protect him.

Where is it? he thought. Had he lost his sense of direction? *It should be coming up any second . . .*

His hand reached out and pushed away some branches . . . and there it was.

The west branch post office sat alone in the moonlight. Dhevic looked for signs of police, saw none, then jogged to the building, using shadows for cover. There were no cars in the lot—would there be maintenance people here this late? *I'll find out in a real soon,* he thought. He opened a tattered briefcase, extracted his lock picks, and was in through a back door in little more time than it would take to open with the key.

Dhevic stepped inside and closed the door behind him.

The coffee was helping her feel better, even after the grisly recollection.

"You're right, though," she said at the table. "I'm sure he would've left the motel once I got away."

"Sure, but now that I've got an APB out—plus your description of his vehicle—every cop in the county is going to be looking for him. There's no way he can get away."

"God, I hope you're right."

"Relax, I *am* right." He poured more coffee for them both, then grabbed the phone again. "Let me call in and get a status report."

Jane went to the kitchen sink while Steve was on the phone. She needed some cold water in her face. It livened her, as she'd hoped, but it also sharpened the images of her memory: Doreen in Dhevic's bathtub. She could hear Steve talking in the background:

"Yeah, dispatch, it's Chief Higgins again. I need a status report on that APB . . ."

The strong flashlight beam roved over the darkened aisles, feeders, and collators. *Just doesn't feel right up here,* Dhevic thought. It would be an easy vibe. He spotted a door, hoped it led to the basement, and when he opened it, he was right. The only problem, now, was going down there.

I better not be afraid of the dark . . .

His stomach flipped when he began to step down. The darkness was so complete, it seemed to soak up half the flashlight's power. Downstairs was a clutter of shelves and storage bins. Columns of stacked boxes, in the shifting darkness, looked like men standing in wait.

He was scared, yes, but when his head began to hurt, he knew he was getting close.

There, he thought.

The beam hovered over a crawl space.

Dhevic got on his knees and began to crawl in.

Jane walked to the window in Steve's dining room, still playing over her thoughts. She didn't know where to start, what to do next; too much had happened for her to assess anything with any logic. "Good work," Steve was saying into the phone in the kitchen. "I can't believe it. And he had some of Doreen Fletcher's clothes in the car with him? That's rock-solid."

Jane's eyes widened.

"I can't believe we got him so fast," Steve said. "That psycho son of a bitch. Book his ass and put him in the detention center. I'll be down shortly."

Steve hung up. "Jane, great news. One of my mobile units arrested Dhevic a few minutes ago. He was heading for the interstate—"

Then Steve's look of confidence corroded into a frown of failure. He was looking directly at Jane.

Jane had the dining room phone to her ear. She slowly lowered it.

"Really? And who told you that? The dial tone you've been talking to the whole time?"

"How did you know?"

"I never specifically told you it was Doreen."

Steve signed. "Smart girl, stupid me. But I kept you strung along long enough."

Jane's heart felt like it was twisting in her chest. "Why? You've been lying about this whole thing from the start? Why?"

Steve smiled sheepishly. "Well, not from the start. Just a few days ago, actually. When I met the Messenger . . ."

The crawlway was hot; cakes of dust stuck to the sweat on Dhevic's hands and face. A panel at the end of the cubby was pushed out, leaving a maw of utter black. Would a Rive be waiting for him? *I'd be able to see it,* he thought. *Or at least I hope so.*

It was hard to remain fearless; nevertheless, he crawled right up to the stinking opening and reached in.

What would he do if something reached back?

He closed his eyes and felt around. *Yeah, if they'd used the striker to open a Rive, I'd definitely know by now . . .*

There was nothing.

Then his hand landed on something:

A box.

Don't count your blessings, he told himself. He pulled the box out. It was just a standard cardboard shipping box, oblong in shape. Its flaps stood open; Dhevic shined the flashlight in, and—

My God. This is it.

The iron striker of the *Cymbellum Eosphorus* lay at the bottom of the box. Dhevic grabbed it, kneed backward until he was out of the crawlspace.

But when he stood up and turned around, he could plainly see that he was no longer in the post office.

Jane shirked into the corner. *I guess this is it,* she thought with amazingly little fear. *This is the end.*

"I was looking around in your west branch the other day," Steve said, "just looking for any clues or evidence, anything that might give me a lead as to how your employees all became connected to a cult, and, well, I found it. I found it in the basement . . ."

The Rive opened before Dhevic's eyes. He was standing at the threshold, that narrow strip of antireality that exists between two worlds. To his back was his own world, to his front a byway to the abyss.

Dhevic looked across the blood-red sky, saw the black church in the pestiferous valley. Tall pale things encroached, tumid sex organs swinging at their groin, enlarged fruitlike heads, stick-thin limbs, all showing black veins beating beneath translucent-white skin.

Dhevic stepped back. *Can they cross?* he wondered, face glazed by sweat. *Does the Rive allow them to cross from there . . . into here?*

"No, but you can cross from here to there," a voice informed him from behind.

Hands latched on to him; Dhevic couldn't jerk loose. The striker fell to the basement floor and rolled away. Chuckling and shrieks of glee resounded about his head. Dhevic was turned in place, forced to glimpse his attackers: all human, all dead. Martin Parkins, Marlene Troy, Sarah Willoughby, Carlton Spence, and others he didn't know. Inhuman traits had infused into their features—this close to the netherworld—tiny horns sticking out from their foreheads, grins full of fangs. The clawed hands gripped Dhevic as surely as chains.

Sarah and Marlene and several other women were nude, breasts gorged from excitement, nipples erect. As the men held Dhevic upright, the women's hands caressed Dhevic's groin.

"Get his pants off," Sarah urged.

"Let's get it out," Marlene panted. "I want to bite it off."

"Save that for the spermatademons," Carlton Spence ordered, gesturing with his eyes toward eager things that waited just across the threshold.

Dhevic was turned about again; a hand clenched in his hair pushed his face out, a half-inch away from the plane. Beyond, the pallid creatures slavered for him, some male, some female, some both. When Dhevic's head and shoulders were pushed fully through, bone-thin arms wrapped round his neck and puttylike lips sucked onto his. The cold demonic tongue pushed through his teeth then dropped like a live snake to the bottom of his belly.

More claws grabbed him and pulled him all the way through.

He was laid out on steaming earth, his shirt pulled open, evil fingernails scratching crimson threads into his flesh, forming a campanulation . . .

The figures huddled around him, intently kneeling. When his genitals were touched through his slacks, they withered from revulsion. The tongue was retracted from his gut and then a penis like a foot-long maggot was thrust before his face. Dhevic squirmed.

Does a child of God go to heaven if he dies in hell? he wondered. He closed his eyes, to shut out the grinning, primeval faces above him, and then he muttered the first intercession to come to mind, from The Gospel According to John . . .

" 'God is love, and those who abide in love abide in God, and God abides in them. There is no fear . . .' "

The sudden cannonade of shrieks threatened to implode his eardrums. The monstrous hands flew off him, the equally monstrous bodies crawling away on their knees in total horror. Some preferred to rip out their own throats and hearts rather than hear holy words in the most unholy of places. Others crawled away, vomiting black blood.

Dhevic stood up and smiled at them, held out his hands. "I live to love and serve the Lord on High. I am his unworthy servant forever."

Groans and bellows, like surf, rose up. A final prayer finished them, from *Psalms*: " 'But truly God has listened; he has given heed to the words of my prayer.' "

The creatures that hadn't yet killed themselves died then, at those final words, their bellies exploding, their eyes shooting out.

Dhevic could feel his aura beaming bright around his head, when he stepped back through the Rive.

Then the Rive closed.

Dhevic looked around, and—

"Yeah, I found it in the basement, Jane," Steve was explaining, stepping closer. "That's where I met Doreen

Fletcher, by the way, she came down to bring up some vending supplies. Cute little thing, huh? Raping her and cutting her throat was fun, but it was even more fun doing it in Dhevic's motel, so *you'd* think he was part of it, and so we had dead-on evidence against him. We didn't even know where Dhevic was staying until the state police gave us a line on his check card."

"So Dhevic isn't part of this?" Jane said, lower lip trembling.

"No. His only Lord and Master is God, and I'm going to send him to meet God very soon."

"And now you're in the cult."

"It's not a cult." He kept stepping closer. "It's a congregation, Jane, a joyous one."

"And you're going to give a choice, right? I can join your congregation, or die?"

"Unfortunately . . . no. The Messenger has already made his mind up. For his message, Jane, his message to the world."

"What's the message?"

"Atrocity, abomination, everything in the human heart that's black and wrong and negative. Anything that exists as an antithesis to God. Simple. And tonight, *you* will help serve the Messenger. You will be part of his next message."

"Is that so?"

"Yeah. When I strangle you in front of your kids, and then strangle your kids."

Martin, Carlton, Marlene, Sarah, and everyone else lay dead. Foul steam rose off the askew bodies. Dhevic expected an onslaught when he stepped back through the Rive, but—

My prayer, he realized. Just words, but words charged by faith. They worked in both worlds.

So it was over?

He picked up the striker from the floor, hefted it in his hand. Then he gathered his things and left the building. As he stalked back through the woods to his truck, the familiar pinpoints of pain flared at his temples. Behind his closed eyes he saw crackling fringes of bright white, and in his head came the rising sound of something like rusty hinges—

And he saw one last thing.

It seemed as though Jane had stopped breathing completely as she watched Steve step closer. There was only one light on in the kitchen, over the range; the dimness appeared to be merging with something— something immediately behind Steve.

A shadow?

No, it's . . .

But what was it?

Something was tainting Steve's features—perhaps it was Jane's fear, or so many powers of suggestion. She remembered little of what Dhevic had told her, some aspect of possession, something called machination. Was Steve really being manipulated by a bodiless spirit? Some entity that merged its mind and borrowed the possessee's flesh? Could that really be happening?

It really is, she knew now. *Dhevic wasn't lying about any of this . . .*

"Oh, I forgot to show you this, didn't I?" Steve said next, the form deepening behind him. He opened a closet to the side, one with a narrow door where one might expect an ironing board. There was an ironing board inside, all right, along with a dead body—or, as Jane discerned more clearly, *pieces* of a dead body. Severed arms and legs lay about the torso. There was no blood, and the wounds looked blackened. "Pretty good work, huh?" Steve said. "I did the job with a welding torch, cut her up with the flame while she was still alive."

The sight dizzied Jane. A once-pretty blond woman she'd seen before. Over her bare breasts, florid third-degree burns formed the campanulation of Aldezhor.

"She's not my sister, by the way. She's a stripper from St. Pete I was fucking."

Jane jerked her gaze away, feeling as though she were standing on a precipice.

When Steve spread his hands out to explain further, so did the shadow-boned thing behind him.

"For eons upon eons, the Messenger has walked the earth through us. We fulfill his eternal mission: to deliver the message of hell unto God's domain. It never ends, Jane. It goes on forever."

The shadow's hands were on Steve's hands now, urging them into a pocket, to withdraw a stout folding knife.

"We're going to take you back to your house, force your children to watch as we kill you. Then we'll kill Jennifer, while Kevin watches. Then we'll kill Kevin. We will spread the message. But first . . ."

There was nowhere Jane could go; she was jammed

in the corner. Fighting him would be useless—her heart was faltering, and she felt about to pass out. He was right up next to her now, and behind him Jane could see the other face: smokelike, wavering in form, but she could see its bottomless eyes, its great horns, and the wanton grin.

"But before we do that, the Messenger wants to feel you, he wants to feel all the pleasures of your body. And we're going to do that right now, right here"—he held up the knife—"after I cut my lord's emblem into your skin."

Jane brought her hands to her face with a shriek, shut her eyes and went rigid. Steve tore open her blouse, cut off her bra—

"Behold the Messenger, Jane," flowed a pitch-black voice that was only partly Steve's. "The arrival of the Messenger is at hand—"

He pressed her back against the wall, brought the tip of the knife to her chest, and—

BAM!

The window seemed to shatter before she even heard the shot. Jane fainted on the spot but before she lost consciousness completely, she saw half-a-dozen figures scrambling about the room.

Police.

Chapter Twenty-three

(I)

Landslides of nightmares shocked her awake. She was in a police car, being raced somewhere in the night, red-and-blue lights pulsing above her. The cop driving was a sergeant named Stanton, whom she'd seen around.

Jane's mind felt wiped clean.

"What happened?" she murmured, but then another landslide spilled into her mind and she remembered.

"Steve was shot?"

"Yeah," Stanton said. "I still can't believe it. I guess he was part of this cult thing all along. It's crazy."

Aldezhor, the name creaked in her ears.

The Messenger.

"How did the police know what he was doing?"

"Anonymous tip. We traced the call. Guess where it came from?"

Jane shook her head, having no idea.

"The BellSouth payphone nearest the west branch post office."

Jane felt too fractured to try to make sense of it.

"So we sent every cop on the shift to his house. Through the window one of our guys saw him coming at you with the knife, so that was all she wrote."

She shuddered, recalling the impact and concussion of the shot.

"Where are we going now?" she asked.

"The hospital. The doctor wants to look at you, make sure you're all right. You could be in shock, plus you fell pretty hard."

"No!" she blurted. "I'm fine. I need you to take me to my house! I have to make sure my kids are all right!"

"No can do," Stanton said. "I have my orders. First the hospital, then you gotta come in to make a statement."

"To hell with that!" she shouted, head throbbing. "Take me to my kids," and that's when she noticed that Stanton turned left at the next corner. The sign read HOSPITAL, NEXT RIGHT, and then two hands behind her grabbed her hair and dragged her into the backseat. Jane screamed like screeching brakes.

"Christ, that's annoying," a voice said. "Shut her up, will ya?"

Martin Parkins placed one rotting palm across her lips, pressed down hard, then squeezed her throat till her eyes bulged. More weight arranged itself over her; her blouse was pulled open, her breasts mauled.

329

"Sarah and Marlene at her house?" the voice asked.

"Yeah, they're tying up the kids, getting them ready—"

Jane's heart felt like a grenade whose pin had just been pulled.

"Good. I'm gonna start cutting her now, been *itching* to put the Messenger's mark on these tits. We won't rape her till we get back to her house—I want the kids to see that too."

"I get a piece, don't I?"

A laugh. "Martin, your dick rotted off days ago."

"What about me?" Stanton asked over his shoulder.

"After me, partner."

Jane felt certain she was dying; she *wished* she would die. An insane glance forward showed her the shadow-shape machinating Stanton's hands on the steering wheel, then another glance directly upward showed her Steve, with a bullethole in his head, grinning down, and that's when he brought the knife tip to her bare chest and began to carve in the campanulation—

"—Ms. Ryan? Ms. Ryan."

Jane arched her back in the front seat of the police car, gasping for air as though she'd just been saved from drowning.

"Jesus, what's wrong?"

It was Stanton, next to her, looking very concerned. "Sounded like you were having a whopper of a nightmare."

Her eyes darted, frantic. "Where are we?"

"Your house. That's where you said you wanted to go."

Jane rushed out the car, ran up her drive, and swung open the front door.

"Hi, Mom!"

"Hi, Mom!"

Jane nearly fainted again, from relief. Kevin and Jennifer sat contentedly on the couch, watching poodles jump rope on *Animal Planet*.

Both rushed up to her, hugging her. "The police lady said she wasn't sure when you'd be home," Jennifer told her, and then Jane saw the female officer sitting in a chair next to the couch.

"They were good as gold, Ms. Ryan," the officer said. "Everything's fine. I was about to get them off to bed—"

"Not yet, Mom!" Kevin pleaded.

"Yeah, Mom, can we at least stay up and watch the rest of *Animal Planet?*"

Her arms trembled around their shoulders. She wanted to cry and laugh and shriek with joy at the same time.

"Call us if you need anything, Ms. Ryan," the female officer said. "I'll get a ride back with Stanton."

"Thuh-thank you," Jane stammered.

"Good night."

The officer left, after which Jennifer and Kevin practically dragged her to the couch. *They don't know about anything that happened tonight,* she realized, with even more gratitude.

"Mom, can we make popcorn?" Kevin asked.

"Sure."

"I'm gonna make it," Jennifer insisted. "Kevin always does the butter wrong in the microwave—"

"I do not!"

"*Both* of you make it," Jane suggested.

"Good idea!" and then the kids were off to the kitchen.

Just when the comforting silence settled over her, the phone blared. Jane gasped again, clutching her chest. *Jesus! If I don't have a heart attack today, I never will . . .*

She looked at the phone. *Steve,* came the most macabre thought. The undertow of her nightmare in the patrol car was seeping back. But, no, it couldn't be Steve. He was dead.

She let it ring several more times before summoning the courage to answer it.

"Hello?"

"I'm glad you're safe . . ."

Jane recognized the accent at once. "Professor Dhevic . . ."

"I called the police when I was finished at the post office—"

"How did you know what was happening?" she asked, astonished.

When he didn't reply, she felt foolish. *He simply knew,* she realized at once. "Sorry. Dumb question. But thank you. You saved my life."

"It was never actually in jeopardy." Did he chuckle? "Trust me."

"I'm sorry I didn't believe you," she said next. "I thought you were one of them."

"That's understandable, considering what Chief Higgins planted in my motel. But none of that matters now. It's over. And you and your children are safe."

Yes, she finally realized. They were. "What about you? Are you all right?"

"I'm fine."

"Where do you go now? More TV documentaries?"

Dhevic groaned over the line. "Only when my benefactors pay me late."

She paused. "Who exactly *are* your benefactors, Professor?"

"It doesn't matter," he said. "They'll be very pleased when they next hear from me. But I'll be leaving town now, to go somewhere else."

"Did you find what you were looking for?"

"Yes."

Another pause. She didn't know what to say to this man who'd just saved her life.

"So I'm off now, I'm off for the next one. I just wanted to say good-bye."

She couldn't fully understand what he meant. "Good-bye, Professor."

"I'm not a very proficient 'holy roller,' Ms. Ryan, but please take this quote from The Book of Mark to heart. 'Your faith has made you well.' Think about that."

Jane kept the phone to her ear even after the dial tone came on. *Has it?* she wondered. *Has my faith really made me well?*

She supposed she'd find out in time.

But one thing puzzled her. *I wonder what he meant when he said, I'm off for the next one?*

The next what?

Jane hung up the phone.

(II)

Dhevic hung up the phone.

The new motel was little better than the first, but he wasn't complaining. His quest was over for now. His mind felt blissfully quiet—no inklings, not a single presage. He let out a great sigh in his chair behind the little desk topped by a Gideon's Bible. In the briefcase by his feet rested the striker, inert now, harmless against his aura and his faith. Tomorrow his benefactors would meet him at the Tampa airport, and would take the striker to the Security Depository of the Swiss Guards, at the Vatican, and place it in the locked vault for such relics.

He winced when he sipped his carryout coffee from the motel lobby. Behind him, the television babbled innocuously; Dhevic wasn't much for TV but he liked to have the set on for the welcome distraction. But then he heard:

"Welcome to another edition of Satanism and Witchcraft, *America's premier presentation on the occult. Tonight's guests are master psychic Jeremy Hoty; the lucid-dreaming priest, Father Jason Judd; and the world-renown clairvoyant, Professor Alexander Dhevic—"*

Dhevic yanked the television cord out of the wall.

Oh, the things we do for money, he thought.

It had been a relatively short quest this time, yet he felt worn out. Nothing surprised him anymore. He knew, though, that he'd sleep better than he had in a long while. He'd sleep without dreams and without visions.

The prospect enthused him.

His folder lay on the desk, the anonymous engraving of the *Cymbellum Eosphorus*. He looked down at it with a touch of vertigo, and a cringe in the belly. *All done for tonight,* he concluded and got ready for bed. *Five down and one to go . . .*

Another polycarbonate plate lay under the first, supposedly from the same book; below the frame, its title could be seen: *Metallurgous de Aldezhor,* or the metalworks of Aldezhor. Before a fiery furnace, demonic iron smiths forged and hammered star-ended bell strikers on mammoth anvils. There were exactly six such strikers being forged.

Epilogue

Saeed stood in a manner of parade rest, high up in the observation room. Discipline was order, and it was Saeed's job to maintain both for the good of the state. He wore tan trousers, a tan tunic, and black leather boots to the knees. Even though this was a civilian supervisory post, Saeed was allowed to wear his Victory Cross and veteran's bars, which he'd earned with honor as an artillery captain in the Holy War against Iraq. Saeed wore the medals with pride.

Now that there was peace, Saeed was assigned to this important civilian station, the city's central post office—the largest mail-processing center in the country. Down below, through the long window, his handlers manned the sorters and conveyers, focused in their tasks.

A sharp rap came at the door.

"Enter," Saeed said.

The floor supervisor came into the room and stood at attention with a package under his arm.

"What is it?" Saeed asked in authoritative monotone.

"A package, sir. Improperly marked according to postal regulations."

"Set it down and leave it to me," Saeed ordered. "And return to your work. The work of the state is Allah's work."

"Yes, sir," the man said and left.

Packages and mail that weren't properly marked were taken into the custody of the state. Illegibility and a lack of return addresses proved the most consistent violations. Private marketeers often tried to mail opium-base to pickups in the larger cities—a capital crime. It was Saeed's job to properly inspect any suspect package.

What have we here? he wondered.

Saeed wasn't worried. On rare occasions, enemy religious factions would send mail bombs to government buildings, and if this were such a package . . .

Allah will protect me, Saeed felt certain.

He walked to the table on which the package had been placed.

It was an oddly shaped box, oblong. It was wrapped in plain brown paper. There was no return address, and the postmark appeared smeared; Saeed couldn't make out the postal zone it had been mailed from.

He lifted the box in his hands. It had some weight to it—ten to fifteen pounds, perhaps—but it felt oddly balanced.

Saeed opened the box and looked inside.

INFERNAL ANGEL
EDWARD LEE

Hell is an endless metropolis bristling with black skyscrapers, raging in eternal horror. Screams rip down streets and through alleys. The people trudge down sidewalks on their way to work or to stores, just like in other cities. There is only one difference. In this city the people are all dead.

But two living humans discover the greatest of all occult secrets. They have the ability to enter this city of the damned, with powers beyond those of even a fallen angel. One plans to foil an unspeakably diabolical plot. The other plans to set it in motion—and bring all the evils of Hell to the land of the living.

MONSTROSITY
EDWARD LEE

Blue skies, palm trees, and flawless white-sand beaches. Clare Prentiss thinks her new home is paradise, and her brand new job as security chief at the clinic almost seems too good to be true. It is. But the truth is worse than she could ever imagine.

Lurid dreams, erotic obsessions, and twisted fantasies aren't the only things that abruptly invade Clare's life. Is someone really peeping into her windows at night? Yes. Could those grotesque things in the woods possibly be real? Yes. Is Clare being stalked? Yes. But not by anything human. By a monstrosity.

DOUGLAS CLEGG
NIGHTMARE HOUSE

There are places that hold in the traces of evil, houses that become legendary for the mysteries and secrets within their walls. Harrow is one such house. Psychic manifestations, poltergeist activity, hallucinations, and other residue of terror have all been documented in Harrow. It has been called Nightmare House. It is a nest for the restless spirits of the dead.

When Ethan Gravesend arrives to inherit Nightmare House, he does not suspect the horror that awaits him—the nightmare of the woman trapped within the walls of the house, or the endless crying of an unseen child.

Also includes the bonus novella *Purity*!

DOUGLAS CLEGG

THE HOUR BEFORE DARK

When Nemo Raglan's father is murdered in one of the most vicious killings of recent years, Nemo must return to the New England island he thought he had escaped for good, Burnley Island. But this murder was no crime of human ferocity. What butchered Nemo's father may in fact be something far more terrifying—something Nemo and his younger brother and sister have known since they were children.

As Nemo unravels the mysteries of his past and a terrible night of his childhood, he witnesses something unimaginable . . . and sees the true face of evil . . . while Burnley Island comes to know the unspeakable horror that grows in the darkness.